Stolen moonlight kisses

"I was working around to kissing you under the moonlight," he said.

Quickly, he kissed her. At first she was so startled that she didn't feel much of anything, and then she realized that this was a very special kiss. She was aware of her heart pounding.

"Nice," he whispered in her ear. He bent to kiss her again, and this time she slipped her arms around his neck. She didn't think, she just enjoyed his mouth on hers.

Other Romances
you will enjoy:

Winter Love, Winter Wishes
by Jane Claypool Miner

A Winter Love Story
by Jane Claypool Miner

Forbidden
by Caroline B. Cooney

Unforgettable
by Caroline B. Cooney

MALIBU
S U M M E R

Jane Claypool Miner

SCHOLASTIC INC.
New York Toronto London Auckland Sydney

No part of this publication may be reproduced in whole or in part, or stored in a retrieval system, or transmitted in any form or by any means, electronic, mechanical, photocopying, recording, or otherwise, without written permission of the publisher. For information regarding permission, write to Scholastic Inc., 555 Broadway, New York, NY 10012.

ISBN 0-590-20354-1

12 11 10 9 8 7 6 5 4 3 2 1   5 6 7 8 9/9 0/0

Printed in the U.S.A.   01

First Scholastic printing, August 1995

*This book is dedicated with much love
to two wonderful people —
Teddy and Davy DuVivier*

MALIBU
SUMMER

Chapter 1

Amber Wood could see her reflection in the glass panes of the old kitchen cabinets. She wished with all her heart that the face she saw was a little more sophisticated-looking. If only she could get her nose to grow a bit longer or her hair to be dark and striking. The reddish-blond waves and the little nose gave her an innocent look that might be all right in some ways, but she longed for something more dramatic.

She tried smiling and then frowning but it seemed as though her expression did almost nothing to change the cheerful young face that stared back at her. She sighed and wished that something would change in her life. If she looked more mature, she might gain the ability to attract several boyfriends, the way her friend Jessica did. Then her life would be interesting. Amber smiled at the thought of what her parents would say about boys being around all the time. They simply wouldn't like it. But there were other kinds of excitement. Her friend Heather had this wonderful job in California for the summer. She would love to have a chance like that.

"Anything *different*," Amber said aloud and stuck her tongue out at her reflection. It was no good wishing for a new nose and it was no good wishing for excitement. Nothing ever happened around here!

"Amber?" her father's voice bellowed out from the dining room. "What's keeping dinner?"

"Be right there." She picked up the pot roast and started to carry it toward the dining room. The telephone rang and she put the platter down. When she picked up the receiver and said hello, it was her best friend, Heather Jones, on the line.

Heather said, "Hi. I've got some wonderful news for you. For me, too. I got a last-minute invitation to go to France with my grandmother, so do you want my California job?"

Amber felt her knees go weak. California! All her life she'd dreamed of seeing California! Then she remembered that she wasn't the one who would make the decision. She said, "You *know* I want it. But I'll have to ask my parents."

"Ask them today. I have to know right away," Heather said.

"I'll need time to convince my parents. You know how they are," Amber answered. Her heart was still beating fast with excitement and she allowed herself to hope. The idea of spending all summer in southern California — and most of the time on the beach — was so wonderful! "I want this so much that I'll have to find a way to make them give in!" Amber said.

"Amber?" Her mother's voice interrupted the phone conversation.

Amber turned and saw her mother standing at the kitchen door. "Got to go," she said quickly and hung up the telephone. To her mother, she said, "I'm sorry. I'll be right there."

"You know the rules, Amber. No phone calls during meals."

"But this wasn't exactly during a meal," Amber replied.

Her mother shook her head and picked up the pot roast. "I hope the potatoes aren't cold."

Amber followed her mother into the dining room and slid into her seat. Her parents were nice people, but they were really strict about certain things. One of those things was that family meals were a time of pleasant togetherness.

She knew that this was the wrong time to bring up the possibility of a summer job in California so she forced herself to join the general Sunday conversation and say nothing about her great news. Her parents might not think it was such "great news." She was certain that it would be better to broach the subject later.

After dinner, she cleared the table and cleaned the kitchen quickly. Then she joined her family on the back porch. Her brother was painting a model airplane and her parents were sitting on canvas chairs discussing their vegetable garden.

Amber sat down on the porch steps and began, "Heather called just before dinner . . ."

"Is that what took you so long?" her father asked and his voice didn't sound pleased.

"Yes." Amber plunged forward. "She was going to work as an *au pair* this summer."

"A pair of what?" her younger brother Timmy asked.

"*Au pair*," Amber explained. "It means mother's helper in French." Then she directed the rest of her explanation to her father. "She was supposed to help her cousin Madeline Harvey in Beverly Hills, California, with her eight-year-old son. The boy has some learning problems, I guess, but he's basically all right. Anyway, Heather was going to go out there and spend the summer with her as an *au pair* and then she got an offer to go to Europe with her grandmother." Amber paused and took a deep breath before she began again. "So now I can have the job. The Harveys will pay my way and all my expenses and fifteen hundred dollars for the summer. I promised to let them know right away."

There was a very long silence as her mother and father stared out over the garden and then her mother asked, "What does Mr. Harvey do to be so rich? And are there other children?"

"He's John Harvey. He used to be an actor and now he's a director and producer. There are three other children but two are boys who are older. There's a thirteen-year-old girl but I wouldn't have to take care of her."

"Seems like between the mother and the thirteen-year-old they could manage one young child. How old is the boy?" Her mother seemed to be thinking things over and that gave Amber some hope.

"Eight. His name is Kyle and he's been in special schools for two years. But he's still not able to read and Heather says he doesn't talk much. They want someone to spend time with him and help him with his communication skills. It would be great experience for me since I'm going to be a speech teacher." When they didn't say anything, Amber added, "I guess you think California is a long way from Wisconsin, but I could call home every week and it wouldn't cost anything. That's part of the deal. It really is a great chance." She wanted to say even more, but she didn't get the opportunity.

Her father stood up abruptly and said, "Your mother and I will talk about it."

"But I have to know right away."

"The only answer you'll get right away is, 'We'll see,' " her father said firmly.

Her mother asked, "You surely don't think we'd say yes without thinking about it? California is two thousand miles away and you're only fifteen."

"Sixteen. I was sixteen two weeks ago and I have my driver's license. That's lucky because the job requires someone who can drive and Madeline said it was all right if I wanted to come instead of Heather."

"You must call her Mrs. Harvey," her father said.

"Heather says she wants to be called Madeline."

"Heather doesn't know any better but you do." Her father frowned and asked, "Isn't it time to do homework? Final exams coming up. Right?"

Amber bit her lip to keep from pointing out that she was a straight-A student. She knew her parents were doing the best job they could in raising her and her brother, but they were so old-fashioned that sometimes it drove her crazy. And sometimes they treated her like such a baby that it made her furious. On the other hand, they hadn't said no. So she could still hope.

During the next week, Amber did everything she could to keep up this hope. She daydreamed about seeing the Pacific Ocean, and all the wonderful sights in southern California, and tried to learn as much as she could from Heather. Over and over again, she questioned her friend about the Harveys but there really wasn't much information.

"All I know is that they have scads and scads of money and there are two boys in college. The boys are not home a lot, but I hear one is really handsome and the other is really talented. What more could you possibly want?"

"Not much," Amber admitted. "It sounds like the ideal job, all right."

At home, she waited for her mother and father to ask her some more questions but neither of them wanted to talk about it. On Friday, she offered to get Madeline Harvey's telephone number so her mother could call her future employer directly. But her mother said, "I'll have to talk it over with your father some more."

Amber approached her father on Saturday morning and tried to point out the advantages of the extra money. Her father said, "No sense talking about that. I'll have to talk it over with your mother."

On Saturday afternoon, Heather called Amber and said, "Madeline called and said if she didn't hear from you tomorrow, she's getting someone else. Can't you make your folks say yes?"

"I can't even get them to *talk* to me about it," Amber admitted.

"Well, you're running out of time," Heather warned. "Mother says Madeline always gets what she wants and she'll never wait. So it's all over if you don't call tomorrow. I'm sorry."

"It's not your fault my parents are so stubborn," Amber said sadly.

"At least make them *talk* to you," Heather advised.

"Yes, I will," Amber promised. "I'll make them give me an answer tomorrow, but I'm not sure it will be yes."

"Would they really put you off a week and then say no?" Heather's voice was incredulous.

"They'll do what they think is best," Amber said. She knew Heather thought her parents were stuffy, but she wouldn't trade them for Heather's stuck-up mother for anything. Mrs. Jones spent all her time and energy in social activities that didn't count for anything but making her feel important, as far as Amber could see.

"Don't get mad at *me*," Heather protested. "I'm not the one who's stalling."

"No one is stalling," Amber said. "I'll have a definite answer tomorrow and I'll call Mrs. Harvey myself to let her know."

Chapter 2

It was her brother's turn to set the table so Amber stayed out of the way until it was time to eat. As she slid into her seat at the dining room table, she said in a determined voice, "I have to call the Harveys today and tell them whether or not I can go to California."

She tried hard to keep her voice light, but she felt as though her whole future depended on the decision. If they said yes, she'd be on her way to an absolutely fascinating summer. If they said no . . . but she didn't want to think about that.

"It's too late," her mother said. "They want you in a week and you have to buy your airplane fare thirty days in advance."

"Only for supersavers," Amber said. "The Harveys don't worry about budget airfares." When she saw the look on both her parents' faces, she realized she'd said the wrong thing again. One of their main objections to the job seemed to be how much money the Harveys had. Amber thought that was very prejudiced of them, but she knew better than to say so out loud.

There were plenty of rich people in Milwaukee, but her family wasn't a part of that group. But even the rich people were probably a lot more conservative about money than Californians. Amber sighed. Maybe it wasn't surprising that they had a hard time trusting people who would pay twice as much for airline tickets as they needed to. All their lives, her parents had worked hard and saved to take care of her and her brother. They were good people. Besides, they were her parents and she loved them.

"I can't believe you really want to go," her father said as he buttered a roll and popped it in his mouth.

"Of course I want to go," Amber answered. "What sixteen-year-old girl wouldn't be thrilled with a chance to spend the summer in a mansion in Beverly Hills, California?"

"Malibu," Tim corrected. "You said you'd be right on the beach."

"Part of the time. The Harveys have a mansion in Beverly Hills and a beach house in Malibu." Amber ruffled her brother's hair and smiled. "I'll miss you but you're going to camp anyway."

"You could get a job as camp counselor," her brother pointed out. "You said they promised you one."

"Sure and make four hundred dollars for the whole summer. But I'm going to get rich in California."

"I haven't given my permission." Her father speared another potato.

"But you will." Amber smiled and tried to charm him into deciding in her favor. "You wouldn't stand in the way of an opportunity like this. I'll see the Pacific Ocean. And earn a lot of money. Don't forget the money."

"We don't need the money. Your mother and I talked it over. We're going to sell your grandfather's farm and there will be plenty of money to send you and your brother to college in Madison." John Wood's voice betrayed a lot of different emotions and Amber knew he wasn't really certain of the decision. Maybe he doubted that the proceeds would really pay to educate both of his children. Besides, Amber knew they planned to hold onto that farm for their own retirement if they could.

Still, it wouldn't do to talk too much about the money. Her father was sensitive about how much he earned as a supervisor of a printing company. It was a good, steady job but it wasn't making them rich. Even her mother's part-time job as a secretary in the public school wasn't helping as much as they'd hoped. But her father was a proud man so it was better to skip the financial angle.

Amber said, "All my life I've wanted to travel and see more of the world. You know I really want to go out of state to college. I want to go to New York City or maybe even Los Angeles. UCLA has a great education department."

"You talk about all your life as though you were ninety-five-years old. Sixteen years isn't very long to want something, is it?" Her father spoke in a teasing voice but Amber didn't think he was very funny. She bit her lip to keep from replying.

Then her mother said, "Anyway, you don't need a long-distance education to be a speech teacher. The University of Wisconsin is a fine school."

"Of course it is," Amber answered. "But it's in Madison. So if you come from Boise, Idaho, or Carson City, Nevada, it's a great school but I come from Milwaukee. That's only two hours away. There's not much adventure in that — is there?"

Neither of her parents answered her and

Amber knew they were talking silently to each other. They had this way of coming to agreement about something their kids wanted without ever saying a word. Amber watched their faces anxiously for clues to what they were thinking. There was still a big possibility they would say no. If they thought it wasn't good for her, *nothing* would change their mind. They would simply say no and that would be the end of the discussion.

The silence continued so long that Amber couldn't stand it. Although she knew she shouldn't, she couldn't keep from adding, "Besides, if I earn enough money, you can wait and sell the farm when Tim is ready for college. It might even take him through graduate school."

"I don't know why you can't be satisfied with the University of Wisconsin." Her mother sighed.

Her father sounded really cross now. "Your earnings won't help so much, you know. One summer job won't earn enough to pay for four years of college, no matter how rich the Harveys are."

"One thousand five hundred dollars," Amber answered. "That's a lot of money and all my expenses will be paid."

"I don't think it's a good idea," her mother said quietly. "Amber is too young. Too inexperienced to go and live among strangers."

"Mother, they are *not* strangers." Amber tried to keep her voice calm. She didn't want to end up in an argument. That would ruin everything. "You know that Mrs. Harvey is the daughter of Heather Jones's mother's sister-in-law. That practically makes Mrs. Jones the aunt of Mrs. Harvey. And you've known the Joneses all your life."

"I never really liked Carolyn Jones," her mother said quietly. "When we were in school, she used to laugh at the farm kids. She thought she was better than we were because she lived in town and her father was superintendent of schools."

"But Heather Jones is my best friend and she offered me the job. She could have given it to Jessica or Melanie or Diane and they would have just said yes. Instead, she's really embarrassed because I can't say yes or no." Amber was nearly in tears now. At this point, she didn't think she cared much what their decision was. She just wanted a decision!

But that wasn't really true, she reminded herself. She was just frustrated. Her mother's fears seemed so unnecessary. She turned to her father and put her hand on his arm. "Please, Daddy, I want to do this so much."

He frowned and shook his head. "It's not going to be anything like you dream, Amber. You'll work hard!"

"They work hard, too. At least Mr. Harvey works hard." In her heart of hearts, Amber wondered why Mrs. Harvey needed a full-time companion for her eight-year-old son when she didn't have a job herself, but Amber was too worried about getting her parents to agree to think about anything else.

Her mother sighed and asked, "What do you think, John?"

"Wasn't there any dessert?" he answered.

"Chocolate cake." Her mother began to rise from the table and John Wood put his hand on her arm and said, "Amber can get the cake."

"It's still warm. I should cut it," her mother said.

"Amber can do it," her father said.

Amber understood they were going to talk *again*. She couldn't imagine what more they had to say to each other. They'd been over and over all of this. But she rose from the table without objecting. This was a crucial moment and any irritation from her might shift the decision against her.

As she walked to the kitchen, she imagined herself getting on the airplane and flying to Los Angeles next Saturday. That was less than a week away.

A final decision was being made right now — and that thought made her so nervous that she was afraid she'd drop something in the kitchen.

After everything was arranged on the tray, she took a deep breath and murmured under her breath, "Here goes." She carried the coffee and cake into the dining room. As she walked into the room, she felt as though she had been gone for an eternity, but her mother looked at her with a smile and said, "That was quick. I'm glad the cake didn't fall apart."

"I'm going to fall apart if you don't give me an answer," Amber said.

"Sit down, Amber, your father and I have made a decision," Mrs. Wood said.

Amber sat down and looked from one to the other. For the life of her, she still couldn't guess what the decision was. Amber took a deep breath and asked, "Well?"

She bit her lip to keep from crying. She was almost certain now that they weren't going to let her go. All her hopes and dreams about a wonderful summer in California would be permanently frozen into exactly that — dreams. She would end up at Camp Weehaddo where she'd been every year for the last six years. And being a counselor this year wouldn't make it that much better.

"Your father and I," her mother said slowly, "have talked it over and we've decided we want to lay out our ground rules so that there's no mistake about what we expect of you."

"Then I can go?"

"Yes," her mother answered. "But we want you to agree that you'll follow the Wood household rules. That no matter how odd those people turn out to be, you'll keep regular hours, eat well, and call us the minute anything — and I mean *anything* — goes wrong."

"Nothing will go wrong," Amber said. "I'll go call Mrs. Harvey and tell her I'm coming. And then I need to do some shopping. Could we go tomorrow?"

"I thought you weren't going to spend any money," her brother teased.

"Your sister knows what she's doing," her father said. "She's very sensible about money." He still looked worried but he smiled at her in encouragement.

"Thanks, Daddy. I have all my baby-sitting money saved and I just need a few things,"

Amber said. "A new bathing suit and some T-shirts."

"And a few dresses," her mother added. "If you're going to work for movie stars, you'll need some party clothes."

"I don't know," Amber said doubtfully. Privately, she was thinking that what her mother considered "party clothes" would be very out of place in Beverly Hills.

"I'll call Carolyn and Heather Jones and see if they'll join us for a shopping spree. We can have a mother-daughter consultation. Two generations should give you some expert advice."

"Great!"

"I doubt if either of them will understand the Harveys any better," her father said sadly. "People with the kind of money the Harveys have are different."

He looked at his daughter and said, "Promise me you'll stay sensible, no matter what."

Amber put her arms around her father and hugged him and kissed him on the cheek. "Daddy, you don't need to worry about me. I'm going to have a wonderful time and a great adventure. But I'll still be me."

"Just don't let them talk you into being any thinner. Or cutting your hair. Or wearing sunglasses at night. Or calling everyone 'dar-ling.' " He was smiling now and Amber real-ized that it really was decided. She really was going to live in southern California this summer and work for the Harvey family.

Chapter 3

It was only Amber's third airplane flight and the first she'd made alone, but she wasn't nervous. She was too excited about California to even watch the movie they showed on the plane. She spent the long trip dreaming of warm sand, blue oceans, and cute boys.

She had never had a real boyfriend and this was the first year she felt that it was absolutely necessary. But there was no one at her school who seemed special enough. Now she dared to daydream that she would find someone *very* special in California. She tried to imagine what the two Harvey sons would be like. How handsome could the one they said was handsome be? Would he have blond hair and blue eyes? Or would he be tall, dark, and dangerous-looking?

She giggled at her silliness and reminded herself that California beaches were full of good-looking surfers. If she didn't meet some-one on the beach, and the Harvey sons weren't exactly right for her, they would have friends. She absolutely knew this was her summer to meet someone wonderful.

The plane began its descent for landing and Amber sat up straight and looked out the win-dow at the vast stretch of desert below. It was so brown and so bare, she could almost imag-ine she was coming into Saudi Arabia or the Kalahari Desert. Then the landscape changed to miles and miles of houses. Looking below, she could see little dabs of blue in a lot of the backyards of the houses. Swimming pools, Amber thought. As the earth seemed to rush up to meet their plane, she thought, This is the beginning of my real life!

She arrived in Los Angeles ten minutes early and decided to use that time to make sure she looked her best. In the airport wash-room, she looked long and hard at her face as she brushed her hair and put on makeup. Her hair looked a little wild after the four-hour jour-ney, but she knew it was her strong point. People always commented on the strawberry blond color. It was thick and hung down to her shoulders in curls or waves, depending on the weather. Her parents had named her Amber because of the color of her hair.

Her skin looked white but by the end of the summer she would look like a regular Californian. Besides, her light skin and light blue-green eyes were usually admired. She smiled at her reflection. Her face was all right, but no one ever called her beautiful. She was just a nice-looking girl with pretty hair. "You didn't come to California to get in the movies," she said out loud to her reflection. Then she picked up her suitcase and went outside to meet her new life.

As she walked down the long narrow hallway, she hoped that someone would approach her and ask if she was Amber Wood, the new *au pair*. She had no idea who that someone might be since Madeline Harvey had been so vague. It might be Mr. or Mrs. Harvey, or the housekeeper, or one of the two older Harvey boys. The possibilities were so varied that she simply had to trust that whoever it was would find her. She'd described her appearance and promised to wear a blue T-shirt to make it easy for anyone to spot her. Mrs. Harvey — Madeline — she was supposed to call her new employer Madeline — had first said she'd get someone to pick her up, then she'd retreated from the promise and said "she'd try." Amber had permission to take a taxi if no one met her.

Amber waited three-quarters of an hour and decided she must be on her own. She found a taxi easily and gave the driver the address. "One two four four five six Sunset Boulevard, please. That's in Beverly Hills."

"Beverly Hills. You live there?" the driver asked.

"I'm going to live there this summer," Amber answered.

"Relatives?"

"Not exactly." Amber was surprised the driver asked so many questions as he drove through the most congested traffic Amber had ever seen. Amber answered politely, but she was too engrossed in taking in her first impressions of southern California to really converse. Nevertheless, the driver practically had her whole life story by the time they turned off the freeway and started to wind around on a beautiful shady street.

"So you're the summer baby-sitter?" the driver asked.

"*Au pair,*" Amber corrected him. She was certainly going to be more than a baby-sitter. She was going to be a helper to Madeline Harvey and spend most of her time teaching Kyle Harvey.

Amber frowned as the taxi made a sharp right turn and wondered exactly what Kyle's learning problems were. Madeline hadn't wanted to talk about it over the phone. Did that mean that Kyle's problems were so light they weren't worth talking about? Or did it mean that they were so bad that Madeline Harvey didn't want to scare her off?

It was four-thirty now and the sky was so overcast and gloomy that it almost seemed as if the sun was setting. Yet she knew that couldn't be so. She shivered in her T-shirt. It was a lot colder than she'd expected. And the sky was a dull and ugly gray. Amber asked, "Is it always like this? So — so cool?"

"You mean the June gloom?" The driver laughed. "We get our worst weather in June. But it usually burns off by ten or eleven. Today it was all day. Smoggy, too."

Amber's eyes were watering and she wondered if it was the smog or something like regular tears. She hadn't expected to feel so alone. And she had hoped someone would meet her!

They were driving down a long, beautiful street with high gates and long, green lawns. Amber asked, "Is this Sunset Boulevard?"

"Yup. Richest real estate in the United States," the taxi driver said. "Your boss a movie star?"

"Mr. Harvey used to be," Amber answered.

"He was the star of a TV show called *Exceptional Days* for ten years and then he was in the movies and now he's a movie producer."

"John Harvey? He's made a couple of fortunes, hasn't he? I guess he had to, with all those wives."

"He only has one wife," Amber said stiffly. "They have four children."

"Not quite." The taxi driver laughed. "*He* has four children and three or four *ex*-wives. His alimony and child support payments must be horrendous."

Amber sighed and looked out the window. She was certainly glad her father and mother weren't hearing this conversation. If it was true, then the Harveys were very different from her family. And she supposed it was true.

"Here we are," the driver said. There was a high wrought-iron gate with ornate patterns blocking the entrance. The gate was held in place by a soft pink stucco archway that seemed to be supported by two tall stone pillars. On either side of the arch was a high hedge of dark green bushes with bright red flowers. They'd been trimmed in a square shape just like the boxwood hedges she had at home. Only at home the hedges were two feet tall and these were about thirty feet tall.

There didn't seem to be anyone around. The

driver said, "Nobody home. You sure of the address?"

"They're expecting me," Amber answered. "Isn't there a bell?" She could hear the trembling in her voice and she knew it wasn't just disappointment. She was also afraid. What if no one was there? What would she do?

The driver leaned out the window and pushed buttons on a panel. When nothing happened, he pushed again. Finally, he said, "Nobody home. You absolutely sure they're expecting you?"

"Yes. Madeline — Mrs. Harvey said if no one met me I should take a taxi to the house. And this is the address."

"Well, there's nobody home. Guess the servants get Saturdays off or something. You could come back to the airport with me or wait here."

"On the street?" Amber wasn't certain what was the best thing to do, but it seemed silly to go back to the airport.

"You can walk up to the front steps." The driver pointed to a small gap between the tall hedge and the stone pillar. "If you can get through the hedge and if there are no dogs, you'll be fine."

Amber took a deep breath and told herself it was silly to be frightened. She opened the cab door and said, "I'll be fine. How much do I owe you?"

"Fifty dollars."

"Really?"

"Really. I'll give you a receipt. You'll get reimbursed, won't you?"

Amber reached into her purse and took out three twenty-dollar bills. He handed her a scribbled receipt and started to back out of the driveway. Amber realized he didn't plan to give her any change and she called, "Wait a minute," but he pretended he couldn't hear her and was gone in a second.

Amber's face burned with surprise and shame at the way the taxi driver had taken advantage of her. She felt foolish, a little frightened, and angry all at the same time. Then she said, "Oh well," picked up her suitcase, and began to push it through the hedge.

She was pretty scratched up by the time she made it through the hedge, but there were no dogs on the other side. Beyond the long, bright-green lawn, she saw a huge two-story stucco mansion with a red tile roof. It was a kind of pink-peach color and trimmed with soft gray-green shutters. Her first impression was one of immense size. It looked like a large pink box trimmed by the old-fashioned balcony that ran along the second story for the whole length of the second floor. There was absolutely no sign of life and the house didn't look especially inviting. It just looked big.

Amber took a deep breath as she looked around and promised herself she wouldn't be intimidated by the immense size of the house, or by the wide green lawns, or any of the expensive-looking things she supposed were inside the house. Some people had a lot of money and that was that. She was going to be her own self and not be intimidated by wealth. After all, money didn't buy happiness and it didn't make you a nice person, either. That's what her parents always said. Still, the house was formidable. She'd never seen a home this large and the lawns were so wide and deep that she wondered who mowed them.

As she neared the entrance, she noticed that there were two huge clay pots on either side of the walk and these pots held lemon trees. She had to admit that she'd never seen lemons growing in pots. For that matter, she'd never really seen a lemon tree before.

She made her way to the front door of the Harvey house and rang the bell but no one answered. She put her suitcase down and walked around the side of the house to the back.

The backyard was a real surprise. It was so

much more beautiful and inviting than the front. Everywhere she looked there were pots full of petunias and geraniums in full bloom. And there were flowering bushes and trees everywhere, making it seem like a magical place. There were red tiles running from the back of the house all the way to the huge swimming pool.

The beautiful flowers and shrubs delighted Amber and there was a lot of comfortable furniture. She sank into a lounge chair that had a deep padded mattress on it. Then she remembered she'd left her suitcase at the front door. But that was all right, she decided, because whoever came home first would know she was here.

She looked at her watch and saw that it was five o'clock. Someone would be here soon, she was sure. She would just rest until someone found her.

Amber woke at six-thirty and discovered she was still alone. Where could they all be? It seemed so strange that Madeline would tell her to take a taxi and then not be here. It made her wonder if her father was right. Perhaps the Harveys were really going to be impossible. Perhaps she had made a big mistake by coming to California.

By seven-thirty, Amber was hungry and scared. Where were they? Why was she all alone in the backyard of this huge house? Surely there would be a gardener or maid or someone by now? What if the whole thing turned out to be a hoax or something even worse? She shivered and realized that she was getting cold and that it was almost dark. Her T-shirt wasn't enough for this weather.

Suddenly, lights went on in the back of the house and Amber realized they were on automatic timer. She decided to go back to her suitcase and find a sweater. She walked around to the front of the house, opened her suitcase, and pulled out a sweatshirt that said *University of Wisconsin* on it. Right now, she wished she were back in Wisconsin where she knew the rules and knew what to expect.

She decided it was silly to sit around an empty house feeling scared. It was almost as though the action of walking to the front of the house gave her courage to take even more action. She locked the suitcase again and picked it up. She would walk back to the street and see if she could find a telephone. It was true that there weren't any stores or public phones around, but she could walk to a neighbor's and ask for help.

Amber sighed. She had never been so completely on her own before and it was pretty frightening. She decided she would have to call her parents as well as Heather. She didn't want to call home and she hated to tell them she was all alone, but her parents were expecting a call and they had probably already started to worry.

She was about twenty feet down the driveway when she saw a red sports car pull into the entry and the gates begin to open.

A young man was driving the red Corvette. He had very curly light brown hair and little round horn-rimmed glasses. He looked young and Amber's first impression was that he had so much energy it seemed to make the air around him crackle. She supposed some people might think he was kind of cute except he was frowning and looked very angry. He leaned his head out the car and asked, "Who are *you*?"

"Amber Wood, the new *au pair*," she replied. Then she couldn't resist asking, "Who are *you*?" She guessed he was one of the sons — probably not the handsome one — because he certainly didn't look like a movie star. In fact, he looked like a young man with a lot of energy who was in a big hurry.

"I'm Jason Harvey. You're supposed to be at the beach house." He sounded quite annoyed.

"I don't even know where the beach house *is*," Amber snapped. She knew she wasn't making a very good first impression, but he was so rude. If the rest of the Harveys were like this, she wouldn't be staying long.

"Madeline moved everyone over there on Tuesday. Didn't she tell you?"

"I talked to your mother on Sunday. She told me to come here if no one met me at the airport." Amber realized she was about to cry and she hated that.

"She's not my mother."

"Is she your stepmother?"

He ignored the question and asked one of his own, "How long have you been here?"

"Since five o'clock. My plane came in at four. No one met me." She knew her voice sounded defensive, but she really was tired and hungry and Jason Harvey wasn't being very nice.

"Why didn't you call?"

He really sounded angry now and that made Amber respond in an angry tone. "What good would it have done? No one was home. The house was locked and there were no servants around."

"You should have called the beach house," Jason insisted.

"I don't have the number of the beach house. I'm not a mind reader, you know. But if you give me a hint, I'll make the call now."

Jason was still glowering, but he said in a controlled voice, "Not your fault, Goldilocks. Climb in and I'll take you to the beach house."

"My name is Amber," she said stiffly. "I don't want to take you out of your way. Are you *going* to the beach house?"

"I'm going there now, Goldilocks."

"Call me Amber." Now her voice sounded angry. "Amber Wood."

"How old are you, Amber?"

"Sixteen. How old are you?"

Jason laughed shortly and asked, "Are you hungry?"

"I just want to get to my job," Amber answered. "And I need to call home."

"Where are you from?"

"Milwaukee, Wisconsin," she answered shortly. The Harveys certainly didn't seem to communicate much. What kind of a family were they really?

Jason frowned even deeper and asked,

"Going to tell your parents to send you a plane ticket home?" Jason asked. "You don't need to panic. We'll give you a plane ticket anytime you want."

"I just need to check in," Amber said. "I promised."

"I wouldn't blame you if you did go home," Jason said.

"Do you want to get rid of me?" Amber was amazed at how easily she quarreled with this abrupt young man. She reminded herself that he wasn't her boss and that the other Harveys wouldn't necessarily be as rude. She moderated her voice as she continued, "I just want to tell my mom and dad I've arrived safely. It's three hours later in Milwaukee. Could we stop somewhere?"

"You can use the car phone," Jason said. "Is that all of your luggage?"

"I only came for the summer."

Jason laughed and said, "I wonder if you'll make it through a whole week." He reached down and pulled up the car phone, which he tossed onto her lap.

She stared down at the small, handheld receiver and asked, "How do I do it?"

"Just like a regular phone. Push the talk button and then punch in the numbers." His tone of voice said he thought anyone should know that. "Don't they have car phones in Milwaukee?"

She ignored the question and asked one of her own. "Will it reach Milwaukee?"

"It will reach Afghanistan," Jason assured her. "You have any relatives in Afghanistan?"

Amber bit her lip to keep from replying. She made her call and when her father picked up the phone she said, "Hi, Dad, I just wanted to tell you I'm here and all right. I'll call you again tomorrow."

"How was your trip? Your mother will get on the other line," her father said.

"I'll call you tomorrow," Amber said. "We can talk then."

"Amber, are you sure you're all right?" Her father's voice was sharp with concern.

"I'm fine. Just tired. I'll call you tomorrow. Don't worry." She hung up before he could object. The last thing in the world she wanted to do was have a long conversation with her parents while Jason Harvey was listening.

As she handed the phone back to Jason, their hands brushed and Amber jumped. There was something about the contact between them that was like electricity.

If Jason noticed anything, he ignored it. "That was short," Jason said. "But at least you didn't say you were coming home."

Amber didn't reply. She stared out the window of the red Corvette to keep from crying. She certainly didn't want him to know how upset she was. Why was he being so rotten? Was everyone in the Harvey family going to be this horrible? If so, she wouldn't be able to stay.

Chapter 4

By the time she'd composed herself and could trust herself to speak again, they were driving down a steep hill and she could see glimpses of the Pacific Ocean. Though the sun had set, the sky was lit by a three-quarter moon and she could see shimmering light on the water. She couldn't hear the waves, but she thought she could smell the sea air.

"We're here," Jason said. "This is Malibu. The house is one block away. And this is Malibu Colony. The whole beach is Malibu."

"Twenty-seven miles of sand and sea," Amber said. "I read about it in the library last week."

"I suppose you're starstruck like most teenage girls," Jason grumbled. "You probably took the job so you could get in the movies. Do you act? Dance? Sing?"

"I took the job because I'm going to be a

teacher — and because I wanted the money," she answered. "Not that it's really any of your business."

"Cheerful, aren't you?"

Amber ignored him and looked eagerly out the window of the car. They were on Pacific Coast highway, she knew. It was the main street and the ocean was just on the other side of the houses, but there was no more view of the ocean. It was simply a long line of houses placed so close together that it looked as if you could hear everything that went on at the neighbors'. Amber was surprised that the Harveys would choose a beach house that was so close to other people. It also surprised her that it was such a short distance between the Harveys' regular house and their summer home. In Milwaukee, she knew people who had summer cabins, but they were at least two hours away from their regular houses. The distance from Beverly Hills to Malibu was less than thirty minutes.

"This is it. Not as fancy as the neighbors' because my dad bought it for an investment. It's what they call a 'scraper,' but in the summer it's home away from home for the Harvey bunch." Jason pressed a button on his car and the metal gates onto the driveway swung upward. "There's only a three-car garage," he said, "so I have to park on the driveway. Can you drive?"

"Yes."

"I always leave the keys in my car when I'm here," Jason said. "If you need one of the cars in the garage, you may have to move mine. Watch out when you back out onto the road. It's dangerous. And I wouldn't want you to dent my Corvette."

Amber didn't even bother to answer. She certainly wasn't going to move his car if she could help it. In fact, she was going to have as little to do with Jason as possible. He was the most obnoxious person she'd met in a long time.

Jason carried her suitcase in one hand and opened the door with his key. Then he called out, "Madeline! Where are you?"

A tall, beautiful young woman who was wearing white silk pants and a hot pink silk blouse looked up from the couch where she was watching television and said, "Oh, Jason. Who is your friend?"

Jason frowned even deeper and growled. "*This*, my dear stepmother, is no friend. This is your new little helper. Apparently you forgot to tell her you were moving everyone to the beach house a month early."

"Oh, did I?" Madeline Harvey smiled directly at Amber and raised her hand in a gesture of helpless apology. "I'm sorry, Crystal, I hope you didn't have to wait too long."

"Her name is Amber," Jason said.

"My name is Amber," she said at exactly the same time. If she'd liked Jason at all, she would have smiled at their simultaneous response, but as it was she was annoyed at his answering for her.

"Put her in the pink room, will you, dear?" Madeline asked and turned back to her television movie.

"The pink room is noisy," Jason answered. "Give her the guest room. You never have any guests here."

"But we might." Madeline sounded unsure.

"If you do, you can let the guests stay in the pink room. And she's hungry."

"Cook is off," Madeline answered.

Jason was glowering as he said to Amber, "Come on."

She followed him down a short hallway to a large beautiful bedroom with two double beds that shared a decorated headboard. The room also had two rattan straight chairs and a rattan rocker and small table. There was a wooden desk, two dressers, bookcases filled with books and videos, and a television set. It was bigger than any bedroom she'd ever seen.

In fact, it was a whole lot better than the deluxe hotel room they'd once stayed in on their family vacation.

Jason went to one wall and drew the long white damask drapes. "You can hear the surf, but the only way you get a view of the ocean is by stepping out onto your balcony and leaning around the corner. Sorry about that."

"It's very nice," Amber said. In truth, she was overwhelmed by the setting and the beautiful things she saw in the house. She really didn't know much about furniture and paintings, but she had an idea that everything she was looking at was not only pretty, it was very expensive. If this was their beach house, she could hardly wait to see the inside of the Beverly Hills mansion.

"The balcony isn't much," Jason said. "You can use the big deck off the living room unless Dad is entertaining. But they almost never entertain here." He pointed to the small balcony and she walked over to take a look at it.

The balcony was tiny, with just room enough for a large potted plant and a couple of wrought-iron chairs and a table. Just beyond the balcony, Amber could see the wall of the neighboring house that went straight up for three stories. Jason was right, the balcony wasn't much, but the room was large and beautifully furnished and Amber loved it immediately. Jason put her suitcase down and said, "I'll show you the kitchen."

"Is this the pink room?" Amber asked.

"This is the guest room," Jason answered.

"But your mother said I should have the pink room."

"How many times do I have to tell you she's not my mother! Her name is Madeline and she could care less what room you have. This one is better for you."

"I really think I should go into the pink room," Amber said.

"You don't need to think," Jason said shortly. "I'll show you the kitchen."

Amber didn't know what to do. Should she argue with Jason? Should she go back into the living room and disturb Madeline? In the end, she followed Jason down the hall to the kitchen.

The kitchen was long and narrow with a table and four chairs at the end closest to the ocean. Amber guessed you could see the ocean from the kitchen during the daytime. At the other end, there were two huge refrigerators. Jason said, "You can eat anything you want in the refrigerator on the left at any time. Just put the dishes in the dishwasher. You have a dishwasher at your house?"

"Of course." Amber might have said more but she yawned so wide that it was impossible.

"Here's some roast beef and turkey and cottage cheese. You want a sandwich? Ice cream? What?" Jason was pulling dishes out of the refrigerator and putting them on the sink. "Potato salad. Leftover chicken. Lots of stuff to eat. Always have fresh vegetables in the crisper. That's Mrs. Murdock's job — to keep that crisper filled. What do you want to eat?"

"Turkey sandwich is fine. And milk. Is there any milk?"

"Whole milk? Nonfat milk? Two-percent milk?" Jason asked. "Pickles?"

Suddenly, Amber realized she was very annoyed at his bossy manner. He was treating her as though she was about three years old. She said, "Any kind of milk. And if you'll just show me where the bread is, I'll make my own sandwich. And I can clean up, you know. You can go on your way."

"Too late," Jason said. "I stopped into the house to get a jacket before I went to the movies. Movie's almost over by now."

This guy was too much! The one real favor he'd done was pick her up and now he was trying to make her feel guilty about that! She didn't even try to keep from sounding annoyed as she said, "I'd really rather make my own sandwich and I'd rather sleep in the pink room."

"Pink room's no good," Jason answered shortly. "Want olives? Cole slaw? There might be some Swiss cheese somewhere. Maybe in the other refrigerator."

"But you said not to go in there."

"I did," Jason agreed. "Makes Mrs. Murdock mad because she says she can't plan meals but she's shopping tomorrow anyway."

"And besides that, you just do whatever you want," Amber challenged. "Don't you?"

Jason laughed shortly and answered, "I wish. But I have been known to graze in the wrong refrigerator. How's that sandwich?"

"Good." Amber was chewing and drinking milk so she said nothing else until she swallowed. Funny how much better a little food made her feel. She decided to stop quarreling and try to act polite. It didn't really matter how he acted — she knew better. She said, "Thanks, it's a good sandwich and I really can put this stuff away."

"I'll wait," Jason said.

As Amber ate, Jason stared at her and finally asked, "Sixteen, you say?"

Amber nodded her head.

Jason frowned again and shook his head in criticism. "Too young. How did Madeline find you?"

Amber washed the remainder of the sandwich down with the last of the milk and rinsed her plate and glass before she put them in the dishwasher. "She offered the job to my best friend, Heather, who is a relative of hers. When Heather got a chance to go to Europe, I got to substitute. Don't you people ever talk to each other?"

"Not much," Jason admitted. "I'm not here much."

"Too bad." Amber smiled sweetly at that news.

Jason laughed at her sarcasm. "A pretty kitten with claws."

"That's a ridiculous thing to say," Amber replied.

He reached out and put his hand under her chin and tilted her head up and said, "It *is* too bad I'm not around more, even though you may not believe that. Tired?"

Amber jerked her head away and then glanced at the kitchen clock, which said ten. "It's eleven o'clock, my time."

"Best go to bed."

"In the pink room," Amber insisted.

"In the guest room. Madeline won't care.

By now, she thinks it was her idea."

Amber sighed and said, "I'm too tired to fight. I'll talk to her myself tomorrow."

"If you can catch her," Jason said shortly. "Can you find your way back to your room?"

Amber nodded and started out of the kitchen. Before she left, she turned and said, "Thanks. You were a big help."

"You're welcome," Jason answered shortly. He was frowning again and clearly thinking about something else.

Amber found the guest room and was in bed and sound asleep in ten minutes.

At eleven-fifteen, she woke because she heard loud voices arguing somewhere in the house. It frightened her and she listened carefully. She couldn't make out what they were saying, but she could hear that it was a man and a woman and that they were very angry.

She got up and pulled her robe on and walked down the hall, following the sound of the voices to the living room. She stood outside the door and listened to Jason and Madeline yelling at each other. Madeline was crying at the same time she yelled, "You're always picking on me. I'm the adult and you're just a kid!"

"Then act like one!" Jason yelled back. "Kyle needs someone to give him some real help. Not some kid who isn't old enough to take care of herself, let alone Kyle. And another thing . . ." Jason stopped in midsentence and called out, "Who's there?"

Amber ran back to her room as quickly as she could. She had heard all she needed to hear. Just as she'd suspected, Jason wanted to get rid of her. And she had been right, he was a *really* rude person.

Chapter 5

Amber woke at seven. She felt guilty for sleeping so late, and she hurried through her shower and dressing. It was seven-thirty when she left her room and went into the main part of the house. This morning, she realized the whole house was a huge one story rectangle that covered the whole building lot. The bedrooms were lined up along each side of the hallway. Nearer to the street, were the laundry room, garage, and driveway.

The large living room spread over almost the full width of the house with only a small portion devoted to the thin kitchen. The living room had red tile floors, which were covered with Oriental rugs, and there was a blend of leather and wood furniture dotted throughout the space. Most of the furniture clustered around a gigantic television set that was flanked on both sides by bookcases.

There was an outside deck with white wrought-iron furniture, and huge planters with geraniums in them. From the living room, Amber could see that the deck staircase led directly to the beach. The whole front of the house was glass and there was a magnificent view of the ocean.

She stepped out onto the porch and opened her arms wide, greeting the day with joy. The beach stretched before her, long, wide, with white sand and a huge blue expanse of ocean. There was nothing but beauty and delight wherever she looked. She was happy to be in California! Happy to be in Malibu. *This is going to be a wonderful summer,* she said to the wind as she hugged herself tight. She slipped back inside the house, moving toward the kitchen with a happiness and a calm joy about the day that was coming up. Whatever came along, she could handle it.

A young girl was sitting at the kitchen table, reading a magazine. She was wearing a striped T-shirt, riding jodhpurs, boots, and a bowler hat. Her light brown hair was long and straight and pulled back in a ponytail and she had exactly the same kind of little round horn-rimmed glasses that Jason wore. She looked up from her magazine and said, "Hi. You the new baby-sitter?"

"I'm Amber Wood." Amber nodded her head.

"You have to fix your own breakfast," the girl said. "Mrs. Murdock gets here at nine and she only makes lunch and dinner — not that anyone actually sits down and eats together or anything. But at least you don't have to cook your own."

"What's your name?" Amber asked. "And where did you get that cereal?"

"Catalina Louise Harvey." The young girl made a face and added, "I'm named after an island — can you imagine that? What if they'd been on Bermuda or the Canary Islands when I was born. Do you think they'd call me Onion or Birdie or something?"

Amber didn't think she was expected to respond to the question. She had an idea that this young woman was used to delivering monologues.

The girl didn't wait for Amber to say anything, but switched the subject back to the kitchen. "You only have to make your own coffee on Sundays and Mondays. Madeline always stays in bed till the cook gets here and John — that's my dad — goes to the office

51

when he's in town. Do you drink coffee?"

"Sometimes," Amber answered. "Do you?"

"No. I drink purified water and herbal teas. I'm a healthy type. Besides, you don't have to cook water and all you have to do is boil it for tea. Anyway, you can call me Catty if you want. You don't have to call me Catalina Louise. In fact, I won't answer if you do. Shall I call you Ambi? As in Ambidextrous? You'll have to be ambidextrous to keep up with the Harvey bunch, you know."

"I think I'll have some coffee and toast," Amber said. She put two slices of bread in the toaster and opened cupboards until she found single packets of instant coffee. She laughed. "See — no cooking involved. I found instant coffee. May I use some of your hot water?"

"Madeline says you come from a normal family, is that true?"

"More or less." Amber smiled at the young girl's question. "I have one mother and one father and one brother. I guess that makes us pretty normal."

"Does your family eat breakfast together?" Catty asked. Her voice changed as she asked the question. The bounce was gone and there was a wistfulness in the question that told Amber that Catty was a lonely young girl.

Amber shook her head. "Not anymore. My

mom has a job in the mornings and my brother goes to school half an hour before I do. So I fix breakfast for my mom and me, and my father and brother have to fix it for themselves. I guess around here, breakfast is pretty much everyone for himself."

"All meals are everyone for himself around here," Catty said. "Sometimes we have dinner together but mostly someone is gone somewhere. My dad works late a lot."

"Well a lot of modern families go their separate ways. My family is pretty old-fashioned."

Catty ignored her and went on, "It's especially bad in the summer because no one has a real schedule. Of course, I have my horses and my brothers have their school. Have you met my brothers yet?"

"I met Jason."

"He's the best," Catty said. "You'll like him the best — everyone does. But Brett is very handsome. I hope you're not the kind of silly boy-crazy girl who just falls for a good-looking face. I suppose at your age it's normal to be boy crazy but I hope you still have good sense."

It was hard for Amber to imagine she wouldn't like Brett better than Jason, but she didn't see any reason to get into any of that this morning. She decided to change the subject. Amber asked, "How old are you, Catty?"

"I'm thirteen. I'm very grown up but I'm not boy crazy. I'm simply very wise for my years. How old are you?"

"Sixteen." Amber laughed and said, "And I'm not sure I can claim wisdom as one of my virtues. But I am a good student."

Catty jumped up and said, "It's eight o'clock. My ride will be here." She ran from the room, leaving her dishes on the table.

Amber finished her toast and coffee and then discovered she was still hungry. She went into the refrigerator, hoping Jason's instructions were correct and that she really could eat anything she wanted. As she looked through the refrigerator, she wondered what they did with all the leftover food they must have each week. She knew enough about cooking to know that you couldn't have this kind of food on hand and never know who was coming to dinner without a lot of waste.

She took some cottage cheese and a nectarine. Then she cut up the fruit and sat down to eat it, along with another cup of coffee.

She reminded herself that she was here to enjoy the summer and take care of Kyle, not to sit in judgment on the Harvey lifestyle. I'm just going to have to adjust to this opulence, she thought and then she giggled at the thought. It should be very, very easy to adjust to wealth like the Harveys'.

Just as Amber finished cleaning her dishes, Madeline Harvey came into the kitchen and smiled. Amber was dazzled by the beautiful woman's smile. She had one of the warmest, most lovely smiles Amber had ever seen. In fact, Madeline was absolutely beautiful with her long lean body and her deep-red hair, which, this morning, she wore pulled back with a big white bow.

Amber noticed that Madeline was wearing a white silk shirt and pants with white thong sandals. Her only jewelry was a pair of large white pearl earrings. She looked like a movie star and Amber wondered if she had been one before she married. She knew Madeline didn't work now.

"There you are, Crystal . . ."

"My name is Amber."

"Yes. Well, I'm a bit absentminded, my dear. Don't be surprised if I call you Pearl or Coral or something else from time to time." She smiled again and said, "You don't look like a Jade or Opal but Crystal does suit you. There's so much light around you, my dear. I'm certain you'll be a wonderful *au pair*."

"I hope so," Amber responded. "I hope we can talk a little bit about exactly what you expect from me. And a little bit about Kyle."

"Of course. I have to leave now so you just introduce yourself to Kyle when he wakes up and take him to the beach for a while. Then he can watch television. Or you can take the car — you can always drive the station wagon if Cook doesn't need it — and go to the movies."

She waved her hand and said, "Have a great day. Will you tell Cook that I want only lean chicken or fish served until further notice? No more red meats, please. It isn't good for us."

Madeline flashed another wonderful smile at Amber and turned from the room. Amber stood looking after her, wondering exactly how she was supposed to take care of Kyle with no more direction than this.

Amber started to wipe off the kitchen counter when an older woman came in and said, "I'll do that. You the new baby-sitter?"

"Amber Wood," she said.

"My name's Mary Murdock," the woman responded. "But some people around here just call me Cook. Can't be bothered to learn my name even though I've been here a year."

"Madeline — Mrs. Harvey — asked me to ask you not to serve red meat until further notice," Amber said.

"Madeline Harvey doesn't eat anything and

she doesn't pay me," the cook said. "Her husband does. So I'd be a fool to take orders from anyone but him, wouldn't I?"

"All right, Mrs. Murdock," Amber said stiffly. "I've given the message." She was beginning to feel very sorry for the way everyone treated Madeline. Jason yelling at her last night was still a shocking memory, and now the cook didn't pay any attention to her orders. Poor Madeline — no wonder she was so vague.

"Kyle up yet?" Mrs. Murdock asked.

"I haven't seen or heard him."

"You'd better get him up," Mrs. Murdock said. "The house cleaners will be here in a minute and they'll want to get into his room."

"All right," Amber said. "Which is his room?"

"He's in the blue room. One down from the white room where you are."

"I'll get him," Amber said. Then she stopped and asked the older woman, "What's he like?"

"Kyle? Poor little guy's too quiet but he's not much trouble. He needs a friend — that's all."

"Doesn't he have any friends?" Amber asked.

"Not that I know of," the cook said crossly. "I never see anyone make any effort to see that he sees other children. In fact, I never see anyone worry about him much at all. You have to keep him out of my way. I've got my menus to plan and I have to go into Beverly Hills to buy groceries." She frowned at Amber and asked, "They tell you to use the station wagon?"

"When you don't need it."

"I need it most of the time," Mrs. Murdock said quickly. "You never know when I'll have to run out and get some milk or something."

Amber managed a smile and once again walked through the living room to the wing of bedrooms. She found the door beyond hers and knocked loudly. When there was no answer, she knocked again and called out, "Kyle?"

Again there was no answer so she pushed the door open and went inside the room. A young boy was sitting on the floor, rolling his small cars along the tiles. She was pleased to see that he looked like a perfectly healthy eight-year-old. He had dark brown hair and a cute face with a pointed chin and big brown eyes. He was actually a darling-looking little boy.

She sat down beside him and said, "Hi Kyle. I'm Amber. I'm your new baby-sitter and I'm going to be here this summer. I'm going to be your friend."

The boy didn't respond and Amber wasn't sure he had actually heard her. She asked, "Kyle, can you hear me? Do you want me to talk louder?"

When there was no response, Amber raised her voice and said in an almost shout, "I'm Amber. I'm going to be your friend."

"Don't yell at him and don't make promises you can't keep." Jason spoke from the open doorway.

Amber was so startled that she jumped and then she turned to face Jason. "Please don't interfere."

"I won't if you promise not to yell. He hears you. Kyle just doesn't always feel like talking. Do you buddy?" Jason's voice was softer as he looked down on his little brother. Then he bent over and pulled Kyle to his feet. He put Kyle's face between his two hands and turned it toward Amber. "This is Amber. She's your baby-sitter today. You stay with her and do what she says. Okay, buddy?"

Kyle nodded his head and asked in a small voice, "You leaving?"

Jason nodded. "Summer school. Remember, I told you about it? But you'll have some fun with Amber. Okay?"

"Okay."

Jason took Amber's hand and placed Kyle's in it. He said, "You don't need to yell. And you don't need to expect a response. Just lead him physically and if he doesn't want to go, don't make him. He is not deaf and he is not stupid. He just doesn't communicate much. And don't think you're going to push him around and change him. This is not a movie called *The Miracle Worker* — it is real life. Got it?"

"You are the rudest human being I have ever met," Amber said in anger.

Jason shrugged. "Haven't got a lot of time. I've got a ten o'clock class. And make sure you both use sunscreen on the beach."

"I'm not an idiot, you know."

Jason looked directly at her. His eyes were brown with green flecks. He was smiling and for a minute, Amber thought he was almost pleasant-looking.

"I've taken good care of my own brother for years," Amber added.

"Well, taking good care of my brother won't be the same," Jason said and then he frowned again. He glanced at his watch and said, "I'm out of here. You have money?"

"Of course I have money!"

"I mean, Harvey money. Did Madeline give you any?"

"No."

Jason reached in his pants and pulled out his wallet. He took out two twenty-dollar bills and handed them to her. "I'll make sure that Dad gives you your own account when he comes home this weekend. If you need anything, ask me. Don't ask Madeline."

"Of course I'll ask Kyle's mother," Amber snapped.

"Then you'll have to go to one of Madeline's séances. Kyle's mother has been dead for years."

"So Madeline is . . ."

"Wife number four. My dad's not crazy about living alone." Jason laughed at the idea. "To give him his due, two of his wives did die. He's only got one he pays alimony to."

"And that's your mother?"

"No," Jason said shortly. "That's Brett's mother. Brett is the other brother."

"Catty told me about him," Amber responded.

"You'll probably fall madly in love with him," Jason said and his voice indicated that he thought they might deserve each other. "He's handsome and polite and all the things I'm not.

On the other hand, if you need help, you'd better call on me."

"I'm not going to need help. And I'm not going to fall for your brother."

As she watched Jason walk away, Amber realized that she was really very, very angry with him. And underneath that anger was a lot of fear about whether or not she was capable of doing the job. A whole summer with the Harveys seemed like a long time if they were as weird as she was beginning to suspect. Of course, Jason was obviously the troublemaker in the bunch. Maybe the others would be a help to her when she got to know them. She took a deep breath and took Kyle's hand. "Come on, Kyle," she said. "We're going to get you some breakfast and then we're going to have fun."

Chapter 6

Breakfast wasn't a success but she did manage to get Kyle to eat a piece of toast and drink half a glass of milk. Mrs. Murdock assured her that was a lot for the early morning hours and Amber decided to be satisfied with that for the first day.

At Mrs. Murdock's suggestion, she packed a lunch of peanut butter and jelly sandwiches and fruit juice in little cardboard boxes. She put the sunscreen and her book in the beach bag and took Kyle's hand, walking out the side door of the kitchen and down some stairs to the beach. He carried a large metal dump truck and a small shovel.

Of course, she had been aware of the pounding of the surf and had seen the ocean from the deck this morning. She wasn't, however, prepared for the startling size of the ocean that stretched for miles and miles on either side of them and out to a horizon line that she could barely make out because the blue of the sky and the blue of the sea were almost the same color.

She stood quite still for a long time, simply letting the beauty and grandeur of the Pacific Ocean sink in. Everything seemed so different up close. The sand was so white and the sky and ocean were so blue. Amber was most surprised by the smell of the salty air. Somehow, she'd imagined the sea would smell more like the way it smelled when it rained, but the Pacific Ocean smelled like salt and lemons. It was a wonderful smell.

"Isn't this beautiful!" she exclaimed. Kyle didn't say anything but he tugged at her hand so she decided to believe he was communicating with her. She laughed and said, "You can't imagine how thrilling this is for me. All my life I've dreamed of seeing the Pacific Ocean and we're actually here."

She looked down at the eight-year-old and saw absolutely no comprehension on his face. She explained, "We don't have an ocean where I live. We have big lakes but the waves aren't like this and it's all very different. We don't have palm trees either. Where shall we sit?"

Kyle didn't exactly answer but he led her to a small mound of sand directly in front of the Harvey house and they spread their towels out on the warm sand. She pulled out the sunscreen and said, "Let me put this on you, Kyle."

He sat still and let her rub the lotion into his fair skin. She kept up a running commentary about the beach, the sun, the sky, and the ocean. She didn't ask him questions because she'd already found out that he didn't answer her, but she still felt it was probably important to talk to him. If he even noticed, he didn't give any sign and very shortly, he left the towel and went down to the wet sand where he began to dig a hole.

Amber watched him dig for a while. She watched him until she was certain he was going to be all right. He obviously was used to being at the beach and the waves weren't high so she began to read her book. As she finished each page, she looked up, to make sure Kyle was all right. An hour later, she was on page 70 and Kyle was still in the same spot, still digging the same hole.

It was eleven o'clock and the beach began to fill up with people. Amber put the book down and looked out at the crowd. How did they get there? They couldn't all live in these expensive houses. How far did they have to walk to get to this secluded strip of sand?

By eleven-thirty, there didn't seem to be a bare spot on the sand and Amber could see several other children about Kyle's age running and jumping in and out of the waves. Their exuberance showed her how quiet Kyle really was as he continued to dig in his own private world. As far as Amber could see, Kyle wasn't building anything and he didn't seem to notice the other children, or much of anything else that was going on around him.

She called out to Kyle several times, but he didn't seem to hear her. Finally, she walked down to the water's edge where he was digging. She sat down beside him and asked, "Is that a tunnel?" Kyle didn't answer, so she asked, "Would you like some lunch?" Then she said, "Don't you think we should put some more sunscreen on your back?"

When all of these questions brought absolutely no response, Amber remembered that Jason had told her simply to take his hand. She reached out and put one of his sandy little hands in hers and stood up. He didn't resist and when she tugged gently, he stood up beside her. "Let's go eat," she said and led him back to the beach towels.

Suddenly, Kyle broke away and started running toward the house. Amber was so startled by his sudden motion that she stood up also in case she had to run after him. She looked toward the house; she saw that Jason Harvey was standing on the deck.

She picked up Kyle's truck and the towels and walked more slowly toward the house. As she walked, she was conscious of Jason's eyes on her and she was glad she'd worn her new blue bathing suit. She knew she looked good in it and it gave her confidence to face this angry young man.

When she got to the deck of the Harvey house, she was out of breath. Jason frowned and said, "You're sunburned. That's stupid. Why didn't you use sunscreen?"

Amber glowered at him and didn't answer. He wasn't her boss so she didn't have to explain that she had used sunscreen. Her light skin was bound to need lots of protection.

Jason frowned and shook his head. "You're so fair-skinned you'll never be able to spend more than an hour or two on the beach. And that's all Kyle likes to do. You'd better stay inside out of the sun the rest of the day. I'm taking Kyle to the movies. We'll pick something up for dinner. Mrs. Murdock has the afternoon off. Will you see that Catty eats something?"

"I thought you had a class." Amber frowned at him exactly the way he was frowning at her.

"I thought I ought to check on you. Good thing, too, because you're both burned. Another hour and you'd be bacon."

Amber was furious but all she did was ask, "Do you know when your moth . . . do you know when Madeline will be back?"

"Didn't she tell you? She flew to San Francisco to meet Dad this morning. They'll be gone for about three days," Jason answered. "No. I don't suppose she did tell you."

"No." Amber tried to keep the disappointment out of her voice as she said, "I wanted to talk to her — about Kyle and about my duties."

Jason frowned and shook his head. "You won't get much out of her. What do you want to know?"

"What am I supposed to do?" she asked. "Do I talk to him? Or do I let him stay silent? Am I supposed to read to him? And what are my hours? Do I have twenty-four-hour duty or what?"

"Bored with the job already, Goldilocks?"

"Don't call me that!"

Jason laughed and said, "I won't. It's just that you looked exactly like her when I first saw you. Coming up that lawn, looking so scared, as though you'd eaten all the porridge and broken the chairs. I just thought it was funny."

"I don't like to be laughed at." Amber wasn't sure whether she was so upset because Jason was laughing at her or because she was so perplexed about what to do about Kyle. All she knew was that so far, this job hadn't been a lot of fun.

"You ought to take a shower and put on some cream," Jason began. "Maybe take a nap."

"I can take care of myself," Amber snapped. She turned and went toward her room. She couldn't help thinking that Jason was the bossiest person she'd ever met and she really didn't trust herself to say anymore to him. He was so rude but the real trouble was that when she was around him, she was also rude. Whatever made Jason such a monster appeared to be catching!

Chapter 7

That afternoon, Amber slept for three hours and by the time she awoke, Catty was making her own dinner. Amber came into the kitchen just as Catty was lifting spaghetti out of the pan onto her plate. She was using a slotted spoon and the sauce dribbled onto the stove and sink.

"I'm sorry," Amber said. "I was supposed to fix your supper and I fell asleep."

"That's all right," Catty said. She sat with both elbows on the table and slurped spaghetti in as though she were a six-year-old.

"Did you have a good day with your horses?"

"Yes. I'm reading a book now," Catty answered. She finished her spaghetti and picked up her book and walked out of the kitchen. Amber stared at the messy plate, the dribbles on the stove and sink, and considered calling

Catty back to clean up after herself. Then she remembered that she was only hired to watch Kyle and that Catty's irresponsibility wasn't her business. She shrugged, picked up the plate, rinsed it off, and put it in the dishwasher.

As she wiped the counter clean, Catty came back and said, "You don't have to clean up. Mrs. Murdock does that in the morning."

"It's so much easier to do it now."

Catty shrugged and took an apple out of the refrigerator. "Suit yourself." Then she left the kitchen and Amber decided she wasn't really hungry yet. She would wait until later and make herself a sandwich.

She went out on the deck and sat in a chair, watching the sun begin to set. It was a giant round globe of red and the whole sky was streaked with pinks and oranges.

As she sat on the deck, the wind ruffled her hair and caressed her face. She thought that the beach was the most beautiful thing she'd ever seen and she tried to tell herself how glad she was to be in California. She reminded herself that this job was an opportunity to see something of life. She had wanted adventure and excitement and there was no sense getting discouraged so quickly. After all, there was bound to be a period of adjustment.

Then she sighed and wished the adjustment

period would hurry ▮▮▮▮▮▮ over. She was
certain she was still ▮▮▮ about not having
anyone meet her at the airport and Kyle was
certainly very quiet. Madeline was strange and
Jason was bossy and rude. Even Catty seemed
self-centered and spoiled, but she was the best
of the Harvey bunch, so far. Amber began to
wonder what the older brother Brett would be
like. Jason thought she would fall in love with
him — that must mean that Brett was nicer
than his brother. Of course, it wouldn't take
much to be nicer than Jason.

Funny how Kyle clung to his brother. But
then, Jason seemed so nice to Kyle. He really
only seemed to be terribly cross with Madeline
and her. Maybe he doesn't like women, she
thought. Maybe some woman broke his heart
and he's never gotten over it. The idea entertained her even if she did think it was
nonsense.

When the sun went down, it was cool and
the breeze was almost cold. She went to her
room and picked up a sweater, took off her
shoes, and walked out onto her own private
patio. She discovered she could get down to
the beach by climbing over a small fence and
dropping about two feet onto the sand. That
gave her a sense of freedom and privacy that
she needed.

She walked directly down to the water's edge and followed the shoreline about two miles toward the Malibu pier. She didn't dare admit even to herself how good it felt to be away from the Harvey house. She passed a couple of groups of teenagers who seemed to be having a great time and a few lone walkers like herself.

The sun was completely gone by the time she returned to the house and the wind was cold. She knew she could climb back into her room unnoticed but it seemed simpler to enter by way of the kitchen. She brushed off her bare feet and started across the large living room toward her bedroom.

Jason and Kyle were eating dinner in front of the television in the living room. For the first time, Amber realized that the house was laid out in such a way that everyone had to pass through the living room to get anywhere. They might not communicate much, but they had to cross paths several times a day. She tried to walk quickly, so as to cross the wide expanse unnoticed, but it was no good.

Jason called out, "Get a plate and join us. We're having a picnic."

Amber supposed the invitation was really a command so she went into the kitchen and found a plate, fork, and knife and a Coke. She returned to the living room and sat down on the couch in front of the television. There was a big box of fried chicken and cold potato salad on the coffee table. Apparently rich people didn't eat any differently from ordinary ones — at least Jason Harvey didn't.

Jason and Kyle were sitting on the floor in front of the television, watching an old black and white movie. *"Son of King Kong,"* Jason announced as he bit into a chicken leg and grabbed his little brother's arm and said, "Watch out! Here comes the scary part!"

Amber ate in silence, not really watching the movie but letting her thoughts drift. She felt relaxed and peaceful after her long walk on the beach and Jason didn't seem so angry this evening. She liked the way he was with Kyle and she decided to give him another chance. Maybe he would settle down and behave decently if she didn't overreact.

When the movie was over, she asked Jason, "What movie did you see this afternoon?"

"Bambi," Jason answered. "They have a special Disney film festival going on Monday afternoons at school. I've decided to take Kyle to all of them."

"That's nice."

"Bambi" is a little sad," Jason said. "We

thought *Son of King Kong* would be a good balance. Want to see something special? What's your favorite movie?" Jason pointed to the bookcase on either side of the huge television screen. For the first time, Amber noticed that one of them was completely filled with videos. The Harveys had more videos than most people had books.

"I don't know," Amber answered.

"They *do* have movies in Milwaukee, don't they?" Jason offered her popcorn and she took a handful. As she did so, her hand brushed his and she dropped popcorn onto the floor. She was embarrassed and she quickly picked it up and put it on her plate. He offered her more but she shook her head no.

Amber stood up and said, "If you're finished, I'll take your plates."

Jason shook his head and said, "Come on, sit with us a while."

Amber sat back down, but she really couldn't think of anything she wanted to say to Jason.

"Kyle tells me you were reading a book today?"

"Yes," Amber answered. She was a little surprised to realize that Kyle must really talk with Jason when they were alone. Why was her heart beating as though she'd done something wrong? All she'd done was read for a while. Surely that was allowed?

"Kyle, go get me another Coke, will you?" Jason requested.

Amber knew he was going to say something to make her mad, but she wasn't sure what it would be. She steeled herself for whatever he would say as Kyle left the room.

"You're expected to be on duty twenty-four hours a day unless you make special arrangements," Jason said. "Kyle's a good swimmer, but he has this thing about the ocean. I guess he's afraid of it. Anyway, he doesn't like to go in and you shouldn't make him. Stay right by his side if he does decide he wants to swim and watch him all the time."

"You told me that."

"And when he's near the shoreline — even if he's playing in the sand — you're supposed to be watching him. So no reading or fooling around with guys on the beach. All right?"

"What do you think I was doing?" Amber asked angrily. "I didn't talk to anyone and I checked him every time I turned a page."

"Just be careful," Jason said shortly. "You could be reading or get to talking to someone and lose Kyle."

"Kyle sits absolutely still!" Amber could

hear her voice rising in volume. What was it about him that made her sound so strident?

"We hope you'll help him get over that. And another thing, don't talk about Kyle as though he's not in the room when he *is* in the room. It lowers his self-esteem."

"I've only been here one day," Amber protested. "If your brother's self-esteem is low, it can't be my fault."

"I'm not blaming you," Jason said. "I'm explaining. You asked about duties. I'm explaining them."

"I'd rather wait for your mother or father," Amber said. "You act like you're the boss, but you're not much older than I am — are you?"

Jason just frowned and looked out at the ocean.

"How old are you?"

"I'm light years older than you'll ever be," he answered. "Girls like you — I know the type. One of these days you'll be fifty years old and you still won't have a clue."

"And you'll be the same ridiculous windbag you are now!"

Kyle came in with the Coke and looked from one to the other. It was clear he'd heard them yelling at each other. Jason said, "You've made him nervous."

"You're talking about him as though he isn't here," she pointed out.

"Come on, Kyle," Jason said. "Let's go check out your cars." He took his brother's hand and led him away, leaving Amber to stare at the blank television screen.

She was fuming with anger, and she went into her room and slammed the door behind her. She was never going to be able to last a week on this job and she might as well face it. She would just go home tomorrow and admit that she'd made a mistake.

The minute she made a definite decision to leave, she felt better. She packed all her belongings in her bag and then went to the telephone to call her parents and tell them she was coming home. She knew they would be upset, but they wouldn't blame her and they would be glad to see her. She suspected they might even be relieved she was coming home so early. She dialed the number without hesitation, telling herself it was better to get out of this mess early instead of later.

The phone rang and rang and no one answered. Finally, she decided that her parents had taken Tim to camp a day early. They'd talked about taking a short vacation and apparently that's what they'd decided to do. That meant no one would be home till Wednesday night and it was only Monday.

She went out onto her balcony and sat down, tilting her head up so she could see the black sky. Very quickly she began to see that it wasn't all black. It had a deep blue-gray cast that was different from the purple-black of the ocean.

It was certainly beautiful and she began to wish things were different. She hated to leave California after only three days. But things — or more accurately, Jason Harvey — were what they were.

Chapter 8

When Amber woke in the morning she still was determined to leave, but she decided she would have to call her parents first. She didn't want to ask Jason to buy her airplane ticket and she didn't really even know if he had the authority. She would get her parents to buy the ticket and she'd pay them back from the money she already had saved.

Amber sighed and began to brush her long, red-blond hair. She was certain Jason would be happy to buy her a ticket if he could. She stared into the mirror. How could she have gotten into so much trouble so fast? She knew that things were mostly wrong because of the chemistry between her and Jason, but he was the only one who was ever around. She wondered if things would have been different if it had been Brett who picked her up that first day.

She dressed quickly and went into the kitchen. Jason was nowhere in sight so she went into Kyle's room and got him to come out for breakfast. Kyle favored her with a tiny smile as she took his hand and said, "Oatmeal time."

When they got into the kitchen, Mrs. Murdock was just leaving and she said, "Do you want anything special from the grocery store? I'm on my way." Then she frowned and asked, "Can you fix the little one some breakfast?"

"Sure," Amber answered. She turned to Kyle and asked, "Oatmeal?"

Kyle didn't answer but Mrs. Murdock answered for him. "He eats that better than anything. Poor little tyke. Skin and bones. No one cares about him and he knows it. If ever I saw a neglected child, this is it . . ."

"Mrs. Murdock," Amber interrupted quickly, "I think Kyle and I both need a stronger sunscreen. Would you bring us a bottle of number forty-five? And maybe a Chap Stick. It seems as though this air dries out my lips." The cook's constant harping on Kyle's being unloved had to hurt him.

When the cook left the room, Amber made breakfast and served it, keeping up a constant cheerful chatter to Kyle. Then she made a lunch and said, "Come on, Kyle. Let's go to the beach."

They put their towels down in exactly the same place as yesterday and Amber said, "I'd like to take a swim. Come with me?"

Kyle looked kind of scared so she said, "I'll hold your hand. Come on."

She took Kyle's hand and they ran down to the water's edge. The water was sharp and cold and Amber jumped up and down as it lapped her ankles and then up to her knees. She was shivering and she knew she would feel better if she were wet all over so she said, "Come on, Kyle, let's dunk!"

She bobbed up and down and got all wet, but she couldn't persuade Kyle to go any farther into the water than his knees. "I'll hold you," she offered, but Kyle refused by shaking his head.

They fooled around in the shallow water for a while and then he tugged at her hand and she allowed herself to be led out of the water.

Kyle dropped down on the sand and began digging. Amber went back into the water for a while, but she really couldn't swim and keep her eye on Kyle at the same time so she gave up and returned to shore. "Come on with me, Kyle. I need to put more sunscreen on your back."

The little boy went with her to their towels and when they got there, a handsome young man with blond hair and a wonderful smile was sitting right beside her towels. He grinned at her and said, "Hi. You must be the kid's new baby-sitter."

"I'm the Harvey *au pair*," she corrected and, immediately, she was sorry she'd answered at all.

"I'm Mike Fortman," he said and held out his hand.

Amber had to drop down onto her knees to shake his hand. She asked, "Are you a friend of the Harveys?"

"Neighbor," he answered with a big grin. "I live next door — in that white house." He pointed to the three-story white wood-and-glass house next door. It was built on a very narrow lot and seemed to tower over its neighbors. It looked very modern and imposing and expensive.

"Your house blocks my view," Amber said, and then she immediately added, "I'm not complaining. I just mentioned it." Somehow, she'd only thought of the white wall as a block, she'd never thought of people living there.

"You going to introduce yourself?" Mike asked. "You do have a name?"

"I'm Amber Wood," she said. "And this young man is Kyle Harvey."

"Got yourself a good-looking nanny, kid," Mike said comfortably and smiled at the young boy. "Good for you." He reached out to ruffle Kyle's hair but the boy ducked.

Mike looked surprised and then laughed cheerfully. "Where you from, Amber?"

"Milwaukee, Wisconsin," Amber answered. If he was a neighbor, then he wasn't a stranger, she reasoned. Surely it was all right to speak to a neighbor. And he was absolutely the best-looking boy! He wasn't real tall, but he was broad-shouldered and had the best tan she'd ever seen. She guessed that he must spend some part of every day on the beach.

"This your first day on the job?" Mike asked.

"I flew in Saturday. I got the job because my best friend is a sort of relative of the Harveys and she was invited to go to Europe for the summer. So I got her job."

"Lucky me."

Amber stared at him in confusion. Was he flirting with her? That was almost too exciting to be true. It was also very disconcerting. She wasn't sure she even knew how to flirt.

"So what time do you get off? Can I pick you up at six?"

"I don't know." She flushed and explained, "I mean I'm not certain what my hours are yet. I'm not sure I get time off. I think I'm supposed to be there."

"They can't do that." Mike's voice was deep and he rolled his words out, as though he knew a lot more than he was saying. She wondered if he could be an actor.

"Why not?" Amber asked.

"It's against the law," Mike said and laughed. "Anyway, I doubt the Harveys intend to keep you on a slave labor schedule. I'll pick you up at six? All right?"

"Not all right," Amber answered quickly. Then she wished she hadn't been so vehement. "I mean, I'll find out what my hours are." She felt quite young and foolish sitting beside this handsome young man. He was so smooth and so good-looking that she felt much shyer than she usually was.

Mike smiled and when he smiled, his light blue eyes seemed to dance and the laugh lines crinkled in the cutest way she'd ever seen. He had a wonderful smile and a wonderful voice and she liked him. She smiled back at him.

He said, "That's better. I knew you weren't as serious a character as you pretended. I'll bet I'll find out you have a great sense of humor when we get to know each other."

She flushed again, not sure what she should say next. But at least he planned to get to know her!

Amber smiled and wished she could think of something clever to say. Mike was exactly the kind of boy she'd dreamed of meeting in California. Now that she had met him, she was practically tongue-tied!

"Let's go," Kyle said. Amber smiled at Mike and shrugged her shoulders to indicate she was disappointed. She picked up her things and said, "Got to go."

"Can't we make a date?" Mike asked.

"I'll see you here again," Amber answered. "I'm really not sure about my hours." She didn't want to seem too eager. On the other hand, she didn't want to seem too standoffish. She sighed and shrugged again. Then she began to run toward the house. Most of all, she didn't want Jason to be mad at her for not doing her job — which was really silly since she'd decided to leave tomorrow.

She realized she wasn't making sense and she also recognized that part of her confusion came from meeting Mike. Why would she want to go home and miss the chance to get to know him better? There simply weren't boys as cute as Mike in Milwaukee. And he had been flirting with her and he did live next door. So there was a good chance they would see more of each other if she stayed. Of course, there was no way of knowing whether she would really like Mike when she got to know him. No matter what developed, she was certain that Mike was interested in knowing her better. She had to be honest and admit that she was just as interested in getting to know him.

Chapter 9

Mike was on the beach when Amber and Kyle got there the next day and she was really glad to see him. He waved and said, "Over here."

She dropped her towel next to his and Kyle ran down to the water's edge with his truck. Amber knew she looked good in her blue bikini and she was glad she felt pretty as she dropped down onto the sand next to Mike.

"How's the baby-sitting going?" he asked.

"Better," Amber said and she laughed out loud. "Kyle was never the problem. And since all the others are away, it's been very quiet and peaceful."

"You're all alone in the house?"

"Not really," Amber said. "There's a thirteen-year-old girl. I almost never see her because she spends all her time with horses, and then there are two boys in college. One of them is home some and I haven't met the other one yet."

"He probably doesn't know what he's missing," Mike said. "When he gets a look at you, he'll be home every night for supper."

Amber flushed and smiled. She'd never had a boy flirt with her quite this smoothly and she was not ashamed to admit that she liked it. "What about you?" she asked. "Do you go to school?"

"In the winter," Mike said. "I'm at Davis — or at least I will be this fall. I almost went to the University of Florida, but there were too many sharks in the water to suit me. At Davis I can surf and get an education. How about you?"

"High school," Amber admitted. She waited to see what his reaction would be. He didn't seem to mind.

"I'm hoping to go somewhere interesting for college," she said. "What is Davis like?"

"Great school," Mike answered. "Good town, too. Everyone likes it there and it's not too hard to get into. I mean, all the California universities are hard to get into but Davis is easier than UCLA or Berkeley. You might check it out."

"I will," Amber said. Then she rose and

said, "I'd better check on Kyle now."

"Want to take a drive?" Mike offered. "We could go up the coast to Zuma Beach. That's were I usually hang out. Better surf."

"I can't," Amber answered. "I have to stay here."

Mike laughed aloud and said, "The Harveys have really got you on a short leash, haven't they?"

"I have a job," Amber said and then she frowned as she remembered that she was probably leaving the job. But that didn't influence her decision. She had responsibilities and she had to meet them. Mike would have to understand that.

"Come on," Mike said. He jumped up and took her hand and walked down to the water's edge holding her hand. Once there, he squatted down beside Kyle and asked, "How's it going, big boy?"

Kyle continued to pile damp sand into his truck and ignored Mike completely.

"Listen kid, Amber and I want to take a drive. Want to come along?"

Kyle continued to dig and Mike turned to Amber and asked her in a low voice, "Couldn't you just leave him here for an hour or so? He'll be all right, you know."

"I could never do that." Amber was shocked

at the suggestion, but then she decided that Mike probably didn't know anything about children.

"Well how about if we just make a date to meet tonight. What time does the thirteen-year-old get home?"

"Mike, this is my job. I can't just walk away from it." As she spoke, Amber realized that she sounded as though she was planning to stay.

"All right, beautiful girl," Mike said and he leaned over and brushed sand off her cheek. "We've got all summer and I promised some friends I'd meet them down the road. I'll catch you later."

He was leaning very close to her. She wanted to pull away and she didn't want to at the same time. She felt a little uncomfortable and closed her eyes to avoid his gaze. The minute she closed her eyes, he leaned over and kissed her. His lips on hers felt like nothing she had ever experienced before, but she drew away quickly, saying, "I wish you'd let me go."

"I will," Mike said and he was smiling. She looked up into his blue eyes and felt as though her knees were going weak. She felt self-conscious and silly and at the same time. He said, "But I'll be around. You can count on it."

Mike dropped her hand and turned and ran up the sand, pausing only long enough to pick up his shirt and towel and then go into his own house. Amber watched the handsome young man run, noticing how strong his legs were and how broad his shoulders were. She wondered if he had meant it when he called her beautiful.

Just then, Kyle looked up and smiled at her and asked, "Want to dig?"

She dropped down beside him and asked, "Why not?"

Amber was honest enough to admit that it was the kiss that changed her mind. The minute Mike's lips touched hers, she had known that she would give this job every chance.

It was foolish to give up so easily, she reasoned. After all, any job was bound to have its good and bad points. And if Jason was a bad point on this one, then the Harveys' neighbor, Mike, was definitely a good one.

Amber and Kyle had the house to themselves the next couple of days. The Harveys decided not to come back until Friday and Catty was staying with friends. Neither Jason nor the mysterious Brett showed up at all and Mrs. Murdock said she often didn't see either one for days.

Amber used the time to get a little closer

to Kyle. She talked to him a lot and she didn't ask questions unless she had to. Instead, she told him stories about her home in Wisconsin and about her brother Tim. Kyle listened even though he pretended not to and Amber knew she was making some progress.

On Friday morning, it was quite cool and the fog was thick along the coast, but Kyle obviously wanted to go out onto the beach anyway. Mrs. Murdock assured Amber that the fog would "burn off" so they bundled up and went out onto the beach as they were accustomed to doing.

Amber dropped the lunch and her book on their towels in the familiar spot and suggested, "It's too cold to dig in that wet sand. Let's take a walk, okay, Kyle?"

It was still cool and they both had sweatshirts on over their suits. Amber's sweatshirt was bright yellow and oversized. It had a photo of a rock star on the back. It was brand-new and Amber felt self-conscious wearing it, but her friend Heather had insisted she buy it, swearing that it was trendy and would look great on Malibu beach.

They walked a long way and it got hot. Amber stripped off her sweatshirt and then remembered she'd left the sunscreen in the lunch bag. She put the sweatshirt over her shoulders and called out to Kyle, "We'd better turn back."

He pointed to the pier in front of them and said, "Hamburgers."

Since it was the first thing he'd ever directly requested, Amber agreed. She was thankful she'd tucked a twenty-dollar bill into her sweatshirt pocket.

They went out onto the old wooden structure to a hamburger stand at the very end. Kyle pointed again and said, "Hamburger and fries and Coke."

"Please," Amber reminded him. She ordered the requested food for Kyle and a Coke for herself. They found a bench and sat down while Kyle ate his hamburger. He finished it all and Amber asked in an amused voice, "So this is what you really like to eat, huh, Kyle?"

He smiled shyly at her and nodded his head. Amber was delighted that they were actually conversing. She felt as though someone had given her a great gift and she smiled widely at him.

It was hot on the walk back and Amber could feel she was getting burned. She was angry at herself because she'd forgotten the sunscreen. And she was already angry at Jason for what he would say when he saw Kyle's sunburn.

When they got back to their towels, Mike was sitting about ten feet away with several other teenagers. He stood up and came over to her, taking her by the hand and saying, "Hi Amber. Come meet my friends."

It was the first time she'd seen Mike since he'd kissed her and she had been sort of looking for him on the beach since then. Now that he was here, she felt very shy. "Hi," she said and then she flushed and asked, "how are you?"

"We've been surfing in Zuma lately. I made my friends come here so I could see you. I guess I could just go knock on the door of my neighbor's house, but it seemed weird. Can I call you?"

"Sure."

"What's your number?"

"I don't know," Amber admitted. She turned to Kyle and asked, "What's the phone number here?"

Kyle said, "I'm hot. Let's go."

"Find out and tell me tomorrow," Mike said. Then he tugged on her wrist and said, "My friends are waiting. Do you surf?"

Amber laughed and said, "I told you I'm from the midwest. No oceans. Look, I'd love to meet your friends some other day but we've got to go inside now. We're both really sunburned." By this time, Kyle had gone back down to the water's edge and had started digging in the sand. Amber knew she needed to get him home and in the shower before he was too badly burned. She could feel her own skin tightening and burning.

Mike didn't let go of her hand, instead he tugged her toward the group and said, "This is Amber from New Jersey. She's the girl I was telling you about. Want to come to a party tonight, Amber?"

"I'm from Wisconsin," she answered and then she laughed. "At least you got my name right."

Mike smiled at her and again she noticed the darling way his eyes crinkled when he smiled. And he had the whitest teeth she'd ever seen. She looked at his perfectly even golden tan. "Don't you ever get sunburned?" she asked.

"No. I'm used to it," Mike answered. "But you look a little bit like a tourist today. Sit down with us."

Amber turned and smiled at the group. There were about ten kids sitting together, laughing and talking, and none of them seemed to be paying any attention to her or Mike. A couple of girls were playing cards and she noticed how beautiful one of the girls was. She had long black hair and beautiful features. All the kids were nearly as good-looking as Mike and they all had great bodies and golden tans.

"I've really got to go," she said to Mike and tried to withdraw her hand but he held it tight.

The girl with the long black hair laughed and it was a delightful, full laugh. Amber wished with all her heart she could stay and get acquainted with the group because they seemed to be having so much fun. She really missed talking and laughing with her friends, but Jason had been very clear that when she was on duty she wasn't to socialize. She tried to pull away from Mike again, but he held her even tighter.

"Let her go," the girl with the long black hair called out in a definite command. Amber wondered why the girl had spoken. Was she Mike's girlfriend? If so, why was Mike holding *her* hand?

All this time, she had one eye on Kyle who was down by the ocean's edge, digging. She was horrified to see that a big wave came crashing in and splashed all over Kyle, getting him wet and knocking him down. Amber jerked her hand away and said, "I've really got to go!"

When she got down to the sand, Kyle was rubbing his eyes and he obviously had sand in them. He looked surprised, scared, and wet, and for a minute, Amber thought he was going to cry. She wiped the sand from his face with the edge of her T-shirt and said, "I think we'd better go in now."

He shook his head and squatted down to return to digging the same hole, which was now completely filled with water. Amber knew it wouldn't be long before another wave came crashing in on them both. "Tide's coming in," she said.

She squatted down beside him and said, "I'm sorry, Kyle. But we have to go in now. We can come back tomorrow."

He pretended he didn't hear her so she took his hand and led him all the way back to the house. Once there, she insisted that he shower and she put sunburn cream on his skin. With any luck, he wouldn't burn. Then she left him in his room with his cars and went into her own room to repair the damage to her own fair skin.

She was so burned she would probably peel. What was worse, she was so burned that it was very obvious. Her skin on her face looked weird because her eyes were still very light but her cheeks and nose were bright red. She frowned at her reflection and said aloud, "It will be just your luck to have Jason show up today."

He'd been away for two days and she could

only hope he would stay away long enough so Kyle's most recent memory wouldn't be about getting knocked over by a wave. For once, she supposed that Jason would be within his rights to criticize her. Her instructions were that she should be with him all the time he was in the water and she'd done exactly what Jason told her not to — she'd let her social life interfere with her job.

That afternoon, she decided to take Kyle for a short drive up the coast if she could get Mrs. Murdock to part with the car. She went into the kitchen and asked her for the keys to the station wagon. "I'm going to use it," the cook said promptly.

Amber sighed. So far, Mrs. Murdock had resisted every attempt to share the car. It was beginning to look as if she and Kyle were stuck at home and on their own for the summer. She wasn't sure exactly how to keep this quiet little boy entertained all summer. In fact, no one had been in the house all day except Kyle and Mrs. Murdock.

She went back into the living room and asked, "Do you want to play a game? Do you play cards? Monopoly? How about if I read to you? Do you have books?"

Kyle pointed to the huge shelf of videos and said, *"King Kong."* Amber gave up, found

King Kong, and pushed it into the machine. One more movie and it would be time for dinner. And after dinner the sun would be down and maybe they could take a walk on the beach, if Jason didn't come in and take Kyle away from her.

It was Friday evening and Amber had expected the Harveys home. She had also half-expected Brett or Jason to drop by. But no one showed up except Catty who only came by long enough to pick up fresh clothes and go off with her friend again.

"Do your mother and father know where you are going to be?" Amber asked her.

"Does it look like they care?" Catty answered with a toss of her thick ponytail.

"Write the phone number and the name of your friend down," Amber demanded. "They'll be in later and they'll worry."

"They don't care," Catty said. "They let me go wherever I want in the summertime."

"I care," Amber insisted. She planted herself firmly in front of the doorway.

"Ask Brett if you don't believe me," Catty said.

"Brett?"

"Bet you didn't know he was here, did you?" Catty said triumphantly. "When he's here, he's the boss, isn't he?"

"I suppose so." Amber was quite unsure what to do now.

"I'll go get his permission," Catty said. The young girl ran down the hallway and came back with a tall young man.

In the dim light, Amber could see his dark hair and muscular body. He definitely was good-looking. She wondered why he didn't come in and say hello.

Catty demanded, "Tell her."

"Catty can go to the Williamsons'. They're old friends and I know the number," Brett said. He turned and went back to his room, but not before he took a long, cool look at Amber.

Amber couldn't resist asking, "How long has he been here?"

Catty shrugged and said, "He comes and goes. Brett studies a lot. You probably shouldn't disturb him. He's not as friendly as Jason."

Amber didn't say what she was thinking, she simply returned to her movie, knowing she'd lost yet another battle at the Harvey house. But she had to admit that it didn't seem as important as it had earlier this week. Mike sort of balanced out the picture.

She thought about Brett for a moment. Everyone talked about how handsome he was, but he wasn't as good-looking as Mike.

When the movie was over, Amber asked Kyle if he would walk on the beach with her and he said, *"Mighty Joe Young."* She felt lonely and a little scared as she watched the old movie with Kyle. What would she do after they ran out of gorilla movies?

At eight o'clock, she put him to bed and then she went to her room to put some more cream on her tender skin. As she rubbed the cream into her arms and legs she muttered to herself, "I look like a lightly done lamb chop." It felt pretty weird to be talking out loud to herself and she wished she had a friend to call. She and Heather talked nearly every night at home and she had other friends back in Wisconsin — girls like herself who were interested in school and future careers . . . and boys. She thought about calling up Heather, but she remembered she was in Europe and probably unreachable.

Then she thought about Mike and wondered if he could be a friend. He had such a nice friendly smile and seemed to take things easily. He would probably understand if she called and said she was lonely. She called information and asked for the Fortman residence in Malibu and was happy to find out they didn't have an unlisted number. One of the things she'd read about Malibu was that *everyone* had an unlisted number.

She punched in the first four digits of his number and then stopped with her hand in midair. How could she call a boy she barely knew — even one who had kissed her on the beach. And what would Mike think if she called him up and said, "Hi, you're the only person I know in Malibu, so I thought we could talk for a while . . ."

Amber laughed out loud at that idea. She read for a while and went to sleep early, after telling herself she would just have to do the best she could until Mr. and Mrs. Harvey came back from their trip. When they returned, she could talk to them and maybe get some new ideas about how to keep Kyle entertained and happy.

Chapter 10

"But, Crystal, that's why we hired you." Madeline Harvey raised her lovely hands in mock despair, smiled appealingly, and shrugged. At that moment, her husband walked into the room and she turned to him and put one of those hands on his arm. "We're due at the Chomskys' for drinks in an hour. I have to change."

Madeline swept from the room as though she were a ballet dancer moving across a brightly lit stage. Her soft silk pants swirled around her ankles and she wore a long scarf that trailed down the back of her silk blouse. Everything she wore was pale lemon and there were two gardenias in the back of her auburn hair.

Amber sighed. The Harveys had been home two days and she'd finally managed to corner Madeline to talk to her about Kyle. But Madeline obviously wasn't going to be any help. She'd just said, "Do your best," and patted her on the arm. Amber sighed again and she knew that the second sigh was partly because she was beginning to understand that talking to Madeline was like talking to the wind and partly because she knew that she would never be as beautiful as Kyle's stepmother was. She supposed when you looked like that, some things came too easily.

As his wife swept from the room, John Harvey sat down across from Amber and crossed his legs and took a sip of his drink. "So how do you like California, Crystal?"

She was annoyed. She had already tried to talk to him about Kyle and he'd told her to talk to Madeline. Now he seemed to be making polite conversation. John Harvey looked like an older, handsomer version of his son Jason. The most disappointing thing about him was that he didn't seem to have as much interest in Kyle as Jason did. She corrected him sharply, "My name is Amber."

"I thought Madeline called you Crystal?"

"She did. My name is Amber and I love California but I don't know what to do to keep Kyle entertained. It isn't good for him to watch movies five or six hours a day, you know. And we can only stay on the beach a few hours.

He's not interested in games or having me read to him or anything much. I'm really worried that I'm not doing my job."

"Kyle was always a quiet little guy. And he likes movies. I wouldn't worry about it." John Harvey picked up a magazine and thumbed through it.

Whenever she looked at John Harvey, she was reminded of Jason. He had that same restless energy that his son had and although he'd always been very courteous, he always seemed to wish he were somewhere else. Amber had the feeling he would be better off on a tennis court or in a business meeting than in his own home. And he was apparently not any more prepared to help her with Kyle than his wife was.

Amber wondered what made a man like that have such a big family. He must be about the same age as her father. He had to be in his mid-forties and her father was forty-six, but the two men were so different that it made her want to laugh. John Harvey was wearing stylish clothes and he was as trim as a teenager. His hair had no gray at all in it and she suspected he'd had a facelift, his handsome face was so unwrinkled. Why did a man have a family if he didn't want to be a grown-up?

"I guess you could use some money," he

said and put his hand in his pocket and pulled out three one-hundred dollar bills.

"Mrs. Murdock won't let me use the car," Amber said. "I can't spend three hundred dollars on the Malibu pier."

"You probably could if you tried." John laughed and pushed the money into her hand. "I'll tell you what — I'll tell Mrs. Murdock she has to give you the car on Tuesdays and Thursdays. How's that?"

"She'll say those are her shopping days." Amber blinked back the surprising tears in her eyes. She wasn't sure why she was so upset except Kyle was a nice little kid and she wanted to do a good job. It just seemed so hard to be a part of this family. No one talked to anyone. No one did anything anyone else wanted. No one considered the other. It seemed like an awful place for a kid to grow up.

"Mrs. Murdock will do what I say," John Harvey said confidently. Then he stood up, reached out, and pulled Amber to her feet, saying, "We'll talk to her right now."

He put his arm around her shoulders as they walked into the kitchen and said, "Mrs. Murdock, I've told Amber that she can use the car on Tuesdays and Thursdays, for certain. Will that be all right?"

"Of course, Mr. Harvey. I've always told her she could use it anytime," the cook replied very easily.

"I'm sure you've been very generous, but I think Amber will be more comfortable having definite days. Then she can plan some outings for Kyle. And if you need any errands run on the other days, you might ask her to do them for you. I want her to get around and see a few things. She's a relative of my wife's and I certainly want her folks to know we treated her well. Don't you agree?"

When John Harvey smiled, it was a big, contagious smile that stopped all conversation. He wasn't through charming the cook though. He asked, "What's for supper?"

"Lamb and potatoes."

"My favorite. Shame I have to go out. Will you save some for me for tomorrow?"

"Certainly, Mr. Harvey. I cooked it especially for you."

"Well, make sure my little cousin gets some of her favorite dishes while she's here." John Harvey took Amber's hand and led her out of the kitchen. Once in the living room, he looked at his watch and said, "Got to go."

"I'm not really your cousin," Amber volunteered. "My best friend, Heather is a relative of Madeline's but she couldn't come. I took her place."

"Well I'm proud to claim you as a cousin anyway," John Harvey said and his eyes twinkled so much that she wondered if he'd been making that story up for the cook or if he simply didn't care.

"You're doing us a big favor," John Harvey said seriously. "I hope you'll be happy here. My boys are in school and Catty's too young and Madeline . . . Madeline isn't very maternal, I'm afraid. She's a delightful companion, of course, but she doesn't want children of her own. So we've agreed to raise the ones we've got and let well enough alone. I think we're both looking forward to the time when they'll all be gone. Of course, Kyle is only eight . . ."

"John, let's go." Madeline appeared in the doorway. Her dark auburn hair was loose around her shoulders and she wore a black silk dress that was cut low. The long, tight skirt was slit on one side up to the middle of her leg. She wore only diamond earrings and rings. Amber thought she was the most beautiful woman she had ever seen. She also thought she was the strangest adult she'd ever known.

John Harvey's visit to the kitchen made quite an impact on Mrs. Murdock. Dinner that evening was very different. The cook went to a lot of trouble to make sure that everything was set out well and she served Amber and Kyle on the dining room table, which was at the end of the long living room nearest the kitchen. Amber wanted to laugh at how nice Mrs. Murdock was to her, but she kept a straight face and said "please" and "thank you."

About halfway through the meal, Jason and Catty came in and Mrs. Murdock set two more places. Catty slid in to her chair and said, "This is great — how did you guys rate?"

Amber didn't know quite what to say.

"This is good food," Catty said. "Old Murdock does a lot better when John is around." Catching Amber's look out of the corner of her eye, she asked, "You don't call your dad by his first name, I'll bet."

"No, I don't."

"And do you have an older brother who acts like a weirdo?"

"No. I have a younger brother — Tim. He's your age and I wouldn't call him weird."

"Do you think he'd like me?"

"Not until you stop smelling like horses," Jason said. "You can't be a *femme fatale* without taking a bath, Catty."

"I'm talking to Amber." She turned and looked at Amber directly and asked, "What about it? Would your brother like me?"

"Yes, I think he would," Amber said. "I like you."

Catty turned and said triumphantly to her brother, "See, she does so like the people in this family. It's only you she doesn't like." To Amber, she added, "Jason says you won't stay long because you don't like us. But you like me and you like Kyle, don't you?"

"Of course I do. Could we change the subject?"

Catty went on, "Did you know that Jason will be a great director someday, soon maybe. He's eighteen already."

Jason glowered and Amber laughed out loud. "I *knew* you weren't a lot older than I am!"

"I'm a lot older in experience and I'm in college," Jason said.

It was the first time she'd seen him the least bit unsure of himself and she loved it. She asked, "So, are you a freshman or what?"

"He's a what," Catty answered for him. "Jason is a genius and this is his third year of school. He went to UCLA when he was sixteen on some kind of program."

"Film program," Jason explained. "I did a small movie and got a special acceptance."

"That's impressive," Amber admitted reluctantly. "I'm sixteen and I'll be a senior next year. I'll be seventeen when I finish high school."

"You're right on schedule," Catty said. "He's the one who's off track, so to speak. And then there's Brett, who is only a sophomore and he's a year older than Jason. Of course, as my dear brother Brett is fond of saying he's 'studying a real subject.' "

"Where does Brett go to school?"

"UCLA. They both go to UCLA I'm going to go there, too. All the Harveys go there. My father worked his way through UCLA when he was a poor boy from Eagle Rock. Ask him, he'll tell you all about it . . . by the hour."

"How far away is your school?" Amber asked Jason directly because he really did look uncomfortable and she was getting a bit tired of Catty's strident voice.

"About twenty minutes away," Jason said. "I'll give you my number. I should have done that the first day. Sorry."

"So you have a room on campus?" It was a relief to have an actual conversation with Jason and she was trying hard to get along with him.

"Apartment," Catty corrected. "It's got a refrigerator and everything."

"Room," Jason said. "Room with a refrigerator and big screen TV. All the amenities."

112

"Does your brother Brett live with you?"

That was apparently a very funny question because Catty laughed loudly. Jason and Kyle smiled in amusement. "I guess not," Amber answered for herself. "Where does he live?"

"In a fraternity house," Catty said and she slapped her leg and hooted. "I've got a brother in a fraternity house. Weird, huh?"

"Not if he likes it," Amber said.

Catty pushed her plate away and leaned back on the legs of her chair. She said to Jason, "You promised ice cream."

"There's ice cream in the freezer," Amber offered.

"No. I want a big double-dipper cone with sprinkles."

"Okay," Jason agreed. He put his hand on Kyle's head and said, "Let's go." Then he turned to Amber and asked, "You come, too?"

"No thanks. I'll stay here and clear the table and put the dishes in the dishwasher," Amber said.

"Mrs. Murdock will do it," Catty protested. "Just leave it."

"She's gone home and it will be a big mess if we leave it."

"Yeah, but it will be Murdock's mess," Catty pointed out.

"We'll all help," Jason said. "And then you can come with us."

"That's silly," Catty protested. "Let Murdock do it. She gets paid for it."

"It will only take a minute," Amber said.

"I guess you're *good* at housework," Catty said in a voice that didn't make it sound like a compliment.

"You'd better learn how to do dishes yourself," Amber snapped.

Jason ordered, "Catty, get the rest of the stuff off the table and bring it in the kitchen. Then we can go eat peanut butter and bubble gum ice cream with marshmallows on it."

"All right, but I get to sit in the front seat of the car," Catty answered.

"Kids in back," Jason said.

"Then I'm not going," Catty said.

Amber wondered if Catty could possibly be jealous of her. It was almost impossible to believe, but Catty always seemed to be struggling for her brother's attention. Maybe even a slight thaw in the cold war between Amber and Jason was threatening to her.

When she thought about things from Catty's point of view, she could see why she was so crazy about Jason. She obviously was a kid who wanted and needed a lot of attention and her parents certainly weren't around much. So

Jason was her only source of attention. Amber's opinion of Catty softened. "I promised Kyle I'd sit in back with him," Amber said quickly.

"Then that's all right," Catty said. "I'll go after all."

Chapter 11

The ice-cream parlor was packed with people and it took almost thirty minutes for their number to come up on the tiny little machine on the counter. Amber was fascinated by the mixture of people who were inside the ice-cream parlor. Among them was a beautiful young woman she was certain she'd seen many times on television, but since no one seemed to notice, she decided she must be mistaken.

The crowd was mostly young and casual. A lot of them were dressed in cutoff Levi's or bathing suits, but a few were wearing expensive sports clothes. Amber was sorry she'd worn the yellow sweatshirt with the rock star on the back.

When they were finally served, there were no chairs so they walked out onto the sidewalk and down the street a bit until they came to a small cement block wall they could sit on while they ate their ice cream.

When they were finished, Jason gave Catty a twenty-dollar bill and said, "Why don't you guys go back and get a quart of bubble gum ice cream for the house?"

"We don't need ice cream for the house," Catty protested.

"You always like bubble gum and Mrs. Murdock never buys it," Jason said.

"The line is too long."

"It won't be so long now. It's almost nine o'clock. Go on, Catty, get the bubble gum ice cream and take Kyle and let him pick whatever flavor he wants." Jason's voice made it a definite command.

Catty took the money and said, "Come on, Kyle. Let's get out of the way so Prince Charming can declare his love to Cinderella."

"How would you like to walk home?" Jason growled. He really sounded annoyed with Catty this time.

"What are you so cross about? It's obvious you want to be alone with her — funny — I would have thought you'd go for someone a little more glamorous."

"Get in the car," Jason said grimly. Then he turned to Amber and said, "Make sure Kyle doesn't get that glop all over my leather seats."

Jason's fury was so apparent that Amber took Kyle by the hand and they got into the backseat of the car without another word. Jason and Catty stood outside for a moment and then Jason nudged Catty into the front seat.

They drove home in absolute silence until Catty said in a bright voice, "I guess this is what they mean when they say the atmosphere is so thick you could cut it with a knife."

No one laughed and Jason said sharply, "Just be still, Catalina Louise. We'll be home soon."

"Then what? Are you going to put me on a diet of bread and water? Chain me to the wall in the dungeon of our Malibu castle?"

"We'll discuss this at home."

"After Cinderella turns into a pumpkin and the mouse goes to bed." Catty's voice was no longer bright. It was sullen.

When they pulled into the driveway, Jason got out of the car but he motioned to Catty to stay where she was. As Amber and Kyle got out of the backseat, he said to his brother, "See you tomorrow, Kyle."

"Are you going to spank Catty?" Kyle asked. He didn't seem too disturbed by the prospect.

Jason frowned and asked, "Do you think I should?"

"Yes."

"Well, I won't," Jason said shortly and then he bent over and hugged Kyle despite the chocolate ice-cream smears. "See you tomorrow."

As Amber put Kyle to bed, she went through the evening in her mind. As far as she could see, Catty was just being Catty. She still didn't understand what it was that set Jason off but she decided she would probably never understand the Harvey family so it really didn't matter.

The next morning at breakfast, Catty was as cheerful as usual. She said, "I am hereby apologizing to you. I'm sorry I called you Cinderella. From now on, if you need any help, just call on me. I aim to please."

"Thank you, Catty. I really wasn't upset, you know. I just thought it was a joke."

"It is not a joke to treat the people who are working for you with discourtesy. All directors learn to value the skills of the cameramen and the grips as much as the stars." Catty waved her hand magnanimously.

Amber smiled. "Is that what your brother told you after we left?"

Catty made a face. "He also told me he would check with you two or three times a week to make sure I was behaving courteously. He thinks you're good with Kyle," Catty explained.

Amber found that she was really pleased to hear that Jason had said that.

Catty followed up the compliment quickly. "And all he wanted to talk to you about was Kyle. He's not interested in you romantically at all."

"That's the best news I've heard all week," Amber said as she stirred her coffee.

"Why do you say that? Do you think you're too good for my brother?"

Amber laughed. "Catty, you are really full of energy and ideas, aren't you? I never thought for one moment that your brother was interested in me and he's certainly not the kind of person I would ever be interested in."

"Why not?" Catty demanded.

"He's just not . . ." She wanted to say he was just not Mike, but as she paused and thought about Mike's wonderful smile and crinkling eyes, she realized it was a lot more than looks. It was simply impossible to imagine Mike and Jason as being the same kind of people at all. Mike was so easygoing and friendly and you always knew where you stood with him. Jason was so — so bossy. He loved his younger brother and sister, she could see that, but he definitely tried to manage them too much. She finally said, "He's not exactly a happy person, is he?"

"Jason? Jason isn't happy? Of course Jason's happy. He has more fun than anyone I know. And he has lots of beautiful girlfriends, too. Some of them are a lot older than he is, but they really like him. I think you're making a mistake if you think my brother isn't romantic or something. Of course, you're not really his type. He likes brunettes, not blonds."

"I'm certain I'm not his type," Amber agreed.

"He always has brunette girlfriends," Catty assured her, "and they all really like him. He really is very romantic when he puts his mind to it."

"I'm sure he is." Amber really didn't want to argue anymore. "I think I just see a certain side of him because I'm Kyle's baby-sitter."

"*Au pair,*" Catty corrected her. "You're an *au pair* and that's very skilled and important work. And we're all very grateful to you."

"You sound like a very cheerful parrot," Amber chided.

Catty seemed confused. "I apologized."

"You apologized for something that I wasn't

upset about. And that should be the end of it. If you really want to please me, you could just be yourself. You don't need to say words your brother put in your mouth," Amber said.

Catty stood up and said, "Got to go." As she left the room, she reminded Amber, "Just make sure you give me a good report."

Amber laughed and asked, "What's he bribing you with?"

"Who?" Catty was all innocence now.

"What did Jason promise you if you were nice to me?"

"Jason would never bribe me," Catty said as she stalked out of the kitchen. But Amber knew better.

Chapter 12

There was a large straw hat on the chest by the entrance when she crossed the living room to Kyle's room. It had a tag on it with her name so Amber decided that Madeline had left it for her.

She was wearing the hat as she and Kyle passed Madeline on their way to the beach and Amber said, "Thanks for the hat."

"Hat?"

"The sun hat. It will give my nose a chance to stop peeling," Amber said.

Madeline looked vague and then said, "Do you have something to wear tonight?"

"Where am I going tonight?" Amber asked. She had been here over a week now and she knew enough not to try and follow the logic in Madeline's conversational jumps.

"There's a party at the Redmonds'. Children invited. John thought you would enjoy meeting

Ray Redmond. Of course, you'll have to keep an eye on Kyle part of the time."

Amber could hardly believe that she was actually going to go to a party where her favorite movie star Ray Redmond would be host. Her voice quavered as she asked, "What should I wear?"

"Oh, something simple," Madeline shrugged. "You did bring a dress?"

"A couple," Amber said. She went to her room and returned with her two dresses. One was a sleeveless cotton print sundress. The other dress was more sophisticated. It was a white sheath with a long straight skirt.

When she saw the look on Madeline's face she said, "This is all I brought. I thought I might buy another while I was here."

"Good idea. I'll tell you what. You and Catty can go to town this morning and select something appropriate. Put it on my bill, of course. In fact, I'll call Irena right now."

Madeline went to the telephone and made a call, "Irena, I'm sending my daughter and her friend to you. They need something for the Redmond party. Not too sophisticated. Cotton or silk. Simple. The older girl is about a size five and could wear a short skirt. She has good legs. Catty — if Catty insists, let her have some dressy pants, but a long skirt would be best." There was a slight pause and then Madeline said, "And pick out something for my little boy. Shorts and a jacket. Size eight. The girls will bring it all home."

Amber stared at Madeline in dismay. When the older woman put the phone down, Amber said, "I'm certain that Catty has already gone to the stables and Kyle is counting on going to the beach."

"Tell Mrs. Murdock to watch Kyle and I'll send Brett after Catty. You wait right here." Then she glanced at Amber's T-shirt and bathing suit and said, "Best dress up a bit more to do your shopping."

Amber was torn between excitement about going to the party and worry about Kyle. She had also hoped she would see Mike on the beach again today. But Kyle seemed okay with being left at home as long as he could watch movies. Amber went back to her room and found her white jeans, white cropped cotton sweater, and white flats.

When she reentered the living room, Madeline was standing beside a tall, handsome young man who looked absolutely nothing like any of the other people in the Harvey family. "You know Brett," Madeline said.

Amber hadn't exactly met him but she nodded her head yes. It was simpler just to say hello. Anything else would have been quite awkward to explain.

Brett nodded his head and smiled slightly. Amber could see him more clearly now. His hair was straight and beautifully cut and combed. His dark brown eyes were framed with arched eyebrows and black eyelashes. He was classically handsome with a straight nose and high cheekbones and a square jaw. He was tall and broad-shouldered. He was wearing a white shirt and khaki pants and he looked like a model in some magazine ad.

"Brett will take you to get Catty and then drop you both off at Saks. You can take a taxi home. No, better call first to see if someone can pick you up. John thinks taxis are so expensive in California. Do you have money?"

"I have two hundred and sixty dollars that your husband gave me," Amber answered.

Madeline frowned. "You might see shoes somewhere. However, I don't want you shopping all over Rodeo Drive. Stick to Saks and let Irena tell you what's best. I trust her. But you might not be able to find shoes there. Here's another three hundred."

"You want me to go downtown with five hundred and sixty dollars in my purse?" Amber could hardly keep the incredulousness out of her voice.

"Bring back the change," Madeline said. "But get what you need to fit in."

Amber's face burned as she realized that Madeline was worried about how she would look at the party. It was especially humiliating because she was standing next to the handsomest young man she had ever seen. She took the money and said, "Excuse me."

Then she went back to her room and put the money in her bra. She might spend it foolishly but she was determined she wouldn't lose it.

Brett drove a sleek little Mercedes sports car and Amber was thrilled to ride along beside him as they went up into the Malibu Hills to the Wilkens Riding Academy. This was as close to her dreams as she was going to get, she decided. Mike was almost forgotten. Riding beside this great-looking college student and going to Ray Redmond's party was actually the content of her dreams. She was so excited that she had a hard time concentrating on trying to talk to Brett. But he didn't seem to want to talk anyway so after a few questions about his school and his fraternity, she let silence reign.

The stables were high up in the Malibu hills and Amber was amazed at how brown and dry everything was. When they got there, Amber said, "It's like a different world, isn't it? From here, you'd think the ocean was a thousand miles away."

"Hot and dry," Brett agreed. "This can be a dangerous place when the fires come."

She had read about the big fires that periodically swept across these mountains, stripping the land of all foliage. "Then after the fires, you get the floods," Amber added. "We saw the mud slides on television last year. Was your house hurt?"

"Not much," Brett answered. "It's on higher ground than some. The storms don't hurt us much, either." Then he asked, "Think you can find her? I need to get back to school soon."

"Oh. You're not going to the party?" Amber asked.

"I may," Brett said. "If I finish my project in time. I'm working on the history of the Civil War."

"That doesn't sound like anything you could finish in an afternoon," Amber said and laughed.

Brett smiled and he repeated his question, "Can you find her?"

"I'll try." Amber flushed at being dismissed so completely and climbed out of the Mercedes. It was hot on top of the mountain and the air was really dry and there was a lot of dust. She went up to a couple of kids standing by a fence. "I'm looking for Catty Harvey," Amber said.

"Check in at the office." The kids pointed to a run-down shack with a big sign that read OFFICE painted in bright-red letters.

Amber was surprised to find Catty inside the office when she pushed the door open. Catty was thumbing through a magazine, drinking a Coke. She looked up and asked, "Something wrong?"

"No. Madeline asked me to pick you up and then we're supposed to go to Saks to pick up something suitable for the Redmond party tonight. Brett's waiting outside."

Catty yawned and said, "I'll bet Brett's thrilled. I'm not going."

"But your mother . . ."

"She's not my mother, you know. And neither are you."

"Don't I remember something about courtesy reports?" Amber asked. "I think I'm supposed to file my first one tomorrow. Right?"

"Right." Catty put the magazine down and followed her meekly out the door. She even sat in the backseat of the Mercedes without any complaint.

Brett didn't say a word as he drove them

down the hill and into Beverly Hills where he dropped them off one block from Saks. As they were walking, Catty asked, "How did you like my brother Brett?"

"He certainly is handsome," Amber said.

"I asked how you liked him, not what you thought of his looks," Catty said. "Everyone knows he's handsome. Handsome isn't so special in this town. So — how did you like him?"

Amber laughed. "I'm not certain what you're really asking. He doesn't talk much. But he seemed okay."

"Did you like him better than Jason?"

"It's not a competition, Catty. Jason is more — Jason is more outgoing. I know that Jason is your favorite because he obviously cares a lot about you, but I did like Brett, too."

"So do you think you'll fall in love with him, now that you and Jason definitely don't have a thing going?"

Amber laughed out loud and hugged the girl. "You really are very funny sometimes, Catty. Would it disappoint you terribly if I picked someone besides Jason or Brett to fall for? Or if I didn't fall for anyone at all?"

"Like our cute neighbor maybe," Catty said.

"How do you know about Mike?" Amber asked her sharply.

"Kyle told Jason and Jason told me. Simple."

"I don't know what your brother said, but what you're thinking is simply not true. I'm not interested in Mike or anyone else."

"Then how come you kissed him?"

"Is that what Kyle told Jason? I didn't kiss him." She didn't add that he had kissed her; instead, she said, "I'm just here doing my job."

"You have a temper, too," Catty observed. "Just about everyone has a temper except Madeline and Brett. They just sort of go away in their minds."

"Is Brett like Madeline?" Amber asked, mostly to change the subject.

"He's not like any of us Harveys," Catty said. "At least he's not much like Jason or me. He looks like his mother who was a very famous movie actress. Lorraine Wilson — remember her?"

"Not really," Amber admitted.

"Glamorous. The last of the glamour girls is what Jason calls her. Jason says she drank and she was beautiful and not very talented. She made a lot of money and John was married to her just long enough to get Brett. Then he married our mother — Jason's and mine. Our mother was John's secretary before they married. Her name was Louise — that's why my name is Catalina Louise. Anyway, she died when I was five months old, but Jason remembers her. He was five."

Amber's heart went out to Brett. The handsome young man seemed so different from his brother and sister. There was more to him than a handsome face, she was sure of that. He was probably shy because he'd had an absolutely dreadful childhood, being shuttled back and forth between his father and mother. And if his mother was half as bad as Catty said, then Brett was obviously a credit to her. Even though he'd been silent, he'd been very courteous and Amber was attracted to his deep, melodious voice even more than his good looks. There was no doubt about it, if she had to choose a Harvey — it would be Brett she'd choose. Compared to Jason, he was a real winner.

"And then you had another stepmother who died?"

Catty nodded. "Kyle's mother. I can remember her a little bit but not very well. Jason says she was a nice woman. She died five years ago when Kyle was three. And now there's Madeline."

They were walking and talking and Amber had a hard time concentrating on anything because there was so much noise and traffic on

Sunset Boulevard. Cars were honking and people were moving fast. Everywhere she looked, she saw women who looked as if they were trying to imitate Madeline, but none looked as good as she did. The women were generally carrying large shopping bags.

Some of the stores they were passing had really interesting things and Amber vowed she would come back here by herself some day and just look around. In the meantime, she continued her conversation with Catty. "Madeline's quite young for so many responsibilities," Amber said.

Catty whooped with laughter and asked, "How old do you think Madeline is?"

"Twenty-five?" Amber guessed.

"More like forty-five," Catty said. "Too bad I'm not speaking to my wicked stepmother. I'd tell her you think she's twenty-five. That would make her day."

"She's certainly *not* forty-five," Amber said. They had entered the department store now and Amber asked, "Do you know where we're going? Someone named Irena?"

"Sure. That's Madeline's best friend. They talk to ghosts together."

"I never know whether or not to believe you," Amber said doubtfully.

"They don't really talk to ghosts, but they

go to a lot of spiritual stuff together. John won't go. And they are good friends. Irena's all right. She's on the second floor."

Irena turned out to be a six-foot-tall woman with thin arms and legs and a smile almost as warm and beautiful as Madeline's. She began by hugging Catty and then insisted on hugging Amber as well, declaring that she had just the right things for both of them. "But first," she said, "let me show you what I found for Kyle." She held up a pair of white linen shorts and a navy-and-white striped T-shirt with a gold insignia on the pocket. "Look!" Irena said, and brought out a navy-blue linen jacket with the same insignia and a little matching captain's cap. "Isn't that just perfect for Kyle?"

Catty looked at Amber and raised one eyebrow. Amber almost laughed out loud. Catty leaned over and whispered, "You'd better hope that Madeline doesn't expect you to dress him in that monkey suit. You'll have your hands full."

"Now let me show you what I found for you," Irena said to Catty.

"Whatever you say," Catty said impatiently. "You pick it out and I'll wear it."

Irena laughed and held up a pale pink silk dress. The dress had tiny white flowers with green leaves sprinkled around on it. It had short sleeves and a long skirt with just the right amount of fullness. "Princess dress for a princess," Irena said. "Try it on."

"I'll take it," Catty said. "I don't need to try it on."

"Yes, you do." Irena led Catty toward the dressing rooms and said to Amber, "We'll be right out."

"I really don't need to try it," Catty protested.

"Your horses will keep. Anyway, Madeline said I was to send you to the beauty salon and have your hair washed next."

"Give me a break!"

"It's tough to be gorgeous, but you will be. You're a natural beauty." Irena laughed and tugged Catty into the dressing room.

They came out in just a few minutes and Irena said, "Now move on over there and ask for Marcella. She's going to give you a French braid with pink ribbons."

"Ugh!" Catty said but she did as she was told.

Once Catty was dispensed with, Irena turned to Amber and surveyed her critically, looking her up one side and down the other. Amber had never had anyone look at her so long and intently and she felt very uncomfortable. Finally, Irena said, "You do have a good figure and good posture. That's a start. Now tell me, what are your ambitions? How do you see yourself?"

"I'm sixteen," Amber said.

"In this town sixteen can mean anything," Irena said. "Tell me about *you*. Do you want to be an actress? A dancer? Perhaps a television personality? What are your dreams?"

"I'm going to teach school," Amber said. "I like children and I like to travel. So teaching will be perfect. My biggest dream is to travel all over the world. I keep clippings of places I'd like to see."

Irena nodded. "Would you like to see the French Riviera? Buenos Aires? The Kremlin? Tell me?"

Amber laughed and said, "In Milwaukee they don't make you answer questions like this just to buy a dress. I want to go everywhere. To Europe for sure, but to exotic places like the Galápagos Islands and Kenya and Afghanistan."

"I make you answer questions because I want to see you talk," Irena said. "Your face lights up and you are more than just another pretty girl. You are someone. I think you are too strong for pastels. Too young for black, and half the women at this party will be in white. I have soft yellow silk pants and a blouse I want you to try. A dark lavender dress and some apricot shorts and a tank top. You will need a jacket with those I suppose."

"I don't think I'm supposed to get shorts," Amber said. "It's a party at a movie star's house."

"Trust me, darling." Irena was leaving as she spoke.

Amber laughed out loud. Irena was the first person she'd heard use the expression "darling" since she got to California. As she waited, Amber walked over to the only rack of dresses in the whole store and looked through them. Most of them were too old for her, but there was a white linen dress that she liked. She picked up the price tag and dropped it like a hot potato. She had never even seen a dress that cost seven hundred and fifty dollars before! Did people really wear things like that?

"Here they are." Irena was holding three garments in her hands. She frowned and said, "The things on that rack are on sale. Madeline would want you to have something fresher."

"How much do these things cost?" Amber demanded.

"Madeline is paying."

"I can't let her pay and I certainly can't afford

seven hundred and fifty dollars," Amber said.

Irena smiled and raised an eyebrow. "How much did you want to spend?"

Amber took a deep breath and said, "I'll look at anything you have under one hundred dollars." She had never had a dress that expensive, but she might never be invited to a movie star's house again.

"These are all under a hundred," Irena said calmly. "They came from the junior department. I only take care of Catty and Kyle because Madeline is my friend and one of my best customers."

Amber relaxed and looked at the clothes. After a minute, she said, "I can't tell. They all look so different from what I have."

"That's the point," Irena said smoothly. "Now let's try them on."

Amber followed the tall woman into the dressing room and allowed her to help her into the clothes. First she tried on the yellow pants. The blouse had a very low neck and long sleeves; it would have looked better on Madeline. The lavender dress was pretty, but it was so short her mother would never allow her to wear it. She tried it on though and she had to admit it looked good.

The short set turned out to be too big and Amber said, "I don't think any of these will work. The dress is cute but it's too short."

"Don't even think about it, darling," Irena said. She disappeared and was back in a minute with a deep-blue silk dress. Amber loved the color and the fabric and she reached out to touch it. "This blue is beautiful. What is it?"

"Sort of a cross between indigo and navy blue. We're calling it 'smokey night blue.' For a young girl like you, it will seem like a substitute for black. It's sandwashed silk. You like it?"

"Soft-looking," Amber answered. There was something about the color that did remind her of the evening sky over the ocean. It had an iridescent quality — the silken fabric glowed without being the least bit shiny. She loved it but she didn't want to commit herself until she asked, "How much is it?"

"Forty-five dollars," Irena said and helped her slip it on. The dress was cut almost exactly like Catty's, except it buttoned all the way down the front. Amber thought it was the most elegant dress she'd ever seen.

Irena insisted she wear it partially unbuttoned to the party, saying, "You should always show off those legs, darling. They're a gift."

"Do these shoes look all right?" Amber asked anxiously. "They're the only ones I have."

"Take the dress and go down to the shoe department. Get the style with a little heel and have them dye it to match. Don't worry about the cost . . . what is your size?" Irena asked. "I'll call ahead and tell Joel what to show you."

Amber told her she wore a size seven and took the dress on a hanger and wrapped in plastic down to the shoe department. The clerk named Joel showed her some white shoes that had a one-inch heel. Amber asked, "How much are they?"

"Twenty dollars," the clerk said promptly.

"I never had shoes that were for just one dress before." Amber said doubtfully. "Are they on sale?"

"They must be," the clerk said. He brought a card and together they picked a shade of blue that would match the dress and she asked, "Are you certain you can dye these today?"

"They'll be at your home by five P.M."

Despite the fact that the shoes were inexpensive, Amber felt very uncomfortable about spending so much money and so she said, "I think I'll skip the shoes. These white ones will look fine. Thanks, but I don't need the shoes."

"You don't want these shoes for twenty dollars?" the clerk asked and he seemed to be about to burst into laughter.

"No, thanks," Amber said and she walked

away. As she went up the escalator to pick up Catty, she decided that she had been within her rights not to spend money on something as foolish as a pair of matching shoes. The dress would be all right next year. She could wear it buttoned up to any dressy event, but the shoes would be an absolute waste of money and she really couldn't justify it.

Amber waited almost an hour for Catty to get her hair done and during that time she sat and read a magazine. She would have loved to go all around the store just looking at the pretty things for sale, but she was afraid she'd run into Irena and have to admit she didn't buy the shoes after all. She knew that Irena would think that was awful and she supposed that Madeline would, too, if she thought about it. But she was counting on Madeline to be too vague to think about it.

When Amber called home, Mrs. Murdock said that no one else was home and she couldn't pick up Amber and Catty. "I've certainly got my hands full with the little one," she complained. Amber bit her lip to keep from saying how little trouble Kyle was but she only said, "Tell Kyle I'll be there soon." The taxi fare was more than the shoes would have cost her, but Amber had been in the Harvey household long enough to understand that the value of money was different for her than for the Harveys.

As they climbed out of the taxi, Catty said, "Now the first thing I have to do is take this silly ribbon out of my hair."

"I like the way she did your hair," Amber said. "I think you should leave it in."

"Do I look gorgeous or silly? Tell the truth," Catty demanded.

"Gorgeous," Amber assured her.

Catty looked so doubtful that Amber hugged her and added, "Trust me, darling."

Chapter 13

Amber dressed Kyle for the party and he didn't complain since she explained to him that everyone would be wearing party clothes and that he could take off his hat and jacket the minute they got there.

When Kyle was ready, Amber went to her room and took a quick shower and put some foundation over her sunburned face. Then she darkened her eyelashes with mascara and put on some lipstick. She even experimented with pulling her hair high onto her head but decided against it.

The new dress looked wonderful and for a moment she was sorry she'd been so stingy about the shoes, but she told herself it was too late to change her mind now. At exactly five o'clock, John Harvey knocked on her door and said, "They just brought your shoes. Are you ready to go?"

"But I didn't buy the shoes . . ."

"We bought them for you," Mr. Harvey said. "You look very nice. Do you like Ray Redmond's movies? We must have a long talk about what you like sometime. You're from the heartland of America and I make movies for the heartland. It's a perfect match — right?"

Amber nodded and stepped into the shoes, knowing that they made all the difference in how she looked. She had been wrong. People would have noticed what shoes she was wearing and she was very grateful to the Harveys for their generosity.

They rode to the party in the Harveys' Land Rover because it had the most room. John and Madeline were in the front seat and Catty and Kyle and Amber filled the back. Amber was slightly disappointed that Brett wasn't coming to the party because she felt he was the one Harvey she would have the most in common with and she hoped to get to know him better. She was relieved and a little surprised that Jason wasn't with them, but she was determined not to worry about anything this evening and just to have a great time. She felt beautiful and she was certain that she couldn't ask for anything more.

She had never been in a Land Rover before,

although she'd seen them in the movies and on television. From the outside it looked like a van but on the inside it was as sleek and expensive as any car she'd ever seen. The seats were leather and the dashboard was some sort of shining material that looked like a very expensive wood.

"So, Amber, how do you like California?" John Harvey asked her for perhaps the tenth time.

"I love it," she answered. And at that moment, she meant it. She felt beautiful in her new dress and she was excited about the party. Kyle and Catty were well behaved and Jason wasn't around to criticize her. All was well.

"The Redmonds live right down the street from us," Madeline said.

After they'd driven for several miles, Amber figured out that Madeline meant right down the street from their Beverly Hills home. And sure enough, they were soon on Sunset Boulevard and they passed the doorway to the Harvey home just before John Harvey swung off onto a side street and pulled the Land Rover up to the gate of a very large and impressive mansion.

"Good evening, Mr. Harvey," the young man at the gate said. "You'll find valet parking at the front of the Redmond house."

John Harvey drove them right up to the door and a young woman took his keys and said, "Good evening, Mr. Harvey. Have a pleasant evening."

Madeline and John Harvey led the way through the front door and into a very large room with marble floors that led out onto a huge covered patio and backyard. Amber worried that her brand-new shoes would slide on the smooth surface, but she soon got used to walking on the marble.

The house seemed to be more like a formal castle than a real house and it was practically empty because everyone was outside on the lawn. There wasn't much furniture, but there were a lot of marble columns and statues all around. The walls were covered with paintings and everything seemed very ornate. Amber couldn't really say she liked it. Madeline Harvey whispered to her, "Dreadful taste, isn't it?"

"I like your house better," Amber said. "But this is certainly impressive."

"Fancies himself a collector," Madeline said. "But he knows nothing and he won't take any advice."

"Children are over there." John Harvey pointed to an area of lawn that had a striped-awning tent and balloons. He said, "You girls take Kyle over and when he's comfortable, you can leave him. Just make sure that security knows he's there. And then you can do whatever you like. Flirt with the young men. No drinking, of course."

"Of course," Amber agreed, but Catty just raised an eyebrow. Amber decided she would have to keep an eye on the thirteen-year-old as well as Kyle. John and Madeline Harvey had already left them and were moving toward a group of people who obviously knew them.

"Neighbors!" Catty said. "You'd think they'd want to meet new people once in a while, wouldn't you?"

Amber clutched Catty's arm and whispered, "Is that Bridget Fonda over there?"

"Yeah, I think so. You like her?"

"I've never seen a movie star before!"

Catty laughed and asked, "Didn't you see Jim Carrey at the ice-cream place the other night?"

"Jim Carrey?"

"Yeah Jim Carrey — the Pet Detective guy."

"I know who he is — but I didn't recognize him. Why didn't you say something?"

Catty shrugged. "I guess I thought you would see him on your own. And I don't know

him so I couldn't introduce you or anything."
She pointed across the lawn toward the bar
and said, "I do know Denzel Washington. He
was in one of my dad's last movies and he's
over there. Do you want to meet him?"

Amber was too shy to say more than, "Let's
see about Kyle first. What did your dad mean
about security?"

"Oh, Dad has this big fear of his kids being
kidnapped. Jason's just as bad. Know how he's
always telling you to watch Kyle? It's this par-
anoia that runs in the family. That's probably
why you got the job. You're a relative . . ."

"I'm not," Amber interrupted. "I'm the
friend of Madeline's relative."

"Well, you come from a good respectable
family and all that. They'd rather fly someone
out from Milwaukee than trust anyone they
don't know and most of the people they *do*
know don't need to work. So you should probably ask for a raise."

"Your family pays me well. So they have
security at parties like this?"

"Sure. That way they can dump the kids and
not worry about them. Bonded baby-sitters."
Catty waved to someone and said, "I see the
cutest boy in my school. He's your age but I
saw him first. See you." She went running
toward a tall, thin boy in baggy shorts and high-

top sneakers with very long brown hair that was partially shaved and the remainder tied in a long ponytail. He looked bizarre but Amber supposed he was stylish.

Amber took Kyle over to the children's tent and hung around a long time while Kyle watched a magic show and then took a turn on a small merry-go-round. When they started to watch the magic show a second time, a clown came up to her and said, "You can leave, miss. We'll watch your brother."

Amber turned and looked at the tall clown with an exceptionally deep voice. He seemed very nice and talked all the time he was blowing up balloons and twisting them into funny animals. She asked, "Are you really a clown?"

"Part of the time," the clown said. "I'm also hired as security for the young people. What's your brother's name?"

"Kyle Harvey," she answered. "He's not my brother but his father wanted me to be certain you looked after him. He's very well behaved and quiet."

"He'll have a good time here," the clown said. "Why don't you go have a good time, too?"

"Thank you." Amber said good-bye to Kyle and drifted around the edges of the party, looking at all the people and trying not to look too conspicuously alone. People didn't seem to pay much attention to her, although one handsome young man offered her a drink and tried to talk to her.

She asked for a Coke and they chatted a few minutes. He found out she was sixteen and worked as an *au pair* and he drifted away. Amber felt like a wallflower and then she reminded herself that she had come to see what a real Hollywood party was like, not to be the most popular girl.

She began to move around, taking in all the faces and listening to snatches of conversations and really savoring the lives of the rich and famous. At one point, a tall blond man came up to her and asked, "Are you having any fun yet?"

"Yes, I am." Amber was pleased that her voice didn't quaver. "Thank you for inviting me, Mr. Redmond."

"Glad you could come," he said and he smiled a brilliant smile as his eyes scanned the crowd. Then he abruptly hugged her and kissed her on the cheek and said, "Have fun and come back soon."

Ray Redmond actually kissed her! She was certain he didn't have a clue who she was, but he definitely kissed her. Wait till her friends heard about that. She realized she was storing up memories of this party to tell her friends next fall and that made even the parts that weren't so much fun seem like fun.

After looking around for a while, she decided that Madeline probably worried too much about how they all looked and what they wore. There were people there in everything from Levi's and tank tops to long formal dresses. Amber had never seen so many beautiful women in her life and some of them didn't look any older than she was. However, she supposed they were older because they were dressed in very sophisticated clothes and had older men as dates.

After about an hour of drifting from one group to another and eavesdropping on them all, she decided that all the Hollywood rich and famous talked about was investments, and the entertainment business. She was bored and it didn't look as though there was anyone her age to talk with. She decided to tour the house. She carried her glass up to the bar and asked for a refill on her Coke and then climbed the stairs up into the interior of the Redmond home.

She looked all around the huge living room and then followed some people into something she heard them call the screening room.

The screening room looked a lot like the kind of libraries she saw in movies about rich people except that one wall had a huge movie screen on it. The screen was as big as the ones in the movie theaters at the Milwaukee mall and there were a few chairs set in front of it. She wondered if Ray Redmond showed movies of his own pictures or of everyone else's on this screen.

A man's voice behind her said, "This is great, isn't it? I want Dad to put in a media room, but he says it's too pretentious."

Amber jumped at the sound of Jason's voice. He was standing right behind her and he had his arm around a tall young woman with dark hair. She had a lot of curls and they covered most of her forehead, making her dark eyes look even bigger and more dramatic than they were. Amber smiled as she remembered what Catty had said about Jason's preference for brunettes. This young woman definitely fit Catty's profile for Jason. He said, "Amber, this is Carlyle Pope from school. This is Amber — she's living with us and helping us out this summer." To Amber, he asked, "Are you having fun?"

She smiled at the standard question that

everyone seemed compelled to ask her. What if she surprised him and told him the truth? What if she said she thought people's conversation was too much about money and she would rather be walking on the beach with Mike?

But of course she answered, "Yes, I'm having fun." Amber added, "I've been eavesdropping a lot. Do you study filmmaking, Carlyle?"

"Yes, that's my major," the tall girl confirmed. "But I'm really interested in writing. Are you a writer? Eavesdropping is a great way to learn to write dialogue, they say."

Amber laughed. "I'm just a tourist, I'm afraid."

"But you are in school. What's your major?"

"I don't have one," Amber answered. "I'm in high school. But I plan to major in education."

Carlyle Pope smiled over her head and said, "That's nice." Then she waved to a couple who were just coming into the party. "Maggie, Tom! I'm over here."

Two couples joined them and Carlyle eagerly introduced them to Jason, saying, "Jason, this is Maggie Armstrong and Tom Perez and their friends, Jimmy and Eva Burns. Maggie and Tom are the ones I told you about who have this terrific screenplay. I was hoping they could talk to your dad. Do you think you could introduce us?"

Jason looked at Carlyle and answered smoothly. "Your friends can show me their screenplay and then I'll pass it on to my father. I can't interrupt his evening."

"But we're all here at the party together," Carlyle protested. "I thought we were friends." She clung to Jason's arm and smiled at him, but her voice was insistent. Amber thought she was pushy and suspected that Jason was annoyed.

"So did I," Jason said. "By the way, may I introduce Amber Wood."

"Are you that girl on *Mad About the Boy?*" one of the men asked her.

Amber wasn't sure what he was talking about and Jason must have sensed it because he said, "*Mad About the Boy* is a new television show, isn't it? Just a pilot and looking for a home?"

"My friend Mary Marshalline wrote it. I thought your friend looked like the girl. No?"

"No," Amber spoke up. "I'm not an actress.

I'm a student and this summer I'm the Harveys' *au pair*."

The women both said, "That's nice," and then they smiled and began to talk among themselves. Amber stood on the sidelines and listened to them as they talked about who was at the party and who hadn't been invited. They made no attempt to include Amber and they seemed to be very pleased that they were on the party list. Jason looked impatient and kept edging away, but Carlyle clung tenaciously to his arm. The group told each other a lot of stories about the other guests.

Amber yawned and then said, "Excuse me." She thought that the older guests' conversation had been boring, but these people were just plain gossips.

After a few minutes, Carlyle Pope said to Jason, "Well, if you won't introduce me to your father, the least you can do is get me something to eat." She linked her arm in his and said, "Let's go."

"Would you like to join us?" Jason asked.

Amber shook her head quickly and said, "Thanks, but I'm going to check on Kyle."

They walked a few feet and then Jason disengaged his arm and came back to Amber and asked, "Is there anyone here you'd like to meet? I know most of them."

"Do you know Tom Hanks?" Amber asked.

"Sure. Want to meet him?"

"No." Amber shook her head quickly. "I was just asking."

"Tom's a nice guy," Jason teased. "But married and a little old for you. I'd think you'd rather meet someone like Luke Perry."

"Is he here?"

Jason laughed and pointed his finger at her and teased, "Gotchya."

Amber blushed and admitted, "I do think he's cute."

"Jason!" Carlyle called to him and she seemed annoyed.

"You'd better go," Amber said. "I don't need to meet anyone. I'm fine just hanging around studying the scene."

Jason nodded and left her. She realized he had been very nice and that they had actually had a decent conversation. She decided it was because he had a girl with him, although, as she thought the conversation over, she decided he hadn't been very pleased with Carlyle's insistence on meeting his father. She wondered if Jason minded having a famous father and thought that someday she would ask him.

When she came back to the main room, John and Madeline were waiting for her. As she arrived, Catty came in with Kyle and announced, "He really liked the clown. And he had the nicest voice. I'll bet he was cute under all that white makeup."

"I hope you're not entering the boy-crazy stage," John Harvey said. "It's too early for that, you know."

"Exactly how old do you think I should be before I'm boy crazy?" Catty asked.

"Amber's just the right age," John answered. "About sixteen."

"Amber's not boy crazy," Catty said quickly. "She's too serious and too quiet."

"She's probably quietly crazy about boys," John said and hugged Catty and smiled at Amber. "Is that so — are you crazy about boys and too serious to show it?"

For a minute, Amber wondered if he had heard about that kiss on the beach, but then she realized he was just being pleasant. She smiled and said, "The only boy I'm really crazy about is Kyle."

"Good girl," Madeline said. Then she said to her husband, "I'd like to drive home, dear."

It was the first time Amber had ever seen

any sign of good sense on Madeline's part. Her husband must have thought the same thing because he handed her the car keys and said, "If you're ready to take the wheel around here, I'm not going to argue."

Chapter 14

Mike was waiting for her on the beach the next morning and he looked sort of mad as he said, "You weren't here yesterday."

"I'm sorry," she said. "I bought a dress to go to a party."

Mike nodded. "I knew you went to a party. I came over last night and a guy told me you were out. He was a good-looking guy. You like him?"

"That's Brett. I barely know him. But he *is* good-looking."

"He's an actor, I guess, like his father before him?"

"No. Brett is the real student in the family. He's a history major and he seems to take it very seriously."

"I thought one of them was an actor." Mike didn't seem to be in a very good mood this morning, but Amber was pleased to believe he was jealous.

"You might be thinking of Jason," she said. "He's in film school, but he's not an actor, either. How about you, Mike? Did you ever think about being an actor?"

"I guess everyone in southern California thinks about it," Mike answered. "But I'm not really that photogenic."

"I'll take your picture one day and test that," Amber teased. "I don't believe you."

"Acting's hard work," Mike said. "It's different if you've got a father in the business already, but for some poor slob like me, it's a tough way to make a living."

"What are you going to do, Mike?" Amber wanted to keep him off the subject of the Harvey boys if she could. "Do you know yet?"

"I'll probably go into business with my mother. She's in real estate. She's made a lot of money buying scrapers and building new ones." He pointed to his house and said, "That goes on the market next summer. So enjoy my company while you've got me."

"Exactly what *is* a scraper?"

"An old house that should be torn down. Like the Harveys'. Why don't they? They're not short of money, are they?"

"I don't think so. They've been very generous to me."

Mike took her hand in his and then began to rub her arm. She said, "Don't do that."

"Why not?"

"Someone might see. Kyle told Jason you kissed me."

"Was Jason jealous?"

"Of course not."

"And was that your first kiss?" Mike teased.

"I don't have to answer that," Amber answered, laughing. She tossed her head and pulled her wrist away from Mike. Then she stood up and said, "I'd better check on Kyle."

Mike was right behind her and he grabbed her hand and they ran down to the shoreline where Kyle sat in the sand, packing his truck with another load. Amber dropped down beside him and said, "Let's make a castle, Kyle."

She and Mike helped Kyle build a castle for a while and then she said, "Want to go for a swim?" Kyle shook his head no but Mike scooped him up and they splashed into the water. Amber ran behind them, shouting. "Don't go too far, Mike."

Mike turned and laughed at her. Kyle was kicking his legs and squirming in Mike's arms. Amber went over and took him away from

Mike, saying in a soft voice, "He doesn't like the ocean much."

"Not like the ocean? How you going to grow up to be a surfer, kid?" Mike reached up and ruffled Kyle's hair, getting seawater on his head and face. Kyle blinked, but said nothing.

"How about if we both hold on to you?" she asked Kyle. "We could walk out a little farther and when you want to go back to the beach, we will."

Kyle didn't actually say no so the three of them went deeper into the water. There was almost no surf at all and that made it easy. Mike held one of Kyle's hands and Amber held the other and they walked way out, almost to her chest. She supposed the water was above Kyle's head but she had no intention of letting him go. She was a strong swimmer and she knew that Mike was even better and Jason had said that Kyle was quite a good swimmer in the pool.

Kyle seemed to enjoy the experience and once he actually laughed out loud. Then a bigger wave came along and he said, "Go back now."

Mike wanted to take him out farther but Amber refused. As the three of them walked back up to the towels, she said, "It's nearly one-thirty. We need to go home now."

"You turning into a pumpkin?" Mike teased.

"Not quite," Amber answered, "but if I stay out much longer I will. The hat is a big help and the sunscreen is working, but I still don't want to stay out too long."

"By the end of the summer you'll be brown," Mike said. He took her hand and looked deep into her eyes, saying, "This is going to be the best Malibu summer I've ever had. How about you?"

"Me, too." Amber laughed and reminded him, "Of course, this is my first Malibu summer."

"Mine, too," Mike said and he grinned.

"You stinker!" Amber said. "I thought you'd lived here all your life!"

"Nope. We moved here in October. I was here at Thanksgiving, Christmas, and Easter. And I got here two weeks ago."

"But you know so many people." Amber wasn't sure whether to believe him or not.

Mike shrugged and said, "I've made a few friends — mostly surfers. But you're my first real friend."

She felt closer to Mike after she learned he was almost as new as she was. It seemed like another reason for them to spend time together and when he asked if he could come up to the house to visit, she said yes.

She reasoned that this was the end of her second week in Malibu and she hadn't had any time off at all. So what was wrong with asking a friend in to visit?

She let Mike hold her hand as the three of them walked up to the Harvey house. Once inside, she gave Mike a Coke and told him to wait on the deck. She took Kyle inside and saw that he showered and changed and then she put him in front of the television set with his favorite movie and came out to sit beside Mike.

"Aren't you going to invite me in?" Mike asked.

"There's only one room and Kyle is watching TV. Do you like *King Kong*?"

"Only one living room? It really is a scraper, isn't it?"

Amber sighed. "Everyone here seems to expect so much from life. I mean they expect a lot of material things. Their house is wonderful just the way it is. It has tile floors and . . ."

"And the deck droops," Mike said as he put his feet out in front of him, crossing them at the ankles and lifting them up on the deck.

Amber was wearing her straw hat and long pants and a long-sleeved shirt so she wasn't afraid of burning. She smiled out at the people on the beach and said, "Some of them look as though they were born in a clamshell, they're so brown."

"We don't have clams in Malibu anymore," Mike said. "But I know what you mean. The ocean always makes me feel as though life is one long vacation." They sat on the deck quite a while, talking about a lot of things but mostly about surfing. Mike didn't seem to want to talk about school or his family and he didn't ask her many questions, either.

Mike asked for a second Coke and when she went into the kitchen she noticed it was almost four o'clock. As soon as Mike finished his Coke, she would send him home, she told herself. She stopped to say hello to Kyle and ask him how he was doing. He was so engrossed in his movie that he didn't even answer.

When she went back to Mike, he said, "Know what? I hate school. I think I'll drop out as soon as I'm old enough to get my real estate license."

"Wouldn't it be better to get an education first?" Amber asked.

"What for?"

"So you could be educated, Mike. You don't want to be a rich dummy do you?"

"If I'm rich enough it won't matter," Mike said. Then he reached over and put his hand on her neck, drawing her close to him, so that her head leaned on his chest. "You wouldn't care how much I know if I'm rich enough, would you?"

"Let me go, Mike." Amber was laughing as she tried to pull away.

"Let her go," a voice came from behind them.

Amber jumped up and flushed red. She said, "Jason, I'd like you to meet Mike."

"Hello, Mike," Jason said coolly. "Amber, could I see you inside?"

"I'll come in, too," Mike said. He stood up, obviously ready to defend her.

She put her hand on his arm and said, "Mike, I have to go now. I'll see you tomorrow."

"Are you going to let him . . .?"

"Please, Mike . . ."

Mike shrugged and smiled. "I'll call you," he promised. Then he looked directly at Jason and said, "Stay cool, man." He jumped over the railing of the deck and Amber and Jason were left, staring in anger at each other.

Jason shook his head and said, "I told Madeline you were too young for the job."

"I wasn't doing anything wrong," Amber said. "I had a friend over for a Coke. Is that really so out of line?"

"Yes, it is. You don't really know him and neither do we. You were supposed to be spending time with Kyle. Having him here is way out of line, but I don't suppose you could understand that."

"I understand that you've been on my back since the day I arrived," Amber said. "You're not fair and you've never been fair to me. Kyle is happy, why can't you be happy?"

"Kyle is only eight. He doesn't know any better. You never should have been hired for this job and I knew it. All you care about is your own interests — mostly that guy."

"You really are impossible!" Amber was shouting now. "I give up. I haven't had a day off since I got here and now I'm about to be fired because I had a friend in . . ."

"He looked like a very close friend," Jason said. He was shouting, too. "And as for firing you . . ."

"You don't have to. I quit!"

"Good! It saves me the trouble of explaining it to everyone. You can leave whenever you want to."

"What will you do about Kyle?" Amber was suddenly sober as she thought about leaving the young boy all alone.

Jason was the only one who could possibly take care of him if she left and he was in school. "Your folks are talking about going to New York next week."

"I'll drop out of school if they want to go. I knew summer school was a bad idea."

"You shouldn't do that. Catty said it was a really special program you're in."

"That's not your worry, is it?" Jason answered. "Go call the travel agency. You can get a plane out tomorrow. On second thought, I'll make the arrangements."

"Let me know when I'm leaving," Amber said. "I'll be in my room."

Chapter 15

Amber threw herself down on her bed and cried. She cried so long and so hard that she was completely exhausted and fell asleep. She woke when there was a knock on her door.

She jumped up, turned on a light, and called out, "Yes?"

"Don't you want supper?" Catty's voice asked.

"No, thanks."

"Can I come in?" she asked.

"I'm not feeling well," Amber said. "I need to go right to bed."

"Could I take your temperature?"

Amber smiled. It was a little difficult to imagine Catty as Florence Nightingale, but it was sweet that she wanted to try. "I'll be fine," she said. "I just need to rest."

"I'm going to stand here until you let me in," Catty warned.

Amber opened the door and Catty moved right in, flopping herself down on the bed and putting her head in her arms. She looked at Amber closely and said, "You've been crying. Did you and Jason have another fight?"

Amber sighed and said, "I'd rather not talk about it. Really, Catty, I want to go back to bed."

"Aren't you going to eat at all?"

"I'm not hungry."

"I'll never let any guy spoil my appetite," Catty said, "no matter how much I love him. What did you and Jason fight about? You did have a fight, didn't you?"

"Yes, we did," Amber admitted. "I'm going home tomorrow."

"That's stupid!" Catty shouted in a very loud and dramatic voice. "You're not going to let a lover's quarrel divide you from us, are you? Jason loves you! Kyle loves you!" Then in a softer, more tentative voice, Catty added, "I like you, too. I hope you don't go — I hope you never go."

"I know you mean well," Amber said, "but I really need to rest. And I am going to have to leave. Jason doesn't love me — he doesn't even like me. He fired me."

"I don't believe it," Catty said. "And even

if he did, I don't believe he can. He didn't hire you, did he?"

"Madeline hired me."

"Then Madeline is the only who can fire you." Catty was triumphantly logical. "So come on out."

"No, I can't." Amber looked in the mirror and saw that her eyes were swollen from crying. She smoothed down her hair automatically and asked, "Will you say good night to Kyle for me?"

"Jason took him for a walk," Catty said. "I was supposed to see if you wanted to eat."

Amber sighed. It was definite then. Jason had decided that she must go and didn't even want to talk to her. He'd probably already ordered her airplane ticket. She felt terrible and wondered how much of the story she would have to tell her parents. She wondered if Mike would care enough about her to ask for her address. Most of all, she hoped she would get a chance to say good-bye to Kyle. Jason was clearly keeping him away tonight, but maybe he would let her see him in the morning. "I'm not hungry. I just want to rest."

"I'm going to call Dad," Catty said.

"Don't do that!" Amber responded.

"I have a right to call my own father if I

want to," Catty said. "You can't tell me what to do."

Amber lay back down on the bed, but she couldn't go back to sleep. After an hour, she rose, put on a sweater, and then she went out on her balcony to look at the sky. She was sitting there when Catty knocked on the door again.

"What is it?" Amber asked.

"I had a tough time getting him. They weren't in Lake Tahoe, they were in Calistoga, but they're coming right home. No one is to make any decisions until they get here. That includes you. And here's a sandwich and milk outside your door."

"Oh, Catty, you shouldn't have called," Amber said.

"Why not?" Catty asked. "I can call anytime I want to. My dad doesn't mind."

"When will they be here?"

"In the morning. Jason has to stay here and wait for them. I guess I fixed him, didn't I?"

"I don't know," Amber answered. She wasn't sure what was going to happen next. She wasn't even sure she wanted to stay if the Harveys asked her to. In fact, she wasn't sure about much of anything.

Chapter 16

Catty knocked on her door at seven-thirty in the morning. She said, "My dad is here and they want to talk to you. Madeline and Jason already had a big fight. Dad called Brett at six in the morning and made him come home. Now we're all having a family conference. They sent me to get you."

Amber groaned and pulled on a T-shirt and Levi's. Even though she'd had plenty of sleep, she thought she looked tired and depressed. She wished her face was a better mask of her emotions, but it wasn't. Anyone who looked at her would know she had been crying.

All the Harveys except Kyle were crowded together at the kitchen table. It was the first time she'd seen five people around the tiny table and she realized it really was too small.

They were drinking coffee and there was a box of cookies open in the middle of the table.

Mr. and Mrs. Harvey sat close together. Brett and Jason sat directly across from them.

When she entered the room, John Harvey said, "Get Amber some coffee, son, and tell her what you have to say."

Brett stood up and gave Amber his chair. She shook her head and said, "I'll stand."

"No, I'll stand," Brett insisted.

"Get a chair from the dining room and sit down," John Harvey said to his oldest son. "If we let you stand, you'll slip away again. You *are* a part of this family."

Brett didn't reply but quickly brought in a dining room chair and made a space between himself and Catty for Amber. Amber sat down quickly because John Harvey was obviously angry. In fact, he sounded a lot like her father did when things didn't suit him.

He frowned at Jason and said, "You have something to say, I believe."

Jason looked directly at Amber and said, "I'm sorry I was so angry yesterday. I had no right to speak that way to you. I was way out of line and I apologize."

Amber flushed and almost felt sorry for Jason. She knew it must have cost him a great deal to be humbled in that way. She nodded and said, "It was my fault, too. I guess I shouldn't have had Mike over."

"Get Amber some coffee, Jason," John Harvey said. His son stood up and went to the stove, bringing back a coffeepot and an empty cup.

"I'll have a bit more myself." Madeline Harvey held out her cup and Jason poured. Madeline looked at her and smiled.

Amber had the idea that everyone expected her to say something but she really didn't know what to say. She simply nodded and sipped her coffee. Madeline looked different so early in the morning, but she was still very beautiful. It was just that there were smudges under her eyes and she didn't seem quite as young.

"We arrived at five-thirty and we've had a little family conference" — John Harvey smiled his famous, movie-star smile — "which we want to continue with your input. Cream, Amber?"

Amber shook her head. She looked at Catty out of the side of her eye, to see if she could tell what was going on. Catty looked pleased with herself, but that could have meant almost anything. Catty loved drama and it was certainly dramatic to get all the Harveys together to talk at seven-thirty in the morning.

Amber waited for what would come next. Brett didn't seem to want to look at her and Amber was doing whatever she could to avoid

Jason's eyes. She couldn't imagine what kind of a wrangle led up to that forced apology, but she was sure he would hold it against her forever.

"First of all," John Harvey said, "we've all agreed that you're doing a fine job and we want you to stay all summer. Agreed?"

He looked directly at Amber and she realized she was supposed to respond. She took a deep breath and said, "I'd like to try it a while longer. Maybe we could say two more weeks. That way, we'll all be sure." Then she added, "It wasn't right for me to have friends over and I won't do that anymore."

"We want you to have friends," Madeline said. "We simply haven't been planning your schedule correctly." She held out her hand and put it on Amber's arm and smiled sweetly. "Jason reminds us that you haven't had a regular day off and I know that makes it difficult to plan a social life."

Amber smiled. She could not quite imagine Mike as a "social life," but Madeline always spoke in peculiar generalities.

"You didn't do anything wrong. You're just the age to be interested in boys," John said. "There's nothing wrong in what you did, but we'd rather you saw your friends on your own time. And now you will have some time so that should work out. Right?"

Amber nodded in agreement.

John Harvey smiled and said, "Good. We've agreed that you can see your young men on your time off. They're welcome here. You pay all your attention to Kyle and Catty — we'd like you to include Catty more since she says she's getting bored with the horses." He looked as though he was wrapping everything up as he sipped the last of his coffee and concluded, "I suspect that Jason was a little off base because *he* wasn't the boy you are interested in, but he'll get over it."

Jason turned absolutely red with anger and Amber really did feel sorry for him. She spoke up. "I doubt that. Jason said what he did because of Kyle. He's very concerned about what is best for Kyle. He really cares."

Now it was Madeline's turn to flush and John Harvey looked uncomfortable, but he quickly said, "The point is — you will stay all summer and Kyle will be well cared for and you will get some time for yourself. How about two nights a week and one day? You can choose the day. Is that all right?"

"That's fine," Amber said. "But if I take a day off, who will watch Kyle?"

"Jason and Brett can help," John Harvey answered promptly and for the first time, Amber understood why they'd insisted that Brett be a part of this discussion. Now she would have two Harvey boys mad at her!

John Harvey seemed pleased with himself and he was apparently certain that everything was all worked out. He stood up and said, "Madeline and I are going to make more of an effort. This is a very creative family and each of us has his own interests, but we love each other. And we all love Kyle." John Harvey smiled again and added, "We're not deliberately neglecting our son, despite what Jason thinks."

"I didn't say you were neglecting him," Jason growled.

"You pretty nearly said that," his father replied. "But your opinion is based on some truth. I'll make it a point to spend more time with Kyle and so will Madeline." He turned to Amber again and said, "While we're here, let's give you a raise. How much are you making?"

"Fifteen hundred," Amber said.

"That's about right," John Harvey said. "We might be able to do two thousand a month but not more."

"It's fifteen hundred for the summer," Amber explained. "And that's a great salary. You don't need to give me a raise."

"I'll double your salary," John Harvey said decisively. He stood up and reached into his pocket as he said, "Say, I've got an idea, why don't you kids all go to Disneyland today? You're up and ready to go. Gates open at ten and it's eight-thirty. Make a day of it."

Catty jumped up and said, "Oh, could we?"

"Take the Land Rover," John Harvey said. "Jason, do you have the time to drive them?"

"I'm in school, Dad. If they'll wait till one o'clock . . ."

"Never mind," John Harvey said, "Amber can drive. Here — have a good time." He handed her several bills and said, "Better wake up Kyle and get going."

"Couldn't I just take the station wagon?" Amber asked. "I've never driven a Land Rover."

"You could have my Alfa Romeo," Madeline offered. "I'm certainly not going anywhere after that all-night ride. I can keep the Land Rover and John can use the Porsche."

"I'd really rather have the station wagon," Amber protested.

John Harvey laughed and hugged her. "I'm more worried about my kids than my car. If I can trust Kyle and Catty to you, I can surely trust you with my car." Then he said, "Tell you what, Jason, you take the Alfa Romeo and give Amber your Corvette."

"Oh please, no!" Amber said. "I know how to drive the station wagon and it's just going to be parked all day. Let us go in that."

John Harvey looked at her quizzically and raised one eyebrow and said, "Jason said you were hardheaded and I believe he knew what he was saying. Take the station wagon and have a good time."

Chapter 17

Kyle complained that he didn't want to go to Disneyland but Catty and Amber somehow got him into the car anyway. Before she had quite digested the morning's decisions, Amber was driving on the freeway to Disneyland.

Catty was elated with the success of her family conference and wanted to give Amber a blow-by-blow accounting of what everyone said. "Madeline and Jason finally told each other what they thought. Dad was the peacekeeper, of course. I guess he loves them both."

"I'm sure he does," Amber said. She discouraged Catty from telling her much more because it didn't seem quite fair. If the Harveys had wanted her at the family conference, they would have invited her.

After Catty spent a few minutes telling her how everyone really wanted her to stay, Amber said, "I said I'd stay for at least two more weeks. Now let's drop this subject and have some fun. Let's listen to the radio."

Catty found a country western station and said, "I'm thinking of giving up horses and doing something else for the rest of the summer. Maybe become a surfer. But I like country western music a lot better than surfing music."

Amber kept her eye on the road and let Catty's chatter roll over her as though it were part of the background noise. She had the exact directions and she knew something about driving freeways now so the trip was an easy one. They were there by ten-fifteen. Amber pulled into a parking space and opened her bag to count the money John Harvey had given her. She had five hundred dollars!

Amber split the money into four piles. She put two hundred dollars in a pocket, one hundred in each shoe, and left one hundred in the glove compartment of the car. At least they wouldn't lose it all in one place.

Catty asked, "What are you doing?"

"Hiding money. Your dad gave me too much."

"You could give some to me," Catty offered.

Amber laughed and said, "If you want something, just ask. I guess he meant us to spend it."

"Of course he did," Catty agreed. "It's good we're late because now we have to take the trolley."

"Trolley?"

"It's not a real trolley," Catty said. "But if you park anywhere except right in front, you get to ride this cute little train into the gates. I guess you've never been here before?"

"No. I've only been in California three weeks and I haven't seen much except Malibu," Amber reminded her.

"We could go a lot of places now that you're staying," Catty said. "Disneyland can be boring but I'll show you around."

They went to the new rides first and then stood in line for the old favorites. There were a couple that Kyle refused to go on, so Catty had to go alone, and each time she grumbled, "We should have waited for Jason. Then I wouldn't have to go alone."

Each time Catty mentioned Jason, Amber got a funny feeling in her stomach. She really felt terrible that he had been forced to apologize to her and she knew he would never forgive her. She was glad she was staying and not really fired, but she knew she would have to sidestep Jason for the rest of the summer.

And it was really humiliating when his father made the crack that maybe Jason was jealous. When she thought back to that family conference, she saw that there wasn't all that much difference in the way John Harvey thought and spoke and the way her own father might have behaved. They both felt they knew a whole lot more about teenagers than they really did.

Most of the day she just enjoyed herself and didn't worry about the future. She bought postcards to send to her family and friends and an instant camera to take Catty and Kyle's photographs. She even asked someone to take a shot of the three of them.

"Are you guys hungry?" she asked about two o'clock. "Where do you want to eat?"

"We always take the monorail to the hotel and eat there," Catty said.

Amber enjoyed the monorail ride and it was fun to visit the hotel but she was a little surprised at the lunch bill. By the time they ordered dessert and drinks, she was almost through her second hundred-dollar bill. If they stayed much longer she would have to take off her shoe.

That's exactly what she did when Kyle found a toy in Tomorrowland and insisted he wanted it. She sat right down on the bench outside the store and took off her tennis shoe and took out the money. A young man standing beside her asked, "You always carry your money in your boots?"

"I know you," Amber said. "You were a clown at Ray Redmond's house last week. Right?"

"Right." He laughed and said, "You recognized my voice, didn't you?"

"Yes," Amber answered. "I remember thinking at the time that you were probably an actor. Are you?" Now that she could see the face that went with the voice, she thought it was very possible. He was attractive with rugged good looks and dark hair and skin. Not handsome like Mike or Brett but really attractive in an athletic sort of way.

"No," he answered. "I'm a surfer and a clown on the side. Name is Tony Valdez."

"Should I know the name?" Amber asked.

"You wouldn't know me unless you read surfing magazines."

A tall, slim girl with long black hair called out, "Tony, over here."

"I know your girlfriend, too," Amber said. "At least a friend of mine knows her. I've seen her on the beach. It really is a small world, isn't it?"

"That's my sister." He waved to her and called out, "Lucia, over here."

The girl drew closer, saw Amber, and laughed. Amber remembered her wonderful laugh and smiled in reply. The girl asked, "What are you doing here?"

"Right now I'm buying a toy," Amber said. "I've got the little boy I take care of and his sister on a trip to Disneyland. What are you doing?"

"Tony's here on business and I'm along for the ride," Lucia answered promptly. "So, do you live in Malibu?"

"I live right on the beach where I saw you," Amber answered. "At least I live there for the summer." She went on to explain to Lucia about her job and then asked, "Do you live in Malibu?"

"We live in the hills," Lucia said. "Fourth generation. Our dad owns a landscaping business and his dad is a retired stuntman. His dad was a gardener and his dad . . ."

"That's enough," Tony laughed. "Come on, Lucia, I've got to see a man about a board."

"My brother might be in a Disney movie about surfing," Lucia said proudly. "I've got to go but it was great to see you."

"Maybe I'll see you on the beach," Amber said.

"Yeah, maybe," Lucia said. "You live right next door to Mike, huh?"

"Yes, I do," Amber said.

Lucia frowned and said, "Mind if I give you some advice? I'd stay away from Mike."

Amber shrugged; there didn't seem to be much else to do. It was too bad the girl was so crazy about Mike that she felt he was her property, but she could understand the attraction. She liked Mike, too.

Lucia smiled and said, "I'll see you at the beach. I could use a new friend."

"So could I," Amber answered. "But I'm sort of on duty on the beach. Maybe we could get together on one of my days off though."

Lucia nodded, flashed her a smile, and then darted after her brother. Amber looked at the girl with the long swinging hair and the deep, hearty laugh and really hoped they could be friends. She supposed it depended on how things went with Mike and how jealous Lucia was.

Amber went into the shop and bought Kyle the toy and then she bought Catty a cowboy hat. She thought both items were overpriced but why should she worry when no one else did?

By four in the afternoon, Amber was certain they had been on every ride in the place. She was overwhelmed with the noise, the heat, and the confusion so she suggested they think about going home. "Oh, no," Catty said. "We can see some shows and then watch the parade. They have a parade every night just at dark. And there are bands. We can stay till midnight."

"No we can't," Amber said. "We'll leave here by seven-thirty at the latest."

"Only seven-thirty?" Catty cried. "Then we'd better get moving. I want to try the Matterhorn again and then I'd like to go through the Haunted House again and there's lots more to buy."

They went on some of the best rides again and watched the parade. It really was a lot of fun to see all the Disney characters marching down Main Street and Amber laughed and clapped as though she were eight years old. In fact, she was a lot more enthusiastic than Catty or Kyle, but they had seen it all many times before. "Jason takes us here a lot," Catty told her.

By the time they got to their car it was almost nine o'clock and Kyle fell asleep the minute they started moving. Amber and Catty sang school songs most of the way home and then they told silly jokes. As they pulled into the driveway in Malibu, Catty said, "First it was Jason and now Dad wants me to spend more time with you. They think you will be a good influence because you're so normal. I don't think you're so normal — I think you're really nice."

"I think you're nice, too," Amber said and she hugged Catty. "Now can you help me get Kyle into the house?"

"I'll take his feet," Catty offered.

"If you take his stuff, that will be a big help," Amber said. "I can carry him."

Chapter 18

Amber slept late the next morning and when she woke, Madeline was in the living room, sipping tea and looking through a fashion magazine. Madeline asked, "Would you like to have today off?"

"All of it?"

"Yes. I'm having a manicure and pedicure and then my day is free. Mrs. Murdock will watch Kyle until I get home. You can run along." Then Madeline looked at her and said, "Why don't you get your hair cut? I'll have my stylist Matsui do it. He's wonderful."

Amber laughed aloud. "I had to promise my father I wouldn't cut my hair if I took this job. I can't go home with short hair."

"Not short hair, my dear," Madeline shook her head. "You would never want short hair. But a trim is definitely in order. I'll make an appointment for you right now."

Before Amber could even protest, Madeline was on the phone making arrangements for an eleven-thirty haircut.

Kyle came out of his room on his own and asked, "Are we going to the beach?"

Amber said, "Oh, Kyle, not today. I have to have my hair cut."

"But we didn't go yesterday," Kyle complained.

Rather than argue with him, Amber asked, "Would you be happy with just an hour at the beach? I have to leave at ten-thirty but we could go down there for a little while."

"That's a great idea," Madeline said. "And maybe we'll all go together. You could take Kyle shopping and then we can all have lunch with Irena. It will be a late lunch, but it will be fun, won't it?"

Amber smiled and said to Kyle, "Go get your swimsuit on." She tried not to notice that her day off had mostly disappeared.

When they got to the beach, Mike sauntered over and asked, "Did the fireworks die down?"

"Oh, Mike, I almost lost my job," Amber said. "I can't talk to you anymore while I'm watching Kyle."

"That's the craziest thing I ever heard,"

Mike said. "You can't go out at night and you can't talk to me in the daytime. They really are slave drivers."

"No, they're nice," Amber said. "And I do have tonight off."

"Good, I'll pick you up at six-thirty."

"All right. Where will we go?"

"The movies or something. Don't dress up."

He reached over to touch her and Amber drew back quickly. "Sorry but I can't be seen with you while I'm on duty."

He didn't look happy, but he did move away, picking up his towel and saying, "Guess I'll head up the coast. See you this evening."

The haircut turned out to be wonderful. Madeline told her stylist exactly what she wanted and between the two of them, they designed a layered cut that showed off the fullness of Amber's hair and made it even more naturally curly. When her hair was washed and dried, Madeline said, "And give her some good shampoo. I notice her color is fading in this bright sun."

Amber tried to pay for her own haircut, but Madeline just acted as though she had never heard of anything so silly. Secretly, Amber was glad she didn't have to pay because she was sure if the salon cut Madeline's hair, they were very expensive. Well, she had to admit she looked great.

Amber took Kyle shopping in a huge toy store and insisted he buy some board games and books. She didn't care what anyone said, she didn't think it was good for him to sit around all afternoon and watch movies.

They met Irena and Madeline for lunch at the Frisky Frog. Amber tried not to look at the right side of the menu as she ordered her lunch. If Madeline wanted to eat in restaurants that charged three dollars for a cup of coffee, that was her choice. I'm just the hired help, not the financial advisor, Amber reminded herself.

Irena and Madeline did most of the talking — mostly about some new painting class they planned to take in the fall. As they were waiting for their bill, Irena asked, "Are you getting lots of invitations to places where you can wear that wonderful blue dress?"

"I have a date tonight," Amber sidestepped the question, "but I think I'll wear a sundress I brought with me."

"I didn't know you had a real date," Madeline said. "I thought your friend would just come over to visit for a while."

"It's just to go to the movies," Amber explained. "The silk would be too dressy."

"I meant I don't know if we should let you go out on a date. Your parents might not approve," Madeline said.

Amber stared at Madeline and wondered what went on in the woman's head. One minute she seemed to expect everyone to be adult and make all the decisions and the next minute she seemed to be reading lines from some old-fashioned television script.

"I wouldn't let her go out with just anybody," Irena agreed.

"Mike isn't just anyone," Amber said. "He lives right next door."

"But we don't know him," Madeline said. "If you want to go out on a date maybe Jason . . . no, maybe Brett would take you."

Amber opened and closed her mouth without saying anything else. She would wait until they got home and then she would talk to John Harvey. That seemed to be the way everyone handled things around Madeline and for the first time, she really understood why.

But to her surprise, John Harvey was inclined to agree with his wife. "This isn't like where you come from," he told Amber. "Just because Mike lives next door doesn't mean he's reliable."

"He's perfectly reliable," Amber said.

"You can't know him well enough," John

Harvey said. "You haven't been here long."

"And didn't Jason say he was undesirable?" Madeline asked her husband.

Amber began to really get mad when she heard that. "Jason doesn't know him," she insisted. "I do. And I'll tell you this much, my parents would trust my judgment."

John Harvey shook his head, "Jason says you have a lot to learn about boys — that you're very young. I trust his judgment."

She stared at the man and thought of all the things she wanted to say to him. Even more important, she thought of all the things she wanted to say to Jason! But she only said, "Why don't we call my parents and see what they think?"

"Perhaps we *should* call them," Madeline said to her husband.

"I'll call them if you want," Amber offered. She was certain her mother would back her up on this. She wasn't so sure about her father, but he wouldn't be home at this time of day.

"Okay, Amber, I'm sure you know what you're doing," John Harvey said. "But I think it would be a good idea if you took one of the cellular phones with you."

At exactly six-thirty, Mike rang the bell and Amber brought him in to meet Mr. and Mrs. Harvey. They shook hands and then Amber said, "I'll just get my purse." She picked up the large white bag that Madeline had given her just an hour earlier. Inside were a lipstick, a comb, two twenty-dollar bills, four quarters, and a miniature cellular telephone.

Chapter 19

Mike held her hand as they walked to the car and he helped her into a big Cadillac, leaning to kiss her on the mouth before he opened the door. Amber hoped that none of the Harveys were watching because she knew the intensity of that kiss would worry them. He was holding her really tight. She squirmed and said, "Let me go, Mike."

Mike laughed and let her go. As he got into the driver's seat, he said, "You look pretty. That a new dress?"

"Sort of," Amber said.

Mike reached out and touched her hair. "Pretty. You look different tonight. More grown-up."

"I got my hair cut."

"You look pretty," Mike repeated.

"Where are we going?" Amber asked.

"Where do you want to go?" he answered.

"How about a drive up the coast to Santa Barbara? It's only an hour away."

"I thought we were going to the movies."

"We can if you want," Mike said. "Only I don't like movies much. Do you?"

Amber laughed out loud. "You're the first person I've met in California who didn't like movies. What do you like to do?"

"Surf. Chase pretty girls like you. I like it best when I catch them. Party."

Amber wished she knew what to say. She really liked being around Mike, he *was* very nice and very cute, but there were times when his attitude worried her. She was certain he was kidding but even if he was joking, it bothered her. Finally she said, "I'm sure you have lots of other interests."

"Don't be too sure," he said and dropped his arm around her shoulders. They sat in silence for a long distance and Amber enjoyed the view as they drove up the coast. She was intrigued by the way the town of Malibu seemed to stretch on and on. She said, "I read Malibu is twenty-seven miles long but I didn't quite believe it. Where's Zuma Beach?"

"About halfway," Mike said. "We can stop there."

The ocean was beautiful when she caught

glimpses of it through the houses and then, suddenly, the houses thinned out and she could see long stretches of sand and sea. "Now this is what I thought Malibu would look like," she said.

"Out here on the dunes there are only a few houses. Look up there," Mike pointed to a cliff ahead of them. "Some of the richest people in the world live right there. That's what I call the good life."

"How can you be so certain that they're happy just because they live in an expensive neighborhood?"

"I'm not certain *they're* happy." He patted Amber's leg. "I'm only certain *I'd* be happy."

They passed a sign that said Zuma Beach and Mike said, "It's too crowded here. I know a better place." They drove on until the landscape became more perpendicular and it was impossible to see the ocean. Suddenly, Mike pulled into a side road. He took the corner so sharply that Amber slid toward him, despite the seat belt she was wearing. He squeezed her tight.

Amber wanted to tell him to lighten up, but she didn't want to make a big deal out of it. She didn't want Mike to think she was too young. On the other hand, she was beginning to think that maybe she was. As they drove down the road, she asked, "How old are you, Mike?"

"Older than you," he teased.

"But how old?"

"Guess."

She knew he was a freshman at Davis and she also knew he wasn't much of a student so she guessed, "Nineteen?"

"Something like that," he agreed.

As they drove down a long, dark dirt road, Amber admitted to herself that her parents might not be crazy about her dating someone three years older than she was. Actually, she wasn't sure what the rules were because the subject had never come up.

You came to California to have fun, she reminded herself. The road straightened out and they came into a secluded little cove. Mike pulled into the only parking space at the end of the road and said, "Let's get out and walk around."

"I can't," Amber said. "My shoes hurt."

"Take them off."

She didn't really want to get out on this deserted beach. It wasn't that she was afraid of Mike, but she felt uncomfortable because it was such a remote area.

Mike got out of the car and went around

back to open the trunk of the car. He was carrying a blanket when he came to Amber's side. His voice was impatient as he said, "Come on, Amber. Don't act like a kid."

He bent down, unsnapped Amber's seat belt, and swooped her up in his arms. Before she knew exactly what was happening, she was on the beach, sitting on a blanket with Mike.

"It's beautiful, isn't it?" Mike asked her. "I really wanted you to see this side of Malibu. Hardly anyone knows this is here. There are caves up above. We could climb in them when we come back in the daytime."

"It is beautiful," Amber agreed. "Doesn't anyone live here?" She was a little bit angry at Mike for insisting they come to the beach, but she had to admit that this cove was a very special place. The wind was up and there were little whitecaps skipping along the surface of the sea. To Amber, it looked as if the ocean was dancing and she said, "Do you come here often?"

"Can't," Mike said. "The road is private and they usually have someone watching from above."

"Is this a private beach? Are we trespassing?"

"Trespassing?" Mike laughed at her concern and put his arm around her and held her close to him. "We're not hurting anyone are we? Don't worry about it."

"Mike, if we are trespassing, I really think we should go."

"Little Miss-follow-the-rules," Mike said. "You can't follow the rules all the time, Amber."

He kissed her again, but Amber really didn't enjoy the kiss. Mike was kissing her so intensely. He was holding her too close. And then his hands began to stray over her body and she pushed him away. "Let me go, Mike!"

He tried to pull her close to him and she pushed him away again. Until now, she'd been unsure about what Mike intended. But now she decided she didn't really like him at all and that he probably didn't even like her, either. "Get your hands off me," she demanded.

He laughed and said, "I've got some beer in the trunk. I'll go get it."

"No!" Amber said. For the first time, she began to feel anxious. "I want to leave here right now!"

"I don't suppose *you* drink beer," Mike said. "But I'm thirsty. Stay right here."

He got up and she wasn't sure what she should do next. The cove was so secluded and she realized that whether she should be or not, she was frightened.

"I want to go home," she called to him in a loud and very definite voice.

Mike just looked at her and laughed. Then he turned and walked toward the car.

She sat on the beach blanket feeling so stupid. She wished she had listened to the Harveys' advice. She wished she had insisted on going to the movies. She wished she'd been a little older and wiser.

She shivered in the night air and tried to decide what to do next. Then she remembered Tony's sister, Lucia, at Disneyland. This was what Lucia had meant! She wasn't jealous! She was trying to warn her about Mike. She had been trying to tell Amber not to trust him. Amber felt ridiculous and she promised herself that when she got out of this mess, she would never make the same mistake again.

But how was she supposed to get Mike off this beach and back to the Harvey house? She certainly didn't want to stay here and she didn't want to go anywhere else with him. He just assumed I was a pushover, she thought, and the idea made her furious.

There was no way out of this cove except back up the road they came down. For one moment, she was grateful to the Harveys for giving her the cellular telephone. She could always call them. But it would be just her luck to have Jason answer and that would be total humiliation. Even so, she decided she probably should call. Then she laughed out loud as she realized that the phone was in her purse in the car. She would have to follow Mike up to the car and confront him. There was no other way.

She took off her shoes and walked through the sand to the car.

As she was walking, she saw headlights coming down the hill. She wasn't sure what was going to happen next, but she knew one thing — she was going to make Mike take her home.

A Jeep blocked the Cadillac and a man got out just as Amber got to the car. The man was carrying a flashlight and he was shining it on Mike's face. Since he'd left his car lights on, Amber could see him clearly and she saw that he was wearing a uniform. Mike was showing him a driver's license.

She walked up and the man said, "May I see some identification, miss?"

"My bag is in the car," Amber said.

She got her bag and took out her driver's license and the man looked it over carefully. Finally he said, "You're a long way from home, aren't you, miss?"

"I'm staying in Malibu this summer and I'd really like to go home now." She looked directly at the guard, hoping he would get her message.

"Where?"

Amber gave him the address and then he asked for the phone number. He wrote them down in his book. The guard turned to Mike and said, "Here's the deal. I'd drive her home myself but I've got my rounds to make. You get this young woman home in twenty minutes. I'm calling her house and she better be there. If she's not home, I'll put out an all points bulletin and we'll find you and press trespassing charges. How does that sound?"

"We weren't hurting anything," Mike said sullenly.

"You're on private property. And this girl wants to go home. You rather come into court?"

"Of course not."

Amber turned to the man, smiled, and said, "Thank you."

Mike looked really mad, but he didn't say anything until they got into the car and drove up the dirt road and onto the highway. Then he said, "You weren't a lot of help back there."

Amber was clutching the bag with the telephone in it just in case Mike didn't drive her straight home. Now that she was out of the embarrassing situation, she had to keep her head together to keep from letting Mike know how scared she'd been. She asked, "Are you taking me straight home?"

"You bet," Mike answered. "You didn't need to sound as though you thought you were being rescued, you know."

Amber said, "I *felt* as though I were being rescued."

Mike glowered and drove her to her door without another word. She got into the house just in time to catch the telephone before anyone else did. The man on the other end of the phone said, "You're home all right?"

"I'm fine. I guess I was fine all along, you know. I had a cellular phone with me."

"You *looked* pretty worried," the man said. "Better stay away from guys like him from now on."

"I will," she promised.

"Have a nice summer vacation," the man said.

As she hung up the telephone, Madeline and John Harvey came into the living room. Madeline said, "You're home early. Did you have a nice time, dear?"

"Sort of," Amber answered. "But Mike and I don't have much in common. I won't be seeing him again."

"That's fine," Madeline said. "You should

only date the finest of boys — a nice girl like you."

"I think I'll just concentrate on sightseeing and skip boys," Amber said.

Madeline looked slightly perplexed and finally she asked, "But what will you do with all your time off?"

"I think I've met a nice girl," Amber said. "She's about my age and she lives in Malibu. Maybe we can do some things together."

Chapter 20

Amber was grateful that Catty didn't quiz her about her date the next morning but Catty was so full of plans that she could only think about herself. "I'm definitely going to give up horses," she said. "I'm going to do something more interesting with my life."

"And what would that be?" Amber asked as she poured milk over her cereal.

"I had a long talk with Jason last night and we agreed that I'm a natural born writer. He said I could use his laptop computer for the summer. I'm going to write. I think I'll start with the story of my life."

"Good thinking." Amber agreed quickly because it did seem that Catty was better suited to writing than to riding horses. She was so talkative and creative, she just might have some talent.

"I'm going to spend more time with *you*, too," Catty announced.

"Good," Amber said. "Only you have to remember I was hired to take care of Kyle. He has to come first."

"I know," Catty agreed. "I can help you take care of Kyle and on your day off I'll watch him."

Amber thought she detected Jason's opinions in Catty's words but she was so happy to get through breakfast without talking about Mike that she just smiled and agreed. "Yes, you are all one family and you do love each other. You're a very close-knit family in your own way, I'm beginning to see that now."

"I guess you don't think we're so weird after all?"

"Just you," Amber teased. "I think the rest of the family is perfectly normal."

"It's better to be creative than normal," Catty said.

Kyle came into the kitchen then and asked, "Can I have breakfast?"

"You may have whatever your heart desires," Amber said. "You dressed yourself this morning, didn't you?"

Kyle smiled proudly.

"That's wonderful." Amber bent to hug him and decided to say nothing about the choice of red print shorts and an orange and green-and-yellow striped T-shirt.

"His clothes really c-l-a-s-h," Catty spelled the last word out.

"It's better to be creative than n-o-r-m-a-l," Amber replied.

She took Kyle to the beach a little earlier than usual to avoid Jason's arrival. Once there, she asked Kyle, "Would you please take a swim with me? I've never been in the ocean swimming and I want to try it."

Kyle quickly shook his head no and said, "You go."

"I heard you are a really good swimmer, Kyle. Why don't you like the ocean?"

"It burns."

"Burns your eyes?"

"Just burns," Kyle answered and he went off with his trucks.

Amber read for a while and then she went down to the water's edge and asked, "How about a nice long walk?"

Kyle shook his head no.

"Hamburger and a Coke." Amber thought she might be able to bribe him, but he said, "I want to stay here."

She decided to be pleased that Kyle was actually talking in full-length sentences today.

She could really see the progress they were making on communication skills and she hoped the others could see it as well.

"Okay, Kyle," Amber said. "Maybe later." She started back toward her towel when she saw Lucia Valdez coming toward her, waving her hand.

Lucia came closer and said, "Good, you're here. I thought I might find you. Look, I wanted to talk to you about Mike. I think you probably thought I was jealous the other day at Disneyland and . . ."

Amber smiled ruefully and said, "You don't have to talk to me about Mike. I went out with him last night and it was awful."

"Did you end up walking home?"

"Almost. Does he always act like that with girls?"

Lucia shrugged and said, "I guess so. I've never been out with him, because my brother Tony warned him to leave me alone, but he has an amazing reputation, considering he's only been here a little while.

"Were you crazy about him, I mean before last night? Is your heart broken?" Lucia seemed genuinely concerned.

"My pride was wounded as much as anything," Amber admitted. "I sort of had to fight to get out of the house — my employers' son told them not to trust Mike. I don't know how he knew."

"Boys know things like that about other boys, I guess."

"Anyway, they weren't so sure I should go and I insisted. That was one argument I wish I'd lost. It was pretty humiliating," she continued.

The two girls were walking on dry sand and Amber pointed to her towel. "I'm over there, but I'm not supposed to be with friends when I'm watching Kyle."

"That's too bad," Lucia said. "I could put my towel over there and if anyone comes down to check on you, I could move quickly."

Amber wasn't sure it was a good idea but she wanted to get to know Lucia better so she nodded in agreement, saying, "I can see Kyle just fine. I'll tell you what. I'll talk to you and look at him the whole time. Kyle never takes any risks anyway, he doesn't like the ocean. In fact, I wish he would take some risks."

Lucia put her towel down about fifteen feet away and then crossed over to Amber's and sat down comfortably. "Now tell me everything that happened," Lucia said. "I'm naturally nosy and it will be good for you to talk about it."

"Promise you won't tell anyone else — not even your brother?" Amber had definitely discovered that Malibu was a small town and if Lucia told her brother, the whole story could easily find its way back to Jason.

"You can trust me." Lucia crossed her heart. Both girls laughed and Amber told her the whole story.

"He's really gross," Lucia said. "Funny, you'd think a guy as good-looking as that would know better than to be so obnoxious. The first time I saw him, I thought he was really cute. Of course, I was only fourteen and my brother wouldn't let me get within ten feet of him."

"So you're fifteen now?"

"Yes, you must be sixteen because you can drive." Lucia sighed. "I can hardly wait till I can drive. I feel so stuck this summer."

"I get a day off each week — at least I'm supposed to. Maybe we could go somewhere."

"Anywhere!"

"I'd really like to go back to Rodeo Drive and look around," Amber said. "The stores seemed really cool." She added, "I'm collecting memories to tell my friends in Wisconsin."

"What kind of memories?"

"So far, I've been to Disneyland and Rodeo Drive. I've had a fancy haircut and I've been to a party at Ray Redmond's house. I saw lots of movie stars there."

"I'd say you were doing pretty well." Lucia laughed. "If you like movie stars, I think my brother Tony knows just about everyone. The Sheen brothers — Charlie Sheen and Emilio Estevez — live right up the road in Broad Beach. So does Bridget Fonda. I mean, they're not exactly his friends or anything, but he meets just about everyone surfing."

"Your brother is really a famous surfer?"

"Yeah. He's a professional now. He's got sponsors and he's been in two movies already. And he gets commercials all the time."

Amber had been watching Kyle very carefully the whole time she was talking to Lucia, and now she saw him get up and start running up the sand. She said to Lucia, "You'd better go now. Kyle must see his brother Jason. That's the only person he runs to."

"Jason must be nice," Lucia said as she stood quickly and dusted off the sand.

"The older brother, Brett, is a lot nicer," Amber said. "He's not home much but he's very polite and more mature. Handsome, too," she added as though an afterthought. "Very handsome."

Lucia laughed and teased, "Aren't you

lucky? Two fabulous brothers in the house where you work. You don't need to worry about meeting anyone else — you've got your pick of the two of them."

"You don't know Jason," Amber said and frowned. "I wouldn't pick him if he were the last man on earth."

"But Brett is definitely in the running?"

Amber shrugged and said, "I don't know him well but . . . look, would you go on over to your own towel. I can see Jason now, so that means he can see us."

Lucia crossed over and called in a loud whisper, "When's your next day off?"

"I'm not sure. They said I could have any day I wanted once a week but you can't really count on them — Kyle's stepmother is pretty vague."

"When you get your day off, can you have the car?"

"I think so. One of them." Amber laughed and added, "I'm scared to drive anything but the station wagon but if you give me your number, I'll call you tonight." She saw that Catty and Jason and Kyle were almost within hearing distance and she lowered her voice. "Just write it down and toss it to me."

"I don't have a pencil."

"I do." Amber began to rummage around her bag but she couldn't find a pencil. "Here they come," she said.

Lucia jumped up and pretended to just be walking by. She said, "I'll write it in the sand. We can pretend we're detectives in a thriller." She laughed and ran down to the sand where she picked up a stick and wrote her number next to Kyle's truck.

Amber smiled and she felt as though she'd known Lucia a long time and that they were going to be very good friends. At least they would be good friends if Jason didn't spoil it.

The minute Lucia left, Amber took a pencil and a piece of paper from her bag and carried it down to the wet sand. She quickly wrote Lucia's number down as she pretended to be collecting Kyle's trucks and shovels. When she returned to her towel, Jason and Catty were spreading towels out next to hers. Catty said, "I got my new laptop and I'll be writing for hours and hours. But first, want to go swimming?"

"I'd love to but I can't get Kyle to go in the water," Amber answered.

"I'll watch Kyle," Jason said.

Catty caught her hand and they ran into the water. Amber was happy enough to run away from Jason. She hadn't really talked to him since their big fight and she was certain he was still angry at her. Nevertheless, she really enjoyed her swim. It was the first time she'd been able to go out beyond the waves and she swam a long distance, until everyone on the sand looked quite small.

Out there, in what felt like the middle of the Pacific Ocean, she was quite happy. She wasn't worried about what Jason was thinking. She had forgotten all about Mike and that stupid experience. She was perfectly at ease and perfectly happy just bobbing up and down on the waves. She felt as though she was a million miles from everyone and everything until Catty swam up to her and said, "You're a good swimmer. Where did you learn?"

"In lakes," Amber answered. "But seawater is different — more waves."

"Want to race?" Catty asked. She began to swim parallel to the water's edge just as fast as she could. Amber knew she could never catch her so she watched until Catty disappeared from sight. Then Amber decided it was time to return to Kyle. Amber dropped down on her towel and said, "Your sister is a great swimmer."

Jason nodded. "You need to put on sunscreen. And where's that hat I gave you?"

Amber laughed. "I should have known you

thought of the hat. I forgot it but I'll go get it as soon as I dry off."

"I'll get it," he said and he ran up to the house. In a few minutes he came back with her straw hat and a six-pack of Cokes. He dropped the Cokes on the towel and said, "I'll help with the sunscreen."

Jason poured some cream on his hands and began to massage her back. She shivered, and then relaxed and let herself feel the softness of the cream. It made her a little uncomfortable to be touched by Jason and after a while she said, "Are you sure you shouldn't switch to medical school or something? I never saw anyone worry so much about other people's sunburns." Once she said it, she wished she could retract her words. She was going to have to learn how to talk to Jason without sounding as though she were picking a fight, if she was to stay for the summer.

Jason ignored her and screwed the cap back on the tube. He opened a Coke and asked, "Why don't you invite your friend over? What's her name?"

Amber thought about saying Lucia wasn't her friend but then she decided she had always told the truth and she wasn't going to stop now. "Her name is Lucia and I was watching Kyle every second I was talking to her."

"Invite her over," Jason said. "She looks nice."

Amber was tempted to say something about the way Jason was willing to change the rules when a pretty brunette was involved. She knew better than to pick a fight though and it didn't really matter that Jason only wanted Lucia to join them because he thought she was attractive. Lucia was her friend and Amber was glad of her company so she went over and invited her to join them.

Lucia jumped up and said, "I guess he's not such a terrible guy, after all."

"He likes pretty brunettes, that's all," Amber said crossly.

Lucia laughed and said, "Don't be bitter. Blonds get most of the attention in this world, you know."

"I'm not bitter," Amber answered quickly. "I'm glad he invited you and I hope you guys get along really well. It will make my summer a lot nicer."

When Lucia met Jason, she said, "I hear you're a great brother. I have a big brother who always took care of me when I was a kid. It was nice."

Jason seemed pleased that someone recognized that he was a good brother and very quickly he was telling Lucia all about his studies and his school. Amber sat rather silently and listened to the two of them talk. She was amazed at how friendly and relaxed Jason sounded when he was talking to Lucia.

Amber asked Lucia to put more sunscreen on her back and Jason said, "I think I'll take a swim before I leave. Anyone want to come along?"

"I will," Kyle answered quickly.

Amber watched Jason run down the beach and dive into the ocean. She saw Kyle miss one beat and then dive in right after his brother. "I've been here three weeks and I haven't been able to get him to put more than a toe in the water," Amber said.

"It's natural for him to want to copy Jason," Lucia answered. "He's nice."

"Kyle? Yes, he's a sweet little boy. I've grown quite fond of him."

Lucia looked at her new friend through a fringe of dark brown lashes. "I meant Jason," she said. "Jason is nice."

Amber shrugged. "I suppose if I'd met him for the first time today I might agree. But trust me, Jason is not nice. He's rude, he's bossy, and overprotective."

Lucia just smiled and said, "I still think he's nice . . . and cute, too."

Chapter 21

For the next week, Amber's routine changed a lot. She and Lucia met on the beach nearly every morning and they laughed and talked while Kyle played on the sand. Some days they talked Kyle into going into the water with them and some days he was too stubborn to budge.

Amber liked having Lucia around because it made her job a lot more interesting and everyone seemed to think it was fine that she'd made a friend. Madeline even suggested they pack a bigger lunch so Lucia could have a part in the picnics.

Catty would join them for lunch and give them a blow-by-blow description of what she was writing on her computer. Catty actually agreed to watch Kyle long enough for Amber to really swim and that made all the difference in her days at the beach — especially since the weather was very hot.

Twice that week, Jason came down to the beach. When he was there, Kyle would go in the water and that pleased Amber even though she was annoyed by the fact that Kyle was so willing to do things for Jason he wouldn't do for her.

"It's natural he should follow his brother," Lucia said. "When I was a kid, I used to think my brother was the best guy in the world. I still do."

"It's just that I'd like Kyle to swim *every* day. And run around like other kids do. I really think it's good for him to do physical things," Amber said. "He spends so much of his time in his own world."

"A lot of kids are like that," Lucia said.

Amber sighed and answered, "I know the Harveys mean well but they just don't seem to find the time to do things with Kyle, so it's up to me."

"I think on your day off we should go shopping," Lucia said. "Sales start around the fifteenth of July. You can pick up great clothes this time of year."

Amber laughed and said, "I don't think I'm going to find Wisconsin school clothes on sale in California in July. We wear wool sweaters and boots and mittens. Remember?"

"I keep forgetting you have to go back," Lucia said. "I wish you could just stay here."

"I think my family would miss me," Amber said. "In fact, my mother sounds like she already misses me a lot."

The next day when Lucia joined them on the beach, she asked, "How would you like some free surfing lessons? Tony has a big hole in his teaching schedule this afternoon. We could take your car and go up to Broad Beach where my brother gives lessons. We can bring Kyle and Catty with us."

"Great idea." Amber jumped at the chance and within thirty minutes they had gotten the keys to the station wagon away from Mrs. Murdock and the kids piled in the car. Catty had her own board and they tied it onto the rack on top.

Broad Beach was about ten miles north of the Harvey house and as they drove Pacific Coast highway, Amber asked in a low voice, "You don't think Mike will be there, do you?"

"It's a public beach," Lucia answered. "You're not going to let him scare you, are you?"

"Of course not," Amber answered, but she really hoped he wouldn't be there.

Tony seemed glad to see them and took Catty out for the first lesson. By the end of one lesson, Catty could stand up on a board and she announced to everyone who listened, "I think I'm a natural for this. Tony thinks so, too."

Lucia insisted on watching Kyle while Amber tried, but Amber didn't have quite as much success as Catty. She fell off the board over and over but she kept climbing on again. After a while, Tony said, "You've got what it takes, but not in one lesson. Do you have a board to practice on?"

"No," Amber said.

"Tell Lucia to give you hers and I'll bring a new one home to her tonight. I've got to get back to work. Good to see you."

Amber nodded and swam into shore. Lucia gave her a great-looking board and said, "You can keep it. Tony will replace it with something even better. He gets free boards from all these companies after him to use their boards. I get my pick of the rejects."

Then Lucia ran back into the surf. Amber sank down on her towel and stretched out in the sun. She was almost asleep when she felt sand dripping onto her bare midriff in a warm line. "Stop that," she said and opened her eyes, fully expecting to see Catty. Mike was standing over her, smiling down.

"Hello beautiful," he said. "Miss me?"

"Mike!"

Amber sat up quickly and brushed the sand off her midriff. Mike dropped onto the warm sand beside her and lightly ran his hand along her arm as he said in a smooth voice, "I asked if you missed me?"

"No, I didn't." Amber was very pleased to realize that was the absolute truth.

Mike laughed lightly and asked, "Are you having fun at the Harveys'?"

"A lot of it is fun," Amber answered. She really didn't want to talk to him. It made her feel silly to be sitting beside him pretending nothing unusual had ever happened between them. On the other hand, he looked so blond, so handsome and so — nice that it was hard to remember that he was such a jerk.

"So how's the kid getting along?"

"He's getting along just fine," Amber answered coolly.

"You sure you don't miss me?" Mike's fingers traced her arm lightly and moved up to her neck. Before she knew it, he had his hand in her hair and was drawing her toward him, gently, softly, and he was smiling.

She realized she was also smiling and that if she didn't watch it, she would soon be kissing Mike. She drew back sharply and said, "No!" Jumping to her feet, she added, "I didn't miss you and I don't want to talk to you."

"But you are talking to me," Mike pointed out with a smile on his face. "Come on, Amber. Don't you think you've carried this innocent-girl-meets-surfing-dude far enough? Are you still mad about the other night? You know, I would never do anything to hurt you — ever."

"Well you did, Mike," Amber answered. "You don't care about me, you only care about yourself."

"You are definitely overreacting. How about you give me another chance?" Mike asked confidently.

For one small second, Amber considered the possibility and then she drew in a deep breath and as she exhaled she said, "No. No more chances. Don't call me because I'll just tell Mr. Harvey to get rid of you. He'll probably call your mother and that will be really embarrassing for everyone."

Mike shrugged and said sullenly, "Don't worry. I won't call you. You're not the only pretty girl in Malibu, you know."

"I know," Amber called over her shoulder as she began running toward the surf. She dove in and swam very deliberately toward Tony, knowing that would get rid of Mike fast.

Amber drove Lucia home and then took Catty and Kyle back to the Harvey house. As she pulled into the driveway, Jason was just pulling out. He said, "I was just going to look for you. You all right?"

"Of course," Amber said. "We had a great time."

Then she smiled and waved her arm toward the surfboards on top of the station wagon. "Catty and I both had surfing lessons. We did really well."

Jason looked a little surprised, a little annoyed and then he said, "That's great. Where's Lucia?"

"I took her home," Amber answered.

"I thought she might stay for supper," Jason said. "Well, I've got to go."

"So long." Amber couldn't help wondering if Jason would have stayed around longer if Lucia had been there.

Chapter 22

When Amber got in the house she told Catty and Kyle to shower and went into her own bedroom to do the same thing. There was a big box from Saks on the bed. Amber opened it and took out a soft amber-colored long dress.

The box also contained gold sandals with ankle straps and a gold bag to match and a small card that said, "In appreciation, from Kyle."

Amber knew the dress was from Madeline and she went out to the living room to find her. Madeline was on the deck, sketching. She wore a long-sleeved white cotton blouse, white cotton slacks, and a large white straw hat with a scarf that tied under her chin. The only color was her bright red sash and her deep ruby lipstick.

"I really can't take that dress," Amber said.

"Did you try it on?" Madeline asked.

"Doesn't it fit? Irena and I thought it would be perfect for you."

"Madeline, I know you mean to be nice, but I really don't have any place to wear these expensive clothes. People don't wear gold sandals in Milwaukee."

"I want you to wear it tomorrow night," Madeline said. "By the way, do you want to invite your friend Lucia? Jason says she's a very nice girl."

"Where are we going tomorrow night?" Sometimes it really irritated her to hear the way everyone accepted Jason's pronouncements as though they were the absolute truth. *Jason says she's a very nice girl. Jason says you have a lot to learn about men. Jason says this and Jason says that.*

"We're going to a party that Marcus Margolis is giving for Lauren Blackmore. She's his wife."

Amber wasn't sure she even wanted to go to another big party where she didn't know anyone, but it would certainly be easier if Lucia came along. "I'm not sure Lucia will have anything fancy to wear."

Madeline laughed. "I'm sure she'll have *something* to wear. Her grandfather is a very famous man. The Valdez family owns a big ranch in the hills. Besides, Jason says she's stunning so whatever she puts on will be just fine."

Amber's face burned with some emotion that she could only think was anger. She wasn't certain why she was so upset. What did she care whether or not Jason thought Lucia was stunning? What Jason thought didn't matter to her one way or the other. "I'll ask her," Amber said.

"I'd like to see the dress on you," Madeline called out as she left the room.

It was the next evening before Amber actually put on the amber dress. She had known by looking that it would fit and look wonderful and so she waited until her hair was dry and her makeup was on before she slipped the gorgeous dress over her head. It felt marvelous and looked even better.

Amber stared at her reflection in the mirror. The dress hugged her body just right, showing off her figure without being too tight. Best of all, the dress was exactly the color of her hair and it glimmered with the same highlights that her hair had. She smiled at the reflection in the mirror and said, "You've come a long way from home, Amber." The glamorous young woman in the mirror smiled back.

Madeline approved of the dress and nodded, saying, "We knew it would be just right. I sent

Jason to pick up your friend. They'll join us there."

"I'll get Kyle ready," Amber said.

"The children aren't going," Madeline said. "The invitation said fourteen and older. Catty is furious, of course."

"Poor Catty."

"Catty will have plenty of opportunities," Madeline said. "And it will do her good to take some responsibility for Kyle."

"You're not leaving her alone with him are you?"

"Why not? She's thirteen."

"But Catty is a young thirteen," Amber objected.

"How old were you when you were left alone with your little brother?" Madeline asked.

"Eleven, but that was different."

"I'm sure it was. Nevertheless, Catty's father and I think it is time for her to take some responsibility." Then she smiled and said, "Besides, Mrs. Murdock is staying late to prepare for a dinner I'm giving tomorrow evening. The children will be included then."

Madeline obviously thought the discussion was over and Amber was relieved that Mrs. Murdock would be there so she made no further objection.

This time they took the Alfa Romeo and Amber sat alone in the backseat. She looked out the window as the car sped up the Coast highway for what seemed like miles and miles. Finally, when they were past Broad Beach and Zuma, she asked, "Is this party in Malibu?"

"Right up the road," John Harvey said. "So how do you like California, Amber?"

"I like it a lot," Amber said almost automatically.

"I guess it's a lot different from Missouri, isn't it?" he asked.

Amber didn't even bother to tell him she was from Wisconsin, not Missouri. Instead, she laughed and said, "Mr. Harvey, Malibu isn't as different as you might think."

"Really?"

"Really," Amber answered. "For instance, all you people in the movie business seem to know each other. It's like you all belong to the same Rotary Club or something."

"That so?" John Harvey seemed amused.

"You don't like outsiders, even if they are neighbors," Amber continued. "But you like my friend Lucia because you know her grandfather. That's just like a small town."

"Her grandfather was a great stuntman. Her father could have been, too, only he hurt his back early on. You ever been to their nursery?"

"No, I haven't."

"It's very impressive," John Harvey said. "Get Lucia to take you up there sometime soon. Good people, the Valdezes."

"That's what I mean," Amber said. "You decide that if one person in the family is good, they're all good. Or if one isn't trustworthy, then none of them are. That's just like Milwaukee."

John Harvey asked, "You see that boy next door anymore?"

Amber wished she hadn't said anything. It was natural for Mr. Harvey to think she was complaining about their resistance to Mike and she was sorry she'd brought the subject up.

She didn't have to answer his question though because they turned and began a slow climb to the top of a hill. The road was only one lane wide and very steep. In between holding her breath over the steep drop, she looked out at the most magnificent view of the ocean that she could ever imagine.

The ground leveled out as abruptly as it had risen and Amber realized they were in the midst of a parking lot that held about one hundred cars. "Marcus just flattened this hill to make it into a parking lot," Madeline said and shook her head in disapproval. "I hope he doesn't expect us to park our own car and walk on all this dirt."

"No, there's someone to park the cars," John Harvey said as he neatly maneuvered right up to the entrance.

An attendant opened the door for Madeline and then helped Amber out of the backseat. He looked at Amber quizzically for a moment and then said, "Have a nice evening."

Amber realized it was the man who'd chased Mike and her off the beach. This must be the house that owned the cove. She blushed a deep red and prayed he didn't recognize her. She followed Madeline and John Harvey into the house. Before they took three steps, they were greeted by Lucia, Jason, and Brett. Amber whispered to Lucia, "I've got to talk to you."

"Let's go to the ladies' room," Lucia said and dragged Amber off very quickly. As they entered, she said, "Wait till you see this place. What's up?"

"The guy who opened the door is the one who chased Mike and me off the beach. I'm sure he recognized me."

Lucia laughed. "Don't worry. Even if he did

recognize you, which I doubt, who would he tell?"

Amber realized the only person she was afraid he would tell was Jason. She knew that was ridiculous so she said, "I guess I over-reacted. Anyway, you look great."

Lucia was wearing a sleeveless bright yellow silk dress with a scoop neck and a very long straight skirt. "I wanted to put a long slit in the skirt," Lucia said, "but my mom said I wasn't old enough."

"Did you and Jason have a good time driving over?"

Lucia looked surprised at the question and said, "I guess so. We just drove. Think we should join the others?"

This party was much, much easier than the last one for Amber. For one thing, she wasn't as overwhelmed by the house. It was just as big and just as fancy, but she'd grown a little more sophisticated in the last month. Also, having Lucia there made it a lot more fun. What's more, Jason and Brett stuck pretty close to them so she didn't have to wander around listening to other people's conversations.

There turned out to be quite a few high school people there because the hosts had a son who was fifteen. He quickly zeroed in on Lucia and spent most of the evening telling her about his video games.

Brett talked to Amber quite a bit and she was pleasantly surprised. He told her all about the Civil War and then, in answer to her questions, he talked about UCLA.

It was the first chance Amber really had to get to know Brett better. Then he said the house had an observation deck and he suggested they go look through the telescopes. Amber quickly agreed. He showed her how to direct the telescope so she could see the ocean. And then he showed her where to look for Catalina Island.

"I don't see it," Amber said. "I guess it's too far away." She was pleasantly conscious of Brett being so close to her. He certainly was very handsome and very nice. If I were interested in boys, she thought, I would definitely be interested in Brett.

He reached over to adjust the telescope and his hand brushed her arm. "You look nice," he said.

"Thank you."

"I guess you and Jason know each other pretty well?" Brett asked.

"Not really," Amber answered. She could

see Jason across the deck at the long table where they were serving food. She wondered if he was unhappy because Lucia was talking to the Margolis boy. Maybe she should try to rescue Lucia.

"I got the impression you were spending a lot of time together," Brett said. "My brother can be a bit much if you don't know how to handle him."

"You mean because he's so bossy?" Amber asked. "He's been nice to me all this week." In her heart she knew it was because of Lucia but whatever the reason, she was happy they'd called a truce. "And he's really good with Catty and Kyle."

"Would you like to visit UCLA sometime?" Brett asked. "I could take you to the library and show you where I work."

"I'd love it," Amber said. Brett smiled down at her and she noticed he had absolutely beautiful teeth. He was just the best-looking boy she'd ever seen — *much* better-looking than Mike. She wondered why she'd ever thought Mike was cute. Brett was as good-looking as anyone at this party and this was a party filled with gorgeous people.

"Good," Brett said. "I think I'll go back to school now. Can I give you a ride home?"

"But we only got here an hour ago," Amber said.

"My orders were to put in an appearance. I've done that."

"Do you hate all parties?" Amber asked.

Brett nodded his head. "All Hollywood parties." He waved a hand to dismiss the scene and said, "This is hardly my element."

"No, I guess not," Amber said thoughtfully. "I suppose you're more interested in your studies?"

"Exactly!" Brett seemed quite pleased to be understood. "You can see this is boring to me, can't you?"

"I suppose so." Actually, it was a little difficult for Amber to imagine anyone being bored at a party where they had carved ice figures of the host and hostess, a full band, and the best-looking group of people she'd ever seen in her life.

"So I'll drop you off at home if you want. It's on my way."

"I think I'll stay," Amber said. "Lucia looks as though she needs rescuing."

Brett nodded stiffly and said, "See you tomorrow."

"You putting in another command performance?" Amber teased.

"Dad's trying to sign Lauren Blackmore for his next movie. That's why they trotted us all out. The beautiful Harveys."

Amber stared after the handsome young man as he made his exit, saying good night to his host and hostess, and then moving gracefully out the door. As he walked through the hallway, a voice asked her, "So did you fall in love with Prince Charming?"

Amber jumped and fell backward into Jason's arms. She jerked away and said, "You shouldn't sneak up on people."

"You would have seen me, but you were so busy staring at Brett."

Unconsciously, Amber rubbed her arm. It was tingling where Jason touched it.

"You hurt?" Jason asked.

"Of course not," Amber answered, "but you do have the most annoying habit of coming up behind me."

"Got to keep your eyes open," Jason said lightly. "You can't go around with stardust in them all the time. Too much romance is bad for your liver."

"What are you talking about?"

"Just talking," Jason said cheerfully. "Did you find Catalina?" Jason asked, pointing to the telescope.

"No," Amber admitted. "Brett tried to show me but I couldn't see it."

Jason bent down and looked through the lens. Then he adjusted some knobs and said, "Try again."

This time, when Amber looked through the lens, she saw the island outlined very faintly against the horizon. "I see it," she said. "I couldn't before. Do you think the light has changed?"

"No, I think my dopey brother adjusted it for his eyes and didn't think about yours. He's very nearsighted, same as I am."

"But he doesn't wear glasses," Amber said.

"He wears contacts, but I guess he didn't have them in tonight."

"Well, they look very good," Amber said.

Jason laughed and said, "The love bug really did bite you, didn't it? Well, it's good that there are romantic people in the world. They're the ones I'm going to make my movies for. Just think, ten years from now you'll be sitting in Oshkosh with your three kids and your husband and you'll see my name on the screen."

"I won't be sitting in Oshkosh in ten years. I'm going to travel all over the world. And as for romantic, you're more romantic than I am, you know."

Jason looked at her and smiled. "Maybe you're right. Now let's go rescue your pal, Lucia. She looks as though she's had about all she can handle of young Mr. Margolis."

Chapter 23

"If all goes well, I'm going to take tomorrow off," Amber said. "Want to go to Rodeo Drive with me?"

"Sure," Lucia answered. The two girls were lying on the beach two days after the Margolis party and Kyle was down at the water's edge while Catty was surfing. It was an overcast day, but Amber had learned enough to know that she could get just as burned in the fog as the sunshine. She was wearing her straw hat and putting sunscreen on her legs. "I'm not going to have much tan," Amber said. "I was kind of hoping I'd be your color by the end of the summer."

"It's my natural color. People don't tan this dark anymore," Lucia said.

"It's a great color," Amber said. "You looked wonderful in that yellow dress at the Margolis party. And you got lots of attention."

Lucia made a face. "All Brandon Margolis talks about is Brandon Margolis."

"Jason likes you, too," Amber said. "You talked to him, too."

"Jason's nice," Lucia answered. "What's Brett like? I noticed you were having a long conversation with him. Do you like him?"

"Serious and nice. Kind of mellow. I like him a lot."

"He certainly is cute. Is that the reason you're suddenly so interested in shopping?"

"I just want to look around," Amber said defensively. "I probably can't afford to buy anything."

"What are you going to do with Kyle?" Lucia asked.

"Catty is going to watch him, exactly the way the Harveys promised," Amber said. "They'll survive a day without me. Look at Catty." She pointed out to the ocean. The thirteen-year-old was standing on her surfboard, riding a wave all the way into the shore. It amazed Amber how much she'd learned from just one lesson.

"Tony invited us out again this afternoon," Lucia said. "He's got time to give you and Catty lessons. I'll watch Kyle."

"Maybe today I can stand up on my board," Amber said and laughed. "Look at Catty go!

Since Tony gave her that lesson, she's turned into a fish."

"She's a natural," Lucia said.

They went to Broad Beach that afternoon and Catty learned to stand on one foot. Amber was able to stay on the board a little better, but she could see that surfing wasn't going to be easy.

On the way home, Catty asked Lucia, "Does your brother Tony have a girlfriend?"

"Sort of. But it's an on-again, off-again romance," she answered. "Tony's twenty-one; he's too old for you, Catty," Lucia teased.

"*Now* he is," she agreed, "but he won't be in a few years. I don't think he'll marry early, do you?"

"No." Amber laughed. "I'm sure he'll want to wait around until you grow up. You two could form a surfing partnership. The Amazing Tony Valdez and the Spectacular Catalina Harvey."

Catty did her very best to cajole her parents into eating supper on the beach that evening, but they wouldn't budge. Then she tried to get them to come down and see her surf. "I'll be spectacular with the backdrop of the setting sun," she promised.

"We're going out to the Chomskys'," Madeline said. "We'll see you some other night."

"Never mind," Catty said haughtily. She was obviously offended. "I'm going out myself. Can Amber drive me over to the big house?"

"What for?"

"I want to get some stuff," Catty said. "My other swimsuit for one thing."

John Harvey reached in his pocket and pulled out a hundred-dollar bill. "Sure. Take Kyle and get some ice cream while you're out. Make a night of it."

"I'd like to take the car tomorrow as well." Amber took the money and continued, "I want to take a day off." She had grown so used to his constant giving of money that she took it almost automatically. It was easier than arguing and she was going to give it all back the day she left.

"Can I come, too?" Catty asked quickly.

"No. I need you to watch Kyle for me."

"Let Madeline watch Kyle," Catty said. "She's supposed to be the parent. I'm just a kid."

"Come on Catty, let's go," Amber said.

"I've changed my mind," Catty said. "I don't want to go anywhere."

"I'd like to," Amber insisted. "I'd like some ice cream and I've never seen the inside of the big house. Is it pretty?" Then she added,

"After we do that, we could call Lucia and see if she and Tony want to go for ice cream." She smiled as she realized that she was trying to bribe Catty just the way Jason did. Hey, whatever works, she thought.

Reluctantly, Catty stood up and said, "Okay, I'll go. I really need my white swimsuit."

The Sunset Boulevard house had several lights in the windows and Amber asked, "Who do you think is there?"

"Probably Brett," Catty answered.

"I thought he was at college. Doesn't he have summer school?"

"I don't know. Maybe he does — but that's his car." Catty had pushed the garage door opener and, as it opened, it revealed a sleek gray Mercedes sports car.

Amber sighed. "I'll never get used to the way you people never know where the others are."

"You shouldn't call people, 'you people,' " Catty said. "Jason says it's rude."

"Right. I'll rephrase."

"Never mind, there's a picture of my real mother on the wall in the house." Catty jumped out of the car and ran into the house as though she couldn't wait to be there.

Catty took Amber on a tour of the Sunset Boulevard house, leading her from room to room and showing off all the Harvey possessions. For the first time, Amber understood why Madeline was so critical of the other big homes she'd been taken to. This home was decorated with absolutely perfect taste and every piece of furniture, every object was exquisite.

It was a fascinating blend of antiques and modern. The overall color of the home was white with white carpets and walls, but there were so many beautiful objects that it was far from boring. Amber wandered from room to room, standing back and admiring paintings or large sculptures that seemed to span all periods and places in the world.

"This seems like the home of a world traveler," she said.

"No," Catty answered. "All this stuff came from Madeline's shop or it was stuff my dad already had."

"Madeline really has wonderful taste."

Catty ignored her comment and went out the back door.

A voice behind her said, "Madeline was a designer before she married John. She still owns part of a shop on Melrose Avenue." The voice belonged to Jason and he didn't seem the least bit surprised to see them.

"Oh, I thought Brett was here." Amber

jumped when Jason spoke, but she was getting used to having Jason show up at odd times.

"Looking for my handsome brother?" Jason asked. "You don't want to look too far or you might find him."

"I wasn't *looking* for him. I just saw his car in the garage. At least, Catty said it was his car. Besides, I don't care if your brother's here or not."

"Don't you? I think you do. Didn't anyone ever tell you that beauty is only skin deep?"

"And I don't like Brett just because he's good-looking," Amber said. "I like him because he's nice."

"He's nice enough when you can catch him," Jason admitted. "But he's not around much. Brett always finds a way to be absent. Haven't you noticed?"

"Whereas *you* are always around." Jason didn't bother her as he used to. She'd learned that his bark was worse than his bite — at least most of the time. Sometimes it was even kind of fun to toss remarks back and forth.

"What are you doing here?" Jason asked. "Besides looking for the Lone Ranger."

"We were just picking up Catty's swimsuit," Amber explained. "Catty showed me around because I haven't seen the house before —

on the inside, I mean. I've seen the outside, of course."

"I remember," Jason said and smiled. "You sure looked scared that first day. You've changed a lot since then. How long ago was it?"

"Four weeks ago," Amber answered. Then she smiled and said, "It's been an interesting four weeks."

"Don't you want to know *how* I think you've changed?" Jason asked.

Amber shook her head, "I'm afraid to ask. Did you see Kyle? He was up in his room looking over his toy collection."

"I'm on my way to school," Jason said. "I just dropped by to pick up a video I left here. We need it for our final project. I only have one more week of school and then I'm out of there. At least for three weeks."

"Be sure and say hello to Kyle before you leave," Amber said. Then she added, "We're going to Lucia's maybe and then to get some ice cream. Want to come along?"

Jason shook his head no. "Sounds like fun but Carlyle is waiting for me. I've got to run. You remember Carlyle?"

"Yes."

Jason laughed. "You sound surprised. I'll bet

you thought I'd dump her after she tried to get me to introduce Dad to her friends."

"She's a pretty girl."

"Your face shows your feelings." He was still laughing. "She's my partner on my class project. I'm stuck with her for another week. As for being pretty — there're a million pretty girls in this town. *I* certainly know beauty is skin deep."

"Anyway, she seemed kind of old," Amber said. When Jason frowned she said, "I know you have lots of older friends but she seemed really old."

"She's twenty-one. Not so old."

They were almost arguing again! She didn't know how it happened that whenever she was with Jason, the sparks started flying. She was determined not to let it happen, so she said, "I really like this house. It's much nicer than the other big houses I've seen."

"How many big houses have you seen?" Jason was smiling again.

"I've seen the Redmond house and the Margolis house. That's not a lot but they were big."

"Indeed they were." Jason was pretty cute when he was smiling like that. Funny how his face could change depending on his mood. It even seemed to her that his eyes changed from dark brown to a lighter, golden color.

"Madeline's got good taste," Jason said. "I'll give her that. See you tomorrow maybe. You and Lucia going to the beach?"

"We're going shopping," Amber said. "I'm taking the day off."

Jason nodded and said, "Good thinking. Say hello to Lucia for me."

He was out the door and Amber turned to climb the stairs and round up Kyle before she called Lucia. Kyle came running down the hall and asked, "Is Jason here?"

"He had to go," Amber said. "He said he'd see you tomorrow." Kyle looked disappointed but didn't say anything. Amber said, "Where's your brother Brett's room? We'll go say hello to him."

Kyle pointed to a room off the hall and Amber knocked on the door. Brett opened it and stood in the doorway. He said, "Hello, Amber, I've been meaning to call you."

"We saw your car so I thought we would say hello," Amber said. "Catty is here and Kyle wants to say hello."

Brett looked down at Kyle and said, "Hello, Kyle. How are you?"

"Fine."

Kyle's voice was flat and disinterested. Amber just didn't understand why Catty and

Kyle played such favorites with their brothers. Neither of them seemed to care even a little bit for Brett and as far as she could see, Brett was always nice to them.

"Are you doing your research?" Amber asked. She really didn't know Brett very well and every time she saw him she had to get over the shock of his good looks again. Today, Brett was wearing a light blue shirt and white linen slacks and he looked as though he might have stepped out of *GQ* or some other men's fashion magazine.

His eyes were smiling as he said, "I'm always doing research on the Civil War. I guess you think I'm sort of dull, don't you?"

"Of course not," Amber answered quickly. "I think history is a fascinating subject." Then she added, "Though I've been meaning to ask you why you're not interested in movie-making like the others. You seem like you'd be a great actor."

Brett shook his head quickly. "Plenty of people want to be actors and I gladly let them do it." He sort of frowned and said, "I'm a serious person, Amber, and I gather you are as well."

"I guess I am," Amber answered slowly. She hadn't really thought of herself as serious, but she wasn't going to talk Brett out of thinking they were alike.

Brett cleared his throat and said rather shyly, "Amber, I was wondering if you wanted to go to a party with me. Friday night."

Amber was pleased and surprised. "I'd love to," she answered. "Where is it and what do I wear?"

"It's at a friend's beach house. Wear anything and bring a swimsuit. I'll pick you up at seven-thirty."

Amber nodded and Brett shut the door. She took Kyle's hand and led him down the stairs. Then she called Lucia and invited her for ice cream. When Lucia said she was expecting company, Amber told her, "You'll never believe what just happened. Brett asked me to go to a party with him."

"What did you say?"

"I said yes," Amber answered. "I was surprised but I'd really like to go."

"What will Jason say?" Lucia asked.

"What does Jason care?" Amber was perplexed by the question.

"You really don't know he's interested in you, do you?" Lucia asked.

"If he's interested in anyone besides himself, which I doubt, he's interested in you,"

Amber said. "He's always asking about you. He wanted to know if you were coming to the beach tomorrow."

"Jason's right about one thing," Lucia laughed softly. "You *do* have a lot to learn about boys."

Chapter 24

The girls went shopping on Rodeo Drive the next day and they both found treasures on the sale rack. Amber bought a pair of black pants that looked great on her and Lucia found a white cotton dress.

They had lunch at Hamburger Hamlet and Amber said, "I can't get over the prices of the clothes at Saks. When I was there before, they had a lot of things for forty-five dollars. This time they were on sale for two and three hundred dollars."

Lucia smiled and asked, "What makes you think they ever had anything for forty-five dollars?"

"That's what my blue dress cost," Amber said. "I paid for it myself." She told her the whole story and even included the part about the dyed-to-match shoes.

"Madeline and Irena tricked you," Lucia

said. "They let you pay forty-five dollars just to keep you happy. That blue dress probably cost over three hundred." When she saw the look on Amber's face she said, "Don't worry about it. They didn't spend a penny more than they wanted to."

"I guess I'm still in culture shock," Amber said. "I read about it in a travel book. You go into a society where the people are living a life that is so different from yours that it puts you into shock. The Harveys' attitude toward money shocks me."

"You'll get used to it," Lucia said. "Let's go to the movies."

"Not another movie! That's all Kyle does is watch movies. Let's go buy him a baseball and bat. Maybe I can get him to play ball tomorrow."

They bought the ball and bat for Kyle and they went to a movie after all. Then Amber went to Lucia's house and ate a barbecue dinner. Tony was out of town on a surfing tour and Lucia's parents seemed very glad to have company. Mr. Valdez drove them all around the ranch, showing off his special landscaping projects and complaining that property values were so high that he really couldn't afford to operate his business anymore.

"You could retire," his daugher said. "You

could sell the business and you and mom could live happily ever after."

"What would we do all day?" her father grumbled.

"Travel. Volunteer for the Peace Corps. Do whatever you want," Lucia said. "It's silly for you to work so hard when the land is worth so much. You wouldn't even have to sell it all. You could just take the offer for the part down at the bottom of the hill and live on the money from that for the rest of your lives."

For the first time, Amber understood that Lucia's family was probably just as rich as the Harveys were. It was funny to think about because the Valdez family seemed so different from the Harveys in so many ways. Mr. Valdez wore Levi's and cotton shirts and worked all day long. Mrs. Valdez did all the cooking and most of the housework and their house was very nice, but it wasn't much fancier than Amber's house in Wisconsin.

When Amber got back to the beach house that evening, Jason was there with the kids. Catty announced, "We didn't miss you a bit. Jason was here all afternoon and he took us all over the place. We even went up to Zuma Beach so I could surf. We saw your friend Mike there. He was with a redhead."

"That's nice," Amber said, trying to keep

any special indication about how she felt about Mike out of her voice or facial expression. She added, "We had a great day ourselves. And I got a tour of the Valdez ranch. It's quite a spread."

"I want to do a movie there," Jason said. "I've got this great idea but I have to wait until I'm far enough along to do full-length features."

"You'd better hurry," Amber teased. "Mr. Valdez sounded like he was going to sell out."

"Probably not," Jason said. "What would he do if he sold?"

"Live happily ever after," Amber said.

"Can't live happily ever after without meaningful work," Jason replied. Then he directed his attention back to the movie he and the kids were watching.

The next morning, Jason was still there and Amber asked, "No school today?"

"I show my class project this afternoon and I'm out of there. You and Lucia want to come to the showing?"

"Sure — at least I'm sure Lucia will want to go. I probably ought to stay with the kids. I had yesterday off."

"Call Lucia and see if she can come. You should probably both dress up — look really grown-up. All right?" Then Jason added, "I'll talk to Catty and get her to watch Kyle this afternoon."

"You and Lucia will have a good time without me." Amber didn't want to be too obvious, but she thought they would probably have a *much* better time if it were just the two of them.

"Could you do me a favor and wear something really sophisticated and gorgeous? Impressive-looking?" Jason asked. "And I'd rather have you both."

"What's this all about?" Amber asked.

Jason looked kind of funny and answered, "I'd really appreciate if you just did what I said and didn't ask a lot of questions. Come on Amber, be a pal."

Amber shrugged and said, "Okay, okay, I'll dress up just to impress your friends."

"Maybe wear that pale green shirt."

"One of the silk ones Madeline gave me?" Amber asked. She had already noticed how Jason paid a lot of attention to things like clothing. He definitely did have a filmmaker's eye.

Amber wore her new wide-legged pants with the pale green silk shirt. She took a lot of trouble to make up her eyes, using mascara to make her lashes look even longer. As a final touch, she added a pair of gold hoop earrings that Madeline had given her last week.

Lucia was gorgeous in her new white dress and white thongs. She wore a white flower tucked behind one of her ears and absolutely no makeup at all. "Why did we have to dress up?" she asked as she got into the Corvette beside Jason. Amber had insisted on sitting in the backseat.

"I just wanted to impress my friends," Jason said.

"That's not like you," Lucia said suspiciously. "I'll bet there's some girl after you and you're trying to get rid of her."

Jason just ignored that comment. "The National Film Institute was founded in 1962," Jason said. "Its sole purpose is to preserve and enhance the art of the film. In the summer they take a few UCLA students, and I was really lucky to get into the intern program here. Some people have waited for years to be admitted."

"You sound like a school brochure or something," Lucia teased. "What's up, Jason? Come on, you can tell us."

Jason just shrugged and fiddled with the radio stations until he found one he liked and then, before they got any more information out of him, they were there.

The National Film Institute turned out to be a huge old mansion that someone had donated.

The large rooms had been chopped up into classrooms and Jason showed them around quickly, introducing them to everyone they met on the stairs. At fifteen minutes to four, he said, "It's almost time for the screening," and he ushered them into a large room that was set up like a movie theater.

A tall dark-haired woman waved to them as she stood in the center of the third row and called out, "Jason, I'm over here."

Jason waved back and acted as though he didn't quite understand the woman. "Isn't that your partner, Carlyle?" Amber asked.

Then she said, "I've got it! I know why we're all dressed up. This is the day that Carlyle gets dumped. Poor Carlyle."

"Don't bother feeling sorry for her," Jason said. He sounded angry and Amber couldn't tell if it was because she'd figured it out or if he was angry that she'd talked in front of Lucia. "Carlyle will always land on her feet."

"That girl is calling to us," Lucia said. She seemed to have missed the previous conversation. "I think she's saving us seats."

"Yes," Amber said. "That's Jason's partner and I'm certain she's saving seats. Let's go down front."

Jason glared at her, but they went to sit with Carlyle. Somehow, Jason managed it so that he was sitting between Lucia and Amber and Carlyle was on Lucia's right. Amber was amused by the maneuvering, but she soon forgot all about it when the films began.

There were six short films of about ten minutes each. One was a comedy with a clown doing some silly stuff that reminded Amber of old-fashioned silent films. Another was a ten-minute film of someone putting on eye makeup. The others tried to tell a story — one took place on the freeway and featured a family who met some obstacles but finally got where they were going. Another was a film about a little girl who was lost in the mall and rescued by a person who was on the first day of work as a security guard.

Only Jason's really seemed like a true movie. It was about a high school boy who wanted to make the school basketball team and failed. He then tried to get a job as a grocery clerk and failed at that. The boy ended up involved in a robbery of the grocery store and then he changed his mind and actually stopped the robbery. In the last scene the boy was asking once again for a job — this time in a 7-Eleven. It was called *If at First*.

Jason's film was so much better than the others that Amber found she was looking at him with new eyes. She said, "I think you really are almost as talented as Catty claims you are. Sometime, I'd like to have you tell more about how you did that."

"Did what?"

"Made a movie that seemed like a real movie. The others seemed like school projects."

Jason smiled and it was obvious he was happy, but some people came up and he had to talk to them. They all went into a large reception room and Jason said, "I'll get us all champagne."

Carlyle said, "I'll go with you." She tagged right along with Jason and they came back very quickly with four cups. Carlyle said, "I didn't think you girls were old enough to drink champagne and I was right. Jason brought you ginger ale."

"I'm drinking ginger ale myself," Jason said.

"I really liked your movie best," Lucia said to Carlyle and Jason. "Did you work on it longer than the others? Or are you just that much better?"

"I think we work really well as a team," Carlyle answered smoothly. "I'm trying to talk Jason into getting his father to give us jobs on his next shoot. We can stay in school and each take half the work. I know it will work out."

Jason just looked at her and didn't reply at

all. Amber asked, "But aren't all movie workers in unions? They don't hire part-time people, do they?"

"No, they don't," Jason said. "And we're not ready yet — neither of us is ready."

"Speak for yourself." Carlyle tossed her long dark hair and said, "I'm definitely ready. I've been waiting for my big break for five years now. I only enrolled in school because I couldn't get in the door any other way. And now that I've got entrée, he won't help me." She pouted her mouth and kissed the air in Jason's direction.

Amber and Lucia were standing back, looking at Carlyle hang on Jason and when she did the air-kissing trick, they both laughed out loud. Then Amber whispered, "What kind of an entrée do you think he is? Roast beef? Lamb chops?"

"Chopped liver," Jason said with a straight face. "I feel like chopped liver."

Both girls doubled over with laughter. Carlyle didn't get the joke, but she had an idea that it was on her. She looked from one of them to the other and shook her head, saying, "What are you children talking about?"

"Chopped liver," Jason answered with a straight face. "Amber asked what I felt like and I said I felt like chopped liver."

"They only have little tiny sandwiches here," Carlyle said. "We could go somewhere else if you're hungry." She turned and said crossly, "Will you girls stop that laughing? People are looking."

Neither Amber nor Lucia could look at Carlyle for fear they would start laughing again. Amber managed to say, "I'm sorry. Jason, we'll wait for you out front."

"I'll go with you," Jason said.

"But we haven't talked to anyone," Carlyle wailed. "There're a lot of people here that I want to meet."

"Just circulate," Jason said. "We're going now."

Once they were out on the sidewalk, Jason said, "I feel like chicken tonight," and flapped his wings in imitation of the silly commercial on television. That made Amber and Lucia start laughing again.

They laughed all the way to Lucia's house and when she got out of the car, she said, "Jason, I really did think your movie was great. I'm sorry if we spoiled your party."

"You didn't spoil my party," Jason said. "You made my day. Tell you what, next time I want a good laugh, I'll call you."

Chapter 25

Brett called on Thursday and asked Amber if she would mind if he cancelled their date. "I have a lot of studying to do this weekend," he said. "Maybe we could do something the week after this one."

"Sure," Amber said.

"I am sorry," Brett said. "It's just that if I don't spend more time on this Civil War stuff, I'll be way behind on my project next fall."

"It's all right," Amber said, but she was really disappointed because she'd never been to a college party.

When she hung up the phone, she called Lucia and said, "Party's off. Or at least, Brett broke our date which means the party's off for me."

"That's great!" Lucia said. "Tony just called and said he had some extra tickets for the cruise after the surfing contest in Oceanside.

There's a big party on a cruise ship and Tony's friends cancelled so he asked if you guys wanted to join us. I'm riding down with him in an hour. There's even a hotel room for you, if you decide in a few minutes. He hasn't called in to cancel their room yet. You and the kids could come down later this evening and we could have so much fun. Can you?"

"I'll check it out," Amber said.

She asked Madeline Harvey's permission to take Catty and Kyle to Oceanside for the weekend. "Lucia says it's the biggest surfing contest in California and Tony has a good chance of winning this year. We could take Kyle on the cruise with us because some of the other contestants have children."

"What time would you be home?"

"We'd drive down tonight and stay over tomorrow night, too. We'd be home early Sunday morning."

Madeline shook her head quickly. "No, I don't think so. I can't say yes to that without checking with John. He's their father, you know. And he's filming on location."

"Can't you call him?" Amber said. "He's only in Lake Tahoe, isn't he?"

"I can't interrupt him when he's filming unless it's a real emergency. I know John and he won't think this is an emergency. If I called, he would just say no. They're starting the actual filming today."

"I think Mr. Harvey wants me to take the kids places. Tony would be with us and he's an adult," Amber said. "But if we can go, I should tell Tony right away. You know, Catty would love it. Tony is her hero and she'd love to see him in competition."

"I'm sorry. I just can't take the responsibility. I'd let you and Catty go," Madeline said, "because Catty is older. But what about Kyle? Cook is off for the weekend and I think Jason's going to visit a friend in Santa Barbara."

"What about Brett?" Amber said. "Couldn't he study here and watch Kyle at the same time?"

Madeline shook her head impatiently. "Jason will always help if he's around." Then she brightened and said, "I'll see if he's gone yet. If you explain how important it is, he will probably change his plans and go with you."

"Oh, don't do that. Please!"

"Why not?"

"It would just change everything," Amber began and then she added, "I don't want to interfere with Jason's plans." Then she had another idea. "Why don't you come with us? You would have a good time on the cruise and you could skip part of the competition if you didn't want to be outdoors all day."

Madeline shook her head quickly. "If you won't let me ask Jason, I'll have to say no. I'm sorry."

Amber nodded. She was glad she hadn't said anything to Catty because she would be heartbroken if she knew how close she'd come to getting to the surfing contest. Amber said, "Don't worry about it. It was short notice and you couldn't help it."

"Couldn't help what?" Jason walked into the kitchen and went to the refrigerator. Biting into an apple, he repeated his question. "What couldn't you help?"

"Amber wants to take Catty and Kyle to a surfing contest in Oceanside," Madeline explained. "To spend the weekend. I said I'd have to ask John, but that I couldn't ask him because he was busy. What do you think, Jason?"

"I think it's a ridiculous idea," Jason answered.

"I thought if you would cancel your plans you might go with them. Or at least watch Kyle tomorrow so Amber and Catty could go alone."

"Amber and Catty are too young to go to a surfing contest with a big crowd. They have no business going that far alone. I'm surprised at Amber for even suggesting it."

"It was your girlfriend Lucia who suggested it," Amber snapped. "Her brother had some extra tickets and she's going. And Tony is twenty-one."

"Lucia knows enough people to go alone. You two would just be a couple of lost little girls in a huge crowd. It's just not a good idea, Amber."

"You're just saying that because you like to be boss," Amber said. "Or maybe because you're afraid if I go that Lucia will meet someone she likes better than you . . ."

Jason was angry now and shouted at her, "Stop talking about Lucia. It's my job to look after my sister. Catty can't go and that's definite. If you want to go alone, I suppose I can't stop you but remember what happened with your pal Mike."

"What do you think you know about Mike?" Amber was really furious at Jason for bringing up Mike. What had he heard? Her cheeks were burning with embarrassment and she was also a little frightened by how angry she could get. She took a deep breath, lowered her voice, and said, "Never mind what you think you know about Mike. That's way off the subject. Besides, I'm a lot more grown-up now than I was then."

"You're the same silly teenager you were when you got off that plane. Only now, instead of falling for an empty-brained creep like Mike, you've fallen for Brett. Not much improvement, you know."

"It's none of your business who I fall for! Ever since I got here you've been on my case. You fired me once . . ."

" . . . I should have fired you but you quit!"

"Keep this up and I'll quit again," Amber threatened.

Madeline broke in, stepping between Jason and Amber and putting her hand on Amber's arm. "Let's not talk about quitting. You can go tomorrow morning. Only just for the day." Madeline interrupted their fight with a wonderful bright smile on her face. "I've got it all figured out. You and Catty can just drive down in the morning and spend the day. I'll watch Kyle tomorrow. Don't worry about it. All I have to do is change my hair appointment and break a lunch date with Irena. And Jason, you go on and go to Santa Barbara. When you come back, this whole quarrel will seem silly to you both."

Amber and Jason glared at each other and then glared at Madeline but no one said anything else. Finally Jason said, "Maybe you're right. A day trip would work and Catty would really like to see the surfing. But you have to promise to bring Catty home by ten in the evening."

"Fine," Amber said. She turned on her heel and went into the living room to tell Catty the good news. She was still so mad at Jason that she didn't want to talk with him, and Madeline had obviously been on her way out of the house.

It was hours later when she was rethinking the whole scene that she realized how decisive Madeline had actually been. Good for her, Amber thought, and if she keeps it up, it will be good for Kyle and Catty. As for Jason, she didn't even care whether or not it would help him to have a more decisive stepmother. As far as she was concerned, Jason was definitely beyond help.

Chapter 26

The surfing contest began at six in the morning so Amber and Catty missed part of it. By the time they arrived at eight, the town of Oceanside was jammed with people in bright-colored shirts who came to see the competition.

They parked in the Sunnyside Motel lot as Lucia had instructed and walked the three blocks to the pier to search for Lucia and Tony Valdez.

They found Lucia talking to a group of people at the end of the pier. "I haven't seen Tony for an hour. I sure am glad to see you two. I was getting tired of fending off boys," Lucia said, laughing.

"Too bad you're so beautiful," Catty said to Lucia. "I think it must be a terrible nuisance. I guess I'm lucky I'm not so beautiful. Not like you or Madeline."

Amber hugged her and said, "You *are* beautiful, Catty. You just don't know it yet."

Catty shook her head and said, "You don't need to tell me lies just to make me feel better."

"You'll see how beautiful you are someday," Amber promised her.

They had to wait a long time for a breakfast table at the outdoor restaurant and when they got it, six gorgeous boys tried to join them while they were eating, but Lucia scared them off by mentioning her brother's name. Then she laughed and said, "I never know whether to be happy or sad that Tony's name carries so much weight."

"Is he nervous?" Amber asked. "Does he think he'll win?"

"He hopes so," Lucia said, "but he really was nervous this morning. The worst part is that he broke up with Anna Lynne last night. They had a big fight and she went home and left us stranded here. So that means he's in a bad, bad mood. Those two fight more than any couple I know except you and Jason."

"Jason and I are hardly a couple," Amber said. She kicked Lucia lightly under the table and they changed the subject. When Catty got bored and went out to see the surfboard exhibition, Amber told Lucia about their latest fight. "He almost fired me again but Madeline saved the day."

"So maybe Madeline's not such a space cadet after all," Lucia said.

"She's not as weird as I used to think," Amber said, "but she's completely unpredictable. I know she wants to be nice, but sometimes I'm not sure she really knows my name. And just when I think she's totally out of it, she does something that makes me think she's okay. She was really sensible last night when Jason and I were yelling at each other. I can't figure her out."

"I imagine being stepmother to that bunch is overwhelming," Lucia said.

"I heard Jason yelling at her the first night I came to California. If that had been my mother or father, I'd still be in my room eating bread and water but Madeline actually seems to like Jason the best. In fact, they all like him best. I don't get it."

"I like him best, too," Lucia said calmly.

Amber was startled by Lucia's statement. Though she'd known from the beginning that Jason was attracted to Lucia, this was the first time Lucia had really admitted that she was also attracted to him. Until now, Lucia had just laughed the idea off. Amber reached out and put her hand over Lucia's and said quietly, "Oh, of course you do. Look, I'm sorry if I said anything to offend you. Of course Jason really is a good brother. I mean, he really tries to be helpful it's just . . ."

Catty ran into the restaurant and called, "They're starting again. Let's go."

They found a spot where they could see the competition very clearly and watched Tony's division with great enthusiasm. As they expected, Tony won the men's division. Lucia was especially happy that it was a unanimous vote. "The higher his scores, the more offers he gets and the more offers he gets, the more famous he gets. Tony won't come right out and say so but I think he'd like to be really famous."

"He could be an actor," Amber said. "He's good-looking and he's got a great voice."

About an hour later, Tony came out to the end of the pier and Catty was so excited that she ran over to him and threw her arms around him and said, "Tony, you were wonderful!"

Flashbulbs went off all around Tony as he was being hugged by the girl. Amber called out, "Catty, come over here. Leave Tony alone." To her pleasant surprise, Catty stepped out of the limelight and rejoined them. They stood on the sidelines and watched as

Tony was interviewed by a television commentator and then posed with his surfboard as the newspaper and magazine photographers took his photo over and over again.

By the time they were finished, it was four o'clock and Lucia said, "We ought to think about getting back to the motel. Did you bring dresses for the cruise? It starts at six-thirty."

"Oh, Lucia, the boat doesn't come back till midnight. We can't stay! I promised I'd have Catty home by ten o'clock."

"That's awful!" Catty wailed.

Lucia agreed with her. "The cruise is the best part of the whole event. And Tony will be so disappointed. I know he'd really like you to be there — he's disappointed about Anna Lynne, for sure."

"I can't," Amber said. "Madeline would have let us stay later, but Jason talked her out of it."

"Catty would love the cruise," Lucia said sadly. "There're always kids her age because a lot of these guys have families."

"What a shame she can't have the fun of going. That Jason — I could kick him," said Amber.

"You can if you want to," Lucia said. She pointed toward the street.

"Jason's here!" Catty called out and started

running down the pier toward the street.

Amber shaded her eyes and said, "She's right. That is Jason. I wonder if there's something wrong."

Catty ran down the pier, calling out, "Jason! Tony won the championship. Tony won!"

She was holding Jason's hand as they got up to where the girls were standing. Jason looked directly at Amber and said, "I drove down here to apologize. I'm sorry. I still don't think you should spend the night, but I didn't have to be so mean."

"We always seem to say more than we intend," Amber answered him. Why was her heart pounding just because Jason was here? What was wrong with her?

"Is there room for me on the cruise?" Jason asked. "Do you have an extra ticket?"

"I promised we'd be back by ten," Amber said. "We can't go on the cruise."

"Yeah, but Dad called and Madeline asked him and he said yes. We decided I could meet you down here. Madeline packed some clothes for you to wear on the cruise. We'll have to drive two cars home but that's all right."

"Are you here because your dad sent you?" Amber asked. She remembered the other time when Jason had been forced to apologize and she didn't think it had worked very well for any of them.

He shook his head quickly. "I'm here because I want to be."

"If you want to leave the station wagon overnight, Tony will drive it home," Lucia said. "His girlfriend drove us down and she got mad and left."

"Perfect planning," Jason said. "How about it, Amber? You ready to kiss and make up?"

"I really want to stay for the cruise," Amber said stiffly.

"But not enough to kiss me?" Jason teased.

"I will," Catty said and she threw her arms around Jason and said, "I'm so glad you came."

Chapter 27

Jason took them all out for drinks at the Chart House. They sat and talked and drank Cokes while they watched the people crowd around Tony and some even asked for his autograph.

"It's a shame his girlfriend isn't here," Jason said to Lucia. "What happened?"

"They had a fight. Frankly, I hope it's all over between them. They've gone out for about two years. She's a nice girl, but every time Tony is in the limelight she gets jealous and picks a fight."

"He needs someone sweet and sensible like me," Catty pronounced. "I'm just waiting for him to mature enough to know it."

"Looks like you've got lots of competition," Amber said. There were three absolutely beautiful girls in bathing suits crowding around Tony and he looked quite happy as he talked with them, turning first to the redhead, then the blond, and then the brunette.

"Your brother is pretty busy," Jason said. "It's a good thing I came down to entertain you girls or you would have been lonely."

"Six guys tried to pick us up at breakfast," Catty announced.

"They were very nice," Amber said quickly.

Jason looked at her and laughed. "So will they be on the cruise? Should I expect competition?"

"I have no idea what you should expect," Amber answered. "But I know I have to get dressed if we're going to make the boat."

"Especially since we only have one room and one shower," Lucia said. "That will take extra time."

"I tried to rent a room," Jason apologized, "but they were all full."

"It will work out," Lucia said and smiled at him.

Amber watched the way they smiled at each other and wished that the day would come when she would have someone look at her like that. Would she ever have someone special in her life? They look as though they really like each other, she thought and although she didn't want to admit it, she felt a slight pang of jealousy.

It was actually fun getting dressed for the

cruise. They took turns with the boys going first and then waiting outside in the car. When the girls were ready, they joined them. Amber was the last one out and she was wearing her blue dress. She was glad when Tony said, "You look radiant."

The cruise ship was crowded with surfer contestants, dignitaries, and their dates. Catty wasn't the only young person there because the junior contestants were invited as well. She quickly fell in love with a group of thirteen- and fourteen-year-olds who entertained themselves by spilling drinks overboard and telling funny jokes.

There were more boys than girls so Lucia and Amber had more than enough dance partners. Lucia laughed and said, "If I ever want to feel popular again, I'll take a cruise."

Jason turned to Amber and asked, "This is a slow one. Want to dance?"

"Can you dance to this kind of music?" she asked. The few times she'd seen Jason dance, the music was fast and wild and that seemed to fit his energy level.

"I was a star student at Mrs. Beeman's dance classes," Jason said. "I can waltz. I can tango. I can polka and I can fake it. What do you do?"

"I fake it," Amber joked. She was in such a good mood she was ready to dance with Jason and have a great time although she wasn't sure why he'd asked her instead of Lucia.

They didn't talk much and she found Jason was a very good dancer. He was just a little taller than she was and his hand felt warm and firm on her waist. "You're easy to follow," she said.

"Don't sound so surprised," he said. Then he brushed his lips across the top of her hair and said, "You look beautiful tonight, Amber."

"Thank you." She missed a step, she was so nervous. Why was Jason kissing her hair? And why did it make her neck tingle?

"You always look great, but that blue brings out your eyes and . . ."

She drew back and laughed. "You sound like you're selling perfume or something. What's up, Jason?"

"I was working around to kissing you under the moonlight," Jason said.

Quickly, Jason kissed her mouth. At first she was so startled that she didn't feel much of anything and then she realized that this was a very special kiss. She loved the feel of his lips on hers. She loved the way he held her and the kiss was deep and long. Her knees felt wobbly, but Jason was holding her close. She felt warm and happy. She was aware of her heart pounding.

"Nice," Jason whispered in her ear and his breath made her shiver with delight. He bent to kiss her again and this time, she slipped her arms around his neck. She didn't think, she just enjoyed his mouth on hers.

Suddenly, Amber remembered where she was. She stepped back from him, putting her hand up to her mouth. "Why?" she asked. She looked into his eyes and they seemed to glow in the evening light. They were a kind of golden brown tonight and for the first time, she realized Jason wasn't wearing his glasses. He must be wearing his contacts, she thought. She'd never noticed how beautiful his eyes were before, but she'd always loved his wonderful smile. "Why did you kiss me?" she asked again. She realized she really was confused by his sudden actions.

Jason smiled and kissed her forehead. He held her close to him and whispered, "Boys are supposed to kiss girls on nights like this. I thought you were the romantic one. Here we are on a starlight cruise, and you're very beautiful." She drew away from him slightly and he pulled her close again, saying, "Because I really like you, Amber, I . . ."

"No." Amber shook her head. "You kissed me because you thought it was the thing to do and maybe you wanted to make Lucia jealous!" She pulled away from him, feeling a mixture of anger and confusion. She tried to sound sensible as she said, "I don't want to be kissed by someone because it's convenient."

"You acted like you wanted to be kissed," Jason pointed out.

"Just leave me alone," Amber answered. "Don't ever do that again."

"You're nuts, you know that?" Jason was suddenly the old Jason again — the boy with the fast temper and short words. She couldn't imagine why she'd even wanted to kiss him.

"I'm leaving!" Amber said. "You'd better go check on your sister before she falls overboard or something."

"*You* go check on her," Jason said. "You're the baby-sitter."

"That's all I am, isn't it? Just the baby-sitter who conveniently has a friend who's rich and beautiful."

Jason looked at her and shook his head in disgust. "Don't say anything else, Amber. You're beginning to sound very silly and a little bit jealous."

Amber turned and ran away, leaving Jason standing in the middle of the dance floor all alone. She didn't see him again until the boat pulled into the dock and then she said, "I'm sorry, but I'm driving the station wagon home. Jason can drive alone or take Catty with him."

"What happened?" Lucia asked.

"Nothing worth talking about." She didn't really understand why she could still feel the softness of Jason's lips on hers. Her cheeks were burning, but all she said was, "Nothing happened. I just want to drive, that's all."

"I don't understand," Lucia said. "You and Jason were getting along so great and now you're fighting again."

"You don't *need* to understand," Amber snapped. "I'm not riding home with him and that's that."

Jason grabbed her hand and pulled her away from the cluster of friends. She said, "Let me go."

"Let me talk," he said in a low voice. "This is really embarrassing and unnecessary. Tony and Lucia need a car to get home and you can ride with me and you don't even have to talk to me. Now give them the car keys and let's go."

"Then I'm riding in the backseat," Amber said.

"Ride where you want," Jason answered. "You sound like Catty. And if you're worried about me — don't worry, I won't ever touch you again."

"Is that a promise?" Amber asked. She was biting her lips now to keep back the tears.

"Of course it's a promise. Now get in the car."

Chapter 28

Jason dropped them off and disappeared for several days. Amber supposed he was in his Westwood apartment although she knew his school term was over. She was happy he wasn't around, but she was surprised that she continued to think about him so much. Memories of the cruise and his kisses simply refused to go away. The more she thought about the way he'd kissed her, the madder she got.

On Wednesday, she woke up and realized she'd been dreaming about that kiss and that made her even angrier. She promised herself she wasn't going to think about Jason anymore — even to hate him — but that turned out to be very difficult. For one thing, Kyle and Catty talked a lot about Jason. For another, the memory of him kept popping up in her mind.

Funny, before she found out what a jerk he was, she'd really liked Mike but she hadn't particularly liked being kissed by him. After Mike's first kiss on the beach, she'd forgotten all about it. She'd always known she didn't like Jason so she couldn't understand why his kiss was so much more memorable. She supposed it was just chemistry.

"When Jason comes home," Catty said, "I'm going to ask him to take us on a beach party. Last spring he took us to a place where you can have a campfire. We cooked hot dogs and it was fun."

"Why don't you ever talk about Brett?" Amber asked. "He's your brother, too."

Catty just looked at her and shrugged. She obviously didn't think the question was worth answering. Later that day, Catty said, "I think I'll call Jason and see if he'll take us on a beach party tonight."

"Don't!" Amber said.

"Why not?"

When Amber didn't answer, Catty said, "You just don't appreciate Jason enough. But don't worry. He's probably out with some beautiful girl anyway — someone who really appreciates him."

"I hope they'll be very happy," Amber replied. "Now why don't you show me that short story you're writing."

Catty did call Jason later that afternoon and

reported that his answering machine said he would be gone for several days. "He's in Santa Barbara," she said.

Amber decided it was good riddance, but she said nothing. As the week progressed, she was a little surprised that Brett didn't call or come by. On the other hand, she decided that with her luck with men, it was just as well to wait until she was thirty-five or so to look for a boyfriend. She was happy to spend her time on the beach with Kyle and Catty without anyone else around.

On Thursday, Catty said, "This is boring. Let's call Lucia and see if Tony will give us surfing lessons."

"I'd rather just hang out on our beach," Amber said. "It's nice just to be together."

"I think it's boring," Catty insisted. "Are you mad at Lucia or something?"

"Of course not." But the truth was that she *was* angry at her friend. Lucia was the only one she'd told about how awful Mike acted that night so she had to be the one who told Jason. Amber was still furious with Jason and since Lucia was so crazy about him, she had a hard time separating them in her mind.

That evening, Lucia called and invited her to go to the movies. "I can't," Amber said. "I'm helping Kyle with his reading."

"But we could go after Kyle goes to bed," Lucia said. "Isn't this supposed to be one of your famous nights off?"

"The Harveys are going out."

"I thought they promised you they would call Jason to baby-sit on your nights off."

"Jason's in Santa Barbara." Why was she glad to know that Lucia didn't know? Sometimes she didn't understand her own reactions to things.

"Then they're supposed to call Brett," Lucia reminded her. "And you told me to remind you to stick up for your rights."

"I'm kind of tired." Amber thought the excuse sounded lame and she also felt dishonest. She said, "The truth is, I'm really kind of mad at you."

"You shouldn't be," Lucia said. "Jason likes *you*, not me."

"I didn't say I was jealous," Amber snapped. "I said I was mad. You told Jason about my hassle with Mike and you promised you wouldn't. He brought it up to prove I was an idiot, just like I knew he would. That's why I made you promise not to tell him in the first place."

"I didn't tell," Lucia said. "Cross my heart and hope to die. Scouts' honor, I didn't tell."

"Then how did he know?"

"I told you boys know things about other boys."

"No, it was more than a guess, he knew what happened and I was mortified. Are you sure . . .?"

"I wouldn't lie to you," Lucia said. "I thought you knew me better than that."

"I do," Amber agreed and she decided to let the whole thing drop. If Lucia said she hadn't told, then she hadn't. It really didn't matter. She worried entirely too much about Jason already. "Why don't you come over for dinner? Then we can watch a movie when the kids go to bed. Do you like *King Kong*?"

"Not much," Lucia said. "My grandfather was one of the gorillas in it and I watched it a lot when I was a kid."

"How old is your grandfather?" Amber asked incredulously. She had seen a photograph of him that he'd sent from Alaska where he was spending the summer. He looked much too young to be in a movie made sixty years ago.

"Grandfather is seventy-eight," Lucia said. "He's just stayed in shape."

"When did he quit working in movies?"

"About twenty years ago," Lucia said. "I think he was the oldest stuntman in the business for about ten years. Then he broke his shoulder and my grandmother said she'd divorce him if he didn't quit. He quit and she divorced him anyway."

"I'm sorry."

"She's happy and he's happy so it all worked out," Lucia said. "So what else have you got besides *King Kong*?"

"We have millions of movies. We can pick one out when you get here. Do you need a ride?"

"My dad will drop me off if you can bring me home."

The Harveys were happy to see Lucia, and John Harvey tried to be especially friendly by saying, "It's nice for Amber to have someone to keep her company while her boyfriend's out of town."

"What are you talking about?" Amber asked.

"I'm sure you miss Jason," John Harvey said. "He'll be home in a day or two. You girls have a nice time. Here's some money for ice cream or something."

Amber took the money automatically and said good night. When they left, she and Lucia went into the kitchen to get supper ready. As they put the dinner Mrs. Murdock had left them in the microwave, Amber shook her head and said, "I've got so much money in my drawer — you wouldn't believe it. Every time

I turn around, he gives me more. I'm going to put it all in an envelope and leave it for him when I fly home. It's easier than trying to tell him I don't need it."

"Why does he give you so much?" Lucia asked.

Amber shrugged. "I guess he feels guilty or something. I mean, he's not exactly a bad father. He loves his children when he thinks about them. Madeline tries, too, but she just isn't cut out for the job."

"The kids are lucky they have Jason," Lucia said. "I wonder who he had when he was young?"

"Do you think John Harvey actually thinks Jason is my boyfriend?" Amber asked.

"Of course he does," Catty spoke up from the kitchen door.

"How long have you been there?" Amber asked. "You shouldn't eavesdrop." She really hoped Catty hadn't heard what she'd said about the Harveys. Amber was always very careful not to say anything disparaging about their parents to the kids.

"I've been there quite a while," Catty said. "I'm practicing to eavesdrop, you know. Jason says all writers are good at eavesdropping."

"Writers may be, but friends don't eavesdrop on each other," Amber said. "But now that you're here, you can help."

Catty didn't seem the least bit upset as she picked up the plates and headed for the dining room table. "I actually came to help," she said. "Don't you think that's an improvement?"

"I do," Amber agreed. "I think you've turned into a very nice person."

They ate dinner and watched a movie called *The Incredible Journey*, then Amber put Kyle to bed. As she read his good night story to him, she thought about the fact that Mr. Harvey believed Jason was her boyfriend. She decided that was probably the reason Brett hadn't asked her to go out again. He didn't want to cut in on Jason. The more she thought about it, the more determined she became that she should put a stop to any ideas about her and Jason.

After she put Kyle into bed, she crossed the living room to go to the kitchen. "Want some popcorn?" she asked Catty and Lucia. The minute she put the popcorn in the microwave, she looked in the family telephone book and dialed Brett's number at the fraternity house.

The popcorn was done by the time she actually got him on the telephone so she said,

"Hi, this is Amber. I was thinking you might like to go somewhere with me tomorrow night. My treat?"

"Where?" Brett sounded surprised.

"Anywhere," Amber offered. Now that she had actually called him, she felt silly. She said, "Maybe you could show me around your school? I've never seen UCLA except to drive around a little."

"I could do that in the afternoon," Brett agreed. "And then we could go to my parents' party together."

"Are they having a party?"

"Dad called earlier this week and said they were having a hundred people over and I had to be there. That's why I was surprised by your invitation."

Amber was suddenly certain that Catty was standing outside the kitchen door, listening to every word. She said, "I'll see you tomorrow. What time will you pick me up?"

"Three," Brett said. "Or three-thirty."

She hung up the telephone and called out, "Catty? Are you there?" By the time she got the popcorn in a bowl and went back into the living room, Catty was seated beside Lucia, looking as innocent as she could. Amber decided not to make a big thing out of it because it would lead to uncomfortable questions.

The Harveys came in just as the second movie ended and Madeline said, "John, why don't you take Lucia home? I want to talk to Amber."

The minute the others left, Madeline sent Catty to bed and she patted the couch pillow beside her. Amber understood she was supposed to sit down beside her.

Amber had no idea what was coming next — Madeline was very unpredictable — but she suspected it might have something to do with the next night's party. She almost hoped that Madeline was going to ask her to give up her day off because she now felt quite awkward about calling up Brett and asking him out.

"I think you've been happy here," Madeline began. "We had a few difficulties at the beginning, but all together, I think we're getting along very well. Don't you think?"

"Yes," Amber agreed. She began to relax. Whatever it was that Madeline was leading up to, it was clear that she wasn't going to say something unpleasant.

"I want to thank you for all the lovely things you've given me," Amber said. "You've really been too generous."

"John and I are very pleased. You've been

good for Kyle and Catty. Jason and Brett think so, too. They agree that you're a very good influence."

Madeline frowned slightly and said, "I'd like to do more for you. Perhaps some new school clothes . . . and maybe some ballet lessons. How would you like to take a few ballet lessons? Very good for the posture."

"I think I'm too old to start ballet, but thanks," Amber said.

"Tennis lessons?" Madeline offered. "We could bring our coach back and he could give Catty a few refresher lessons."

"I'm a pretty good tennis player already." Amber could hardly keep from laughing. Madeline seemed desperate to give Amber something.

Madeline drifted off into space and then came back with a new approach. "I was thinking you are already a part of this family. Perhaps you would like to stay on with us? You could just stay as part of the family. We'd pay you your salary, of course, but you wouldn't actually have to work very hard. You could go to Beverly Hills High School. It's a fine school and you could watch Kyle and Catty when you come home from school, but it would be more like being a big sister than a job."

"You mean not go home?" Amber wasn't

sure she understood what Madeline was saying.

"I know your parents would miss you," Madeline said. "But if we offered you certain advantages . . . you could have your own car. A smaller, nicer car than the station wagon. Maybe a little blue Honda or something. Whatever girls your age want . . . and Lucia is already your friend so you wouldn't be lonely. We'd pay all your expenses and give you your salary. You could save the money for college. What do you think?"

"I'm not sure," Amber said. Her mind was racing as she tried to get used to this new idea.

"Of course, we don't want you to make up your mind without thinking about it and we know you'll be talking it over with your parents. John suggested we might invite them out for a week to meet us if you decide you'd like to stay. Does your family like California?"

"My father was here when he was in the Navy," Amber said. "He liked it, but he was only here about two weeks."

"He was probably in San Diego," Madeline said. "It's nice there, but our area is nicer. If they could take the time off, we could take them on a real tour of the area. How would that be?"

Amber burst out laughing. She couldn't help it and when she finally recovered enough, she tried to explain, "I can't imagine you and your family on a vacation with my family. It sounds like a plot for a movie."

"I guess I don't need to ask which family is the peculiar one," Madeline said. She was trying to smile but Amber could see her feelings were hurt.

Amber put her hand on Madeline's and said, "Please don't be offended. It's not just your family that's peculiar . . . I mean different. My family is really unusual, too. They are the most old-fashioned family of any of my friends."

"Catty says they eat dinner together every night." Madeline smiled ruefully and said, "Just think about our offer. It's a good one. I know your family's not poor, but it would be an advantage to all of them. You have a younger brother they need to educate also, I believe."

"Yes. I know it's a very generous offer, Madeline . . ."

"I was a very poor girl, you know," Madeline said abruptly. "So I understand that we're quite different from what you are used to. Maybe I'm especially different. I suppose your mother can do all those things like cook and bake bread that I've never learned. It's just that I do some things very well and other things not well at all. I do love my husband and his children, you know."

"Madeline, I honestly didn't mean to offend you," Amber said. "I like you and I know you care about the kids. Please, don't be hurt."

Madeline kissed her on the forehead and said, "Well, get your beauty sleep. Must look wonderful for tomorrow night. Is Lucia coming? Did you invite her brother? Do you mind wearing the same dress again? I could call Irena . . ."

"Then you *are* having a party?" Amber asked. "Here?"

"Oh, my dear, no." It was Madeline's turn to laugh. "We couldn't have a hundred people here. We're having a party at home. Did I forget to tell you?"

Amber nodded.

Madeline threw up her hands and said, "Now do you see why I want you to stay through the winter? I have so many things on my mind, I simply let the details get away from me from time to time. Did I tell you we were moving tomorrow?"

"Moving?"

"Moving back to Beverly Hills. I'm so glad I put you in the guest room here because it was the best we had, but at home, you'll have an even better room. It's completely French country and you'll love it. It will suit you much better than rattan. You have a certain elegance of your own that will be set off by the French elegance, you'll see."

Madeline stood up to indicate that the interview was over. Then she added, "Just pack up the clothes in your drawers. We'll have the hanging clothes taken over on hangers, of course. It's a simple move but you might like to know in advance."

"Yes, it's good to know things in advance," Amber said. As she left the room, her head was swimming. It would take her a while to sort everything out.

Chapter 29

Amber called Lucia at eight-thirty in the morning and said, "I'm moving today. They're going back to Beverly Hills and there's a party tonight. I was supposed to invite you and Tony, only no one told me till after you left last night. Can you come?"

"We can't," Lucia said. "My grandfather is coming home from Alaska with his new wife. We're having a big family celebration. I think my parents and aunts and uncles are celebrating because she's only two years younger than he is. My family has been worried he'd find a young wife ever since my grandmother divorced him."

"I can hardly wait to meet your grandfather," Amber said. "He must be really special."

"Come over this afternoon," Lucia offered. "They're leaving for Florida tomorrow morning and they won't be back till Christmas."

"I can't," Amber said. "I have a date with Brett."

"Brett?"

"Brett."

There was a very long silence and Amber said, "Say something."

"Something," Lucia responded.

"I mean it . . ."

"I'll say it once more," Lucia said. "Jason is a great guy and he's crazy about you. There —are you satisfied?"

"Jason is crazy about *you* and he's not wonderful . . ." Amber began and then she said, "But I have some really important news. You'll never guess this. Madeline asked me to stay all year. I don't know if it was her idea or Mr. Harvey's, but they must have talked about it. She thinks I'm good for the kids and they've offered me my own car and the same salary. She even offered tennis or ballet lessons."

"Will your folks let you do it?"

"I doubt it," Amber said. "But it was nice to be asked."

"Would you do it if your folks said okay?" Lucia asked.

"A year at the Harvey house sounds like an eternity, but if Jason and I could keep from killing each other, it would solve my college problems. I'd have enough money to go just about anywhere. That is, if I worked part-time and got scholarships."

"We could have a lot of fun," Lucia said. "I like winter in California a lot better than summer. There aren't as many people on the beaches. We could go to the mountains at Christmas vacation. We could take the kids to the Rose Parade. Wouldn't you like to see it?"

"I would," Amber said, "but I can't imagine Christmas away from my family. It makes me homesick just to think about it."

"Maybe they would come out here," Lucia said. "Sometimes Tony and I go surfing on Christmas Day. We could take your family."

Amber laughed and said, "Know what my family does at Christmas? We go to Christmas Eve service at church and then open presents on Christmas morning. Then we eat turkey and have a few friends in on Christmas night. We sing carols and eat fruitcake. Now you want to take them surfing and Madeline wants to take them on a vacation."

"Why not just take them someplace great like Palm Springs?" Lucia didn't seem to know what Amber was laughing about.

"I'm afraid if I do have a California Christmas, it will be without relatives. I'm just not sure I'm ready to do that. Say hello to your grandfather and tell him I'm sorry I missed him."

"You promise to think about staying this winter?"

"I promise to think about it," Amber said. "But right now I've got to go pack my stuff for the big move."

As she packed her bag, she wondered whether anyone told Jason they were moving today. Would he come home to the beach house and find everyone gone? She shrugged. Jason would figure it out. He was a big boy and he was used to his family.

She dressed carefully for her date with Brett, selecting her new miniskirt, thong sandals, and a blouse Madeline had given her with long full sleeves. She thought she looked very sophisticated and she hoped Brett would, too.

He picked her up at three-thirty and said, "You don't mind dropping by the library for a little while, do you? I have a couple of books on reserve and they just came in. Now that everyone's out of school, I can finally get what I need."

Amber slipped into the Mercedes and they sped off to UCLA library. He led her through the main doors and up to the second floor where the history section was, explaining, "This is one of the finest history libraries in the world. They have a big display of old manuscripts down the hall. Why don't you take a look at it?"

"How long will you be?"

Not too long," Brett said. "The party's at seven and we have to dress."

When Amber looked hesitant, Brett promised, "I'll come after you. The display is right down the hall."

Amber saw that it was five minutes to four when she went into the library museum. She spent a while looking at display cases, faithfully reading the inscriptions under the books and then she went over to a table and picked up a magazine.

For the next hour and a half she tried to focus on what she was reading because if she didn't, she knew she would just let her mind circle round and round about whether or not she wanted to stay in California this winter. On the one hand, she wasn't sure if she could bear to be away from her family so long. On the other hand, she knew it was a great opportunity. Most of all, she knew the decision would probably be her parents', not hers.

At five-thirty, Brett came for her and said, "Sorry I took so long."

As they walked down the marble hallways, Amber was aware that several women passed them by and then turned to stare at Brett because he was so handsome. A couple of them actually smiled, but Brett didn't seem to pay any attention at all. He was more or less in his own world, Amber decided.

The funny thing is that he's so good-looking and he's polite, but when I'm with him, I'm hardly aware that he's around. She remembered what Jason had said once about how Brett would always find a way to be absent. For the first time, she thought she knew what he had meant, but she was determined to at least try and get to know Brett better. She decided she would find a way to break down that wall of reserve. "Tell me why you decided to go to UCLA?" she prompted. "You could have gone anywhere. Didn't you consider an eastern school?"

Brett shrugged. "I was admitted to several, but I chose UCLA when the time came."

"Why?"

"It's a good school," Brett said, somewhat defensively.

"I'm sure it is," Amber quickly agreed. "Are your classes mostly lectures or do you have some smaller classes?" She really wanted to ask him some more personal questions than these, but she felt it would scare him away.

Brett was a nice guy as well as totally gorgeous and she hoped he would be around more and more.

They stopped for ice cream on the way home and Brett actually laughed when she couldn't make up her mind whether to have chunky monkey or peanut brittle. "I thought you'd like vanilla or chocolate," he said as he smiled.

"Does that mean you think I'm dull?" she asked.

He laughed out loud and said, "I guess it means you'll think I'm dull. Chocolate is my favorite."

"Chocolate was my favorite, too, until I met your sister. You should hang around with her more and she'd have you into exotic flavors." Amber watched his face close down as she spoke and she realized that if she wanted to make Brett open up, she'd have to stay away from the subject of his family. Poor guy—he might look as though he had everything—money, looks, and brains—but he obviously was missing out on feeling close to his family.

"We'd better go," Brett said. "We're on a schedule."

"Sure," Amber agreed. Getting to know Brett would take time.

As they got into his car, Brett said, "Dad makes quite a point of all of us showing up on time."

They drove down Sunset Boulevard, and Brett said, "Thanks for being such a good sport. Next time we'll do something more fun. But the manuscripts were interesting, weren't they?"

"Fascinating," Amber said. She sighed and looked out the window, wondering where all her dreams had flown. On the airplane ride to California, she'd dreamed of meeting wonderful young men. She'd met three and Brett was the best of the lot—but he was tough to get to know. Mike had been a total disaster and Jason was . . . Jason was absolutely impossible.

They pulled into the drive of the Harveys' Beverly Hills home and Jason's Corvette pulled in right behind them. "Looks like Jason's home," Amber said.

"Has he been away?" Brett asked.

"He's been in Santa Barbara for a week," Amber said. "You probably ought to say hello to him." She hopped out of the car, not waiting for Brett to open the door, and practically ran into the house. She found Mrs. Murdock in the kitchen and she asked, "Do you know where my room is?"

"How would I know?" the cook answered.

She pointed to a catering truck outside the window and a group of young men and women who were setting up chairs and tables. "I have to supervise this mess," she said. "Ask someone else."

Amber could only think of finding her room before Jason came into the house. She knew she would have to face him eventually, but she wanted to be certain that she was composed and collected before she did. She wasn't ready to spar with Jason.

Chapter 30

The party was very similar to the others she'd attended except that everything was done a little better. The food was more interesting, the band was smoother, and everyone seemed to be having a great time.

Amber was pleased when two or three people spoke to her as though they knew who she was. While six weeks wasn't long enough to really be a part of the family, despite what Madeline thought, she did feel a lot more at home than she had in the beginning.

Catty found her almost the minute she came onto the back lawn where the party was being held. She said, "What took you so long? You were supposed to watch Kyle."

"I took a shower and then I lay down for a few minutes and fell asleep," Amber admitted. "Is Kyle all right?"

"I watched him," Catty said proudly. "And

then Madeline had one of the caterers take him to his room and let him watch television."

"I should go get him."

"No," Catty said. "Madeline said you should enjoy the party. Do you like your new room?"

"It's fabulous," Amber said. "I never saw so many beautiful things in my life. I love the furniture."

"It's nice," Catty agreed. "One thing my stepmother can do is decorate." Then Catty looked as though she was thinking it over and said, "Actually, Madeline can do quite a few things well. She picked this dress for me. Do you like it?" Catty made a mock curtsy to show off her bright red sundress.

"You look great," Amber answered. "Very sophisticated."

"No more hair ribbons," Catty said. "I made her promise. What do you think?" Catty shook her long brown hair which she was wearing loose and straight.

"Beautiful."

"Madeline got me some special shampoo for long hair. It makes my hair shine. I wanted to get some of the shampoo they use on horses, but she said no daughter of hers was using horse shampoo and that was that."

"I'm sure that what Madeline got you was better than horse shampoo." Amber couldn't help smiling at Catty's newfound admiration for Madeline.

"So is there anyone you want to meet?" Catty said. "There're a lot of famous people here."

"I see that," Amber said as she looked around. She saw several movie stars she recognized by names and many more she was certain she'd seen but couldn't place. "Who is that girl talking to Brett?" she asked.

"That's Sunny Perkins," Catty answered. "Her dad is a director and she's a college student. I think they're friends."

"She's beautiful."

"Yeah, but she's not talented." Catty dismissed the young woman with a wave of her hand. "When I'm her age, I'll be beautiful and famous."

"Catty, you've got to learn to be more discreet in the things you say about other people. I'm sure Sunny Perkins is a perfectly nice person."

"Sunny Perkins is a perfectly *boring* person. She and Brett are just right for each other. Look—there's that kid who stars on that new TV series—you know, the surfing one. I think I'll circulate," Catty said.

Catty walked off very purposefully, and Amber laughed out loud when she saw that the girl was aiming for a group that contained several young men about her age. One of them was the kid with the half-shaved head and high-top boots. He was wearing the same horrible surfing shorts and T-shirt he'd had on at the other party.

"Come over this way," Brett called out to her. Amber saw that she had very little choice but to join him and Sunny. She had a drink with them and decided that Catty was absolutely right—Sunny was dull.

"Please excuse me," Amber said, "I want to talk to a few people."

She moved from group to group, enjoying the laughter and feeling free to leave after a few minutes. About nine-thirty, John Harvey found her standing beside the pool house and asked, "How do you like the party?"

"It's the best one yet," she answered honestly.

"Yes. Madeline's great at entertaining. And what have you decided about staying here this winter?"

"I haven't really thought too much about it," Amber answered honestly. "I was so surprised by your offer that I'm still sort of in shock."

"We think it would be a win-win situation," John Harvey said. "You fit in well and you and Jason are so close. We like that. It goes without saying that we think you're just the right girl for him."

"I'm *not* Jason's girlfriend," Amber began, but John Harvey kept right on talking without paying any attention to her protests.

"Kyle is talking more and he seems to be practicing his reading. Catty tells me he's using her computer and that's a good sign. We think you've been a good influence on Catty as well. Of course, she was bound to grow up one of these days but I really think you've helped her. I understand you're a straight-A student and I hope you can help Catty a bit with her studies. She's bright but not much of a student."

"Catty is an independent thinker," Amber said. "Her writing is good, you know. You really should read it."

"I will," the busy director promised, and Amber noticed that he was looking over her head even as they talked. "The main thing is, if you're here the younger kids have some much needed stability. Jason's a help of course, but Jason needs to attend to his own schoolwork. Jason worries too much about the family. And he has great talent."

"Maybe Jason thinks family is more important than filmmaking," Amber said. She realized she was defending the person she disliked most in the world, but she also realized that on this subject, she agreed with Jason.

John Harvey patted her arm and smiled. "It's natural for you to defend him," he said. "I just hope you'll really consider our offer. Beverly Hills High School is famous all over the world and you could have your own car — maybe a little red Mustang. You could see a lot of Lucia even though she probably goes to Malibu High."

"I really will talk it over with my folks," Amber promised him.

"Good, here's Jason now." He waved his arm and called to his son. Jason joined them and nodded stiffly to Amber. His father said, "I want you to show Amber around UCLA tomorrow. If she falls in love with it, maybe she'll want to stay with us permanently. Then, Amber, you could finish high school and go right into UCLA. You could live here and commute. The boys live on campus but a lot of students don't. I commuted from Eagle Rock when I was a student. I worked as a busboy in a restaurant at night and went to school in the daytime. Have I told you about that?"

"I'm certain Amber has heard the story," Jason said with a grin. "But now that you're a famous director, don't you think you should look for one of your guests who hasn't heard it and tell him?"

John Harvey looked confused and then smiled. He said to Amber, "My son thinks my emphasis on my underprivileged childhood is a joke but it's no joke to work your way through college, I can tell you that."

"I'm sure it isn't," Amber agreed.

John Harvey moved away from them, after patting his son on the arm and saying, "So I told Amber you'd take her to look around UCLA tomorrow. You can do that, right?"

"I'd be happy to." Jason sort of clicked his heels together and bowed. "What time shall I pick you up, Madame?"

"I'm busy tomorrow," Amber said quickly.

"Why am I not surprised?"

"You'll have to excuse me now," Amber said. "Catty said she wanted to introduce me to some people."

Later, as she chatted with Ray Redmond and his wife, she wondered why she hadn't told Jason that Brett had already shown her UCLA. It seemed to her that whenever she talked with Jason she ended up wishing she'd said something different.

When the party ended, Amber walked into the house. Brett caught up with her and put his arm around her shoulder and asked her if she'd had a good time. "It was fun," Amber said. "I liked your friend Sunny a lot. Have you known her long?"

"Since kindergarten," Brett said. "I enjoyed spending time with you today." He bent over and kissed her lightly on the cheek and then said, "I'll call you soon."

Before she quite understood what was happening, Brett was leaving by the front door. Jason entered the living room and asked coolly, "Saying good-bye to Brett?"

"I guess so," Amber said. "Where is he going?"

"Maybe back to the fraternity house," Jason said. "He comes and goes like the wind. I heard you ask him about Sunny. Are you jealous of her, too?"

Amber didn't even bother to answer him. She went directly to her room. As she got ready for bed, she asked herself how she could even have thought of staying longer at the Harvey house. When she left in two weeks, she'd never have to see Jason Harvey again and that was the best idea she'd come up with in a long time!

Chapter 31

Over the next two days she thought a lot about the Harveys' offer and she kept coming back to the plain and simple fact that it was a very good one. One year in the Harvey household would almost pay for her college education and that meant her parents wouldn't have to sell their grandfather's farm until Tim went to school.

On the third day, Madeline asked, "Have you talked with your parents yet?"

"Not yet," Amber answered. "But I have to tell you I don't think they'll let me do it. They're pretty strict."

"John and I talked it over and we want you to know you could go home at Christmas. We'll pay your way, of course."

Amber sighed and said, "I'll talk to them today." She really didn't think they would say yes, but she felt she owed it to herself and her family to try. The money was important and she felt silly when she admitted to herself that most of the time she thought about Jason and Brett and her relationship to them, rather than the money. She wished she knew exactly what she felt for Brett. He was certainly nice and she had never seen anyone any better-looking. She liked Brett; in fact, she liked him a lot, but she wasn't sure if she liked him well enough to spend a whole year in California.

On the other hand, she was certain that Jason was a real obstacle to her future if she stayed here. Even when he tried, he was bossy and rude. Whenever she thought about Jason, she got a little agitated and she knew she wasn't going to be able to spend a year under the same roof with him without fire-works. She tried to tell herself that he spent most of his time at college and now that he and Lucia were so close, he would be easier to be around. But the fact remained that Jason was trouble for her, and Jason — on top of the rest of the Harveys — seemed like a lot to take on. It was a long time till June.

Money was important, she thought, and she would go around and around in her mind, sorting through the evidence again and again. Finally, she decided that she should talk to her parents before she thought about it any further.

She called her parents that evening and presented everything as completely as she could. She finished by saying, "They offered to have you come and visit for a few days just to check everything out if you want."

"We don't need to do that," her father said. "We trust your judgment."

"Does that mean I can stay here?" Amber was amazed.

"No," her mother said quickly. "It means we can talk about it and let you know."

By the time Amber hung up, she had the idea that her mother was against the idea and her father thought it might be a wise decision. She told Lucia that night, "I thought they'd be dead set against it but it looks like a split decision. I guess I'll just have to wait."

They talked a little longer and Lucia said, "I feel really sorry for Tony. He and Anna Lynne had another fight and now he doesn't have a date for the Sports Awards banquet tonight."

"I should think Tony would have a line of women after him."

"He does, but I don't think he's going to ask

anyone. Funny how he can be so smart and successful about most things and so stupid about a girl."

"A lot of people are like that." Amber was thinking about her own romantic adventures. She thought about Brett's good-night kiss at the party. What did it mean?

"Speaking of romantic adventures," Lucia said, "I found out why Jason knew what happened with you and Mike on that night you went out."

"What?"

"Tony knows the security guard there who told Mike to take you home. They were at a party together and Mike was there. The guy told Tony about what a jerk Mike was and Tony told Jason. Tony didn't know if you were still interested in Mike or not, but he thought Jason should know."

"I didn't know they even knew each other."

"Tony's three years older than Jason and they run with different crowds but we've all lived in the same town a long time. The Harveys are always in Malibu in the summer so we've always known about them."

"It's just like I told Mr. Harvey," Amber said. "Malibu really is like a small town."

She added rather wistfully, "If I should stay

here all winter, I hope Jason won't be around much. That way we won't kill each other before spring."

"I hope you do stay," Lucia said for the tenth time. They hung up then and Amber took Kyle to the dentist for his annual checkup. When she came back, Jason was there and he said, "Tony Valdez wants you to call him."

"Tony? Is there something wrong with Lucia?"

"It didn't sound like it. He just said he wanted to talk to you."

Amber called Tony and was amazed when he asked her to go to the Sports Awards banquet that evening. "I know it's short notice," he said. "But I don't want to go alone and I'd rather not take Lucia. It's embarrassing to go with someone that everyone knows is your sister. But they don't know you're my sister's friend. They'll think you're a real date. Will you do it?"

"Of course," Amber said and then she added, "I'll have to ask Jason to watch the kids." She turned to Jason and said, "Tony wants me to go to an awards banquet tonight. Will you watch the kids? Are you going to be home?"

"Tony Valdez is too old for you."

"He just needs someone to go with," she said.

"Why doesn't he take Lucia?"

"He wants someone besides his *sister*," she explained. She was trying to be reasonable and she knew she was asking a favor of Jason but as he stood there, looking impatient, she couldn't help saying, "I can't keep Tony waiting. Are you going to say yes or no?"

"Yes, I suppose," Jason answered with a frown. "But he is too old."

"I'll be ready by seven-thirty," Amber said over the phone. She managed to avoid Jason for the rest of the afternoon.

Tony came to pick her up at exactly seven-thirty. Both Jason and Brett were in the living room and Jason invited him in. When Amber came down the stairs, Tony, Brett, and Jason were talking politely about surfing but the atmosphere in the room was definitely strained.

"You look beautiful," Tony said.

"So do you," Amber answered and she laughed because she knew that Jason and Brett would probably hate hearing her say that. Tony did look absolutely handsome in his tuxedo and she knew she made an excellent match in her golden dress.

Jason was frowning and he was standing by

the fireplace with his hands in his pockets. Amber had learned that was a clue that he was not very happy. He asked, "Where did you say you were going?"

"Sports Awards banquet," Tony answered.

"Yes, but where?"

"At the Beverly Hills Hilton."

"What time will you be home?" Brett asked.

"About one or two," Tony answered. "It's a long boring night and I'm one of the guests of honor."

"She's only sixteen," Jason said abruptly.

"*Jason!*" Amber said angrily. "Stop that!"

Tony smiled and nodded and said, "We'll come straight home. Not to worry."

Once outside, Amber said, "I'm sorry for the third degree. The Harveys are kind of funny people. They act like they don't care and then they do this really strict number sort of out of the blue. It's quite confusing. I was so embarrassed. They will have forgotten all about me by the time we're at the hotel."

"No, those boys won't forget you," Tony said. He laughed and said, "I'll bet they're both waiting up for you when I bring you home."

"No," Amber said. "They're not that silly."

"Five dollars," Tony said. "Want to bet?"

"Make it ten," Amber answered.

It was the first time she'd ever spent much

time alone with Tony and she was pleased to find she was almost as comfortable with him as she was with Lucia. For one thing, he had that nice deep voice and when he laughed, it reminded her of Lucia's laugh.

The Hilton hotel and the ballroom where they were holding the awards was spectacular with huge crystal chandeliers and beautiful swirling lights. There were seats for about one thousand people and she sat up on a high stage with Tony and a lot of other sports heroes and their dates. People were really dressed up. Several women had on dresses that were sequined from top to bottom.

"These people are more dressed up than movie stars," Amber whispered.

"Especially the women athletes," Tony agreed. "I guess they want to be known for their looks as well as their ability."

Tony was right about one thing — it was a long, boring evening. They had a singer and several speeches before the awards began. By the time Tony got his trophy it was eleven o'clock. Then the dancing began.

Tony danced with her once and two other people asked her to dance. Most of the time, Amber sat at the table and drank Cokes while Tony talked to people he knew. At one o'clock, he came back and said, "Sorry I left you so long, but I got caught up talking to some movie people. Are you ready to go?"

As they were driving home, Tony said, "I think I've got a speaking part in a movie. Wish me luck."

"Oh, Tony, you don't need luck," Amber said. "You have a great voice and I'm sure you'll be a great actor."

"I'd like to be an actor," Tony admitted. "I'm twenty-one now and my surfing career won't last forever. But if I'm not an actor, I'll probably be able to get a job as a sports announcer or maybe I'll be a boring after-dinner speaker and spend my life on the banquet circuit."

"That sounds just terrible," Amber said with a laugh. "I can't imagine attending many of those things."

"You had a great time, huh? I guess I owe you one. How would you and Lucia like to be *in* the Rose Parade instead of just watching it. I'm going to be on a float for SpeedTime surfboards and I need a few beautiful surfers to ride on the float."

"I can't really surf," Amber said.

"The surfboards and the waves are made of flowers. All you have to do is look good."

"Sounds like fun." Amber laughed at the idea. She imagined how impressed the kids back home would be when they saw her on television and she was suddenly very homesick. "You'd better ask Catty. I probably won't be here," she added.

"I thought Lucia said you were staying in California?"

"I don't know for sure, but I don't think my parents will really let me stay. And even if they say yes, I'm not entirely sure I want to switch schools in my senior year," Amber answered.

They were pulling into the driveway of the Harvey house and Tony said, "It looks like I'm about to win ten dollars."

"They probably just forgot to turn off the lights," Amber said.

"Want to raise the bet?" Tony teased.

"No." Amber laughed. She could see moving shadows in the living room. As the car pulled to a halt, she said, "You don't need to walk me to the door. I can see that Jason is up."

"So he is." Tony laughed. "But you don't have to pay up on the bet. You've already suffered enough for one evening."

He leaned over and kissed her on the cheek. "Thanks, Amber."

When she walked into the house, she said to Jason, "Why are you here?"

"I was just watching a movie," he answered. "Have a nice time?"

"Where's Brett?"

"Your boyfriend went back to his fraternity house, I guess. I'm the faithful type. Did you have fun?"

"Tony was nice. The banquet was boring, just like he said it would be," Amber answered. "Did my parents call?"

"Your mother called. I had a long talk with her."

"You didn't!"

"Yes, I did," Jason said. "We talked about what a nice girl you are and how the offer to stay in California fits right into your plans. She wants you to come home and your father thinks it might be good if you stay. They both think you should make up your own mind."

Amber couldn't believe she was hearing what she was hearing. "You *actually* had this conversation with my mother?"

"Sure, what's wrong with that?"

"I just can't believe she talked about all this with *you*," Amber said. "It's none of your business. Also, it isn't like her."

"Isn't it?" Jason asked. "She was really very friendly. Wanted to know if I was the handsome brother or the good one. Those were her words — not mine. I said since I wasn't particularly handsome, I must be the good one. She said they were going to Camp Weehaddo to pick up Tim and she'd talk to you tomorrow evening. That's the real reason she talked to me, I guess. That, and I'm such a charming fellow."

"Did she really say it was up to me?"

Jason nodded and then he smiled and said, "You're on your own on this one."

Amber was suddenly very tired. She said, "Good night." Then she turned and smiled at him and shook her head, "You are *really* too much. I bet Tony ten dollars you guys wouldn't wait up for me. You cost me money."

"Maybe you could just pay him five," Jason teased. "Only half of the Harvey bunch stayed the course."

She started up the stairs and he called softly, "Amber?"

Funny how when he called her name, it sent chills up her back. She turned to see what else he had to say.

"What are you going to decide? Will you stay here this winter?"

His eyes were beautiful even when he had his glasses on. In fact, the glasses made them shinier and he had such a wonderful smile. She wondered if she stepped down whether he would kiss her again. She wondered if he was thinking about those kisses they'd shared as well. She stood absolutely still and answered his question softly, "I'm not sure. What do you think I should do?"

Jason shrugged and stuck his hands in his pockets. It was a gesture she'd come to know meant he wanted to say a whole lot more than he was going to. "I think you have to make up your own mind," he answered. "You're the only one who knows what's most important to you."

She nodded and went swiftly up the stairs to her new room.

Chapter 32

She asked for the next day off and drove the station wagon back out to the Malibu house. She wanted to be alone and think carefully about what she was going to do. She parked in the gated driveway and walked around the side of the house to the beach.

She took off her shoes and left them on the deck and walked onto the beach. She realized that she already missed the Pacific Ocean and the sound of the waves.

As she walked down the beach, she reviewed her summer in Malibu and decided that it had really been quite wonderful. I'm a success, she thought as she remembered what a quiet little boy Kyle was in the beginning and then pictured him playing baseball with her yesterday evening. There were so many things she felt proud about and she had learned so much. She really loved Malibu, but she wasn't sure she was going to love Beverly Hills.

Her room was beautiful, of course, but it was so formal that she wasn't quite used to it yet. She also found it harder to communicate with the kids in the big house. It seemed as though they were always somewhere else or that they were on different schedules. Kyle had his own television set and Catty was spending all her spare time talking to girl-friends on the telephone.

Would she really like to spend the winter in Beverly Hills? What would it be like to enter a new school as a senior? How much would she miss her friends? The farther she walked, the more she began to think about home. As she walked, she realized that she was getting very, very warm. She longed for the cool fall breezes that she knew were already blowing in Milwaukee. It was late August, this was the hottest day she could remember in California. They said August was usually a hot month and that it could be even hotter in September. At home, it was already quite cool. By Labor Day, there might be frost. The leaves would begin to turn by the middle of September. If she stayed in California, it would always be green. She would certainly miss the fall leaves and the winter snows.

Her Wisconsin friends were probably shopping for school clothes this week, buying new sweaters and jeans. Heather would fly in from France next week and she would be full of stories about her European adventures. Amber reached up to wipe the sweat off her forehead and wished she'd brought her bathing suit. Right about now it would feel good to strip down to her bikini and go dashing into the surf.

Amber began to daydream about winter in California. Would it be warm enough to swim in the Harvey's pool all winter? What would it be like to have no snow at all? She tried to imagine what being in the Rose Parade would be like. She tried to imagine that it would be easy to make new friends at Beverly Hills High. But the longer she walked, the more clear her decision became. By the time she was at the Malibu pier, she knew she would be going home to Milwaukee next week.

She ordered a Coke and sat on the end of the pier for a while, letting the breeze blow across her face, thinking about home. Tim would be there tonight and her folks would be so glad to see him. They would be glad to see her next week as well. It had been a wonderful summer, but she simply wasn't ready to leave home. She wanted to finish school with the friends she'd gone through the past eleven years with and she wanted this last year with her family. She would be on her own soon enough.

If this summer had taught her one thing, it had taught her she loved her family. She wanted to enjoy what she had and really let her parents know how much she appreciated them. Next year she would be on her way to college and from that time on, everything would be different. She didn't want to push the time ahead.

The minute she really decided what she was going to do, she felt lighthearted. She started back to the beach house, but it was so hot now the two miles back began to look more like ten. By the time she'd gone just a little way, she was sweating and out of breath. She looked around and saw that everyone else on the beach was lying still or in the water.

Then Amber laughed and ran directly into the water. What did it matter if she got her clothes wet? They would dry. What did it matter if people thought she was crazy? She was too hot not to go into the ocean. She stood in the water, letting the Pacific Ocean caress her until she was cooled off and ready to start walking again.

The walk back was easier now and each time

she began to feel too hot, she took another dip in the ocean. She walked along the shore, letting the waves lap around her ankles and thinking about nothing at all. This was one of her last days on the beach and she was enjoying it. She bent down and picked up a perfectly formed little shell, remembering that Lucia told her that these shores once were littered with shells before so many tourists came to Malibu. She thought about taking the shell home with her and then decided to leave it on the sand. Let it stay where it belonged — she was going home to where *she* belonged.

When she got back to the beach house, her car was blocked by Brett's. She didn't have a key to the house, so she went to the door and knocked loudly. Brett came to the door and said, "Hi, Amber, I was hoping you were the one driving the wagon."

"Your car is blocking mine," she said. "Were you studying? I'm sorry to bother you."

"You look all wet."

"Yes. I went to the water. I'm pretty dry now though. Can you move your car?"

"Don't you want to come in for a minute? Have a drink? How was your evening with Tony . . . ?"

Amber nodded and stepped into the house. She asked, "So what are you doing here?"

"I usually stay here a lot in the winter," Brett said. "I like it when no one's here."

"The beach is loaded with people. It must be ninety degrees and there's no shade," Amber said. "I think I'll get a glass of ice water," she said and went into the kitchen.

When she came back, Brett was on the deck and he motioned for her to come out with him. She said, "I really don't want to stay long. I was going to go up to the Valdez place after this."

"You can stay awhile with me," Brett smiled and put his arm around her.

Amber caught her breath in surprise. This was the first time Brett had really touched her except for that brief kiss on the cheek. She wasn't sure what it meant and she wasn't sure what she wanted it to mean. She gently backed out of his embrace and took a sip of her ice water. "It's so hot," she said. "I can't believe it's this hot and summer's almost over. They say it could be even hotter in September."

Brett put his arm around her shoulder again and drew her closer. He said, "I didn't like you going out with Tony. Jason convinced me you would go anyway so I kept quiet. But why did you do it? I thought you and I were . . . you know?"

She realized he was very shy, but he sounded so old-fashioned and stiff that it was all she could do to keep from laughing out loud.

She explained thoughtfully, "Tony asked me to go as a favor and he's my friend. That's all it meant." She wondered if Brett was reading more into their relationship than she did. He sounded as though he thought it was up to him whether or not she could go out with Tony.

"I shouldn't have let you go," Brett said and he smiled down at her.

"What do you mean?"

"I came by to take you out for a drive and Jason told me you were going out with Tony. He said he'd given you permission. I said it wasn't up to him to give you permission — "

"He said he'd take care of Kyle for me," Amber interrupted quickly. "That's the kind of permission he meant. Other than that, I didn't need anyone to tell me what to do."

"But you need me, don't you?" Brett said softly and bent to kiss her on the cheek.

Amber was confused. It was true that she'd been hoping that Brett was interested in her, but this sudden possessiveness was really upsetting. How could she get him to back off and not scare him away altogether?

She tried to pull out of his arms and he asked, "You like me, don't you, Amber?"

Amber shook her head and backed away in a panic. She was really amazed at Brett's seriousness and he seemed so awkward about it — as though he were a young boy. She realized that Brett could never be the boyfriend of her dreams and she felt as though she had been leading him on in some way. She was really confused and upset.

Brett moved in closer to hold her tighter and she sort of jerked out of his arms. She said, "Listen, Brett, I don't want to hurt your feelings, but I think you might have the wrong idea about us . . ."

She would never know exactly what happened next but somehow, when she pulled away from him, Brett lost his balance and fell against the deck railing. The railing gave way and Brett tumbled down about six feet into the sand.

Amber was horrified and she leaned over the broken railing calling out, "Are you all right?"

"Of course," Brett said, and he tried to get up but fell down flat in the sand.

Amber ran down the steps into the sand and as she neared Brett she could see he was in pain. There were beads of sweat on his forehead and he seemed as if he were going to cry. She bent over him and said, "Let me look. Did you break anything?"

"Don't touch me!" Brett tried to get up again and collapsed into the sand. He rolled over and groaned and then just lay there.

"I'll call nine-one-one," Amber said.

"No! Just leave me alone. Don't call nine-one-one!" Brett yelled. "I'll be all right in a minute."

"What can I do?"

"Just go away and leave me," Brett said. Then he added, "Don't call anyone. Maybe I can get up now if you help me."

"Brett, I can't help you up. You may have broken something. I really should call someone. Are you bleeding?"

"Don't call anyone! I'm not bleeding!" There were tears running down Brett's face now and Amber realized he'd been trying to get rid of her so she wouldn't see him cry. She said, "I'll get you some water."

Once in the kitchen, she called the Harvey house. When no one answered, she looked up the number of Jason's car phone and dialed that. He answered immediately and she told him what had happened. She finished with, "I don't know what to do. He won't let me call nine-one-one and I'm afraid to help him move."

"I'm only a few minutes away," Jason said. "If he's that determined, he's probably all right. Just keep him still until I get there. Don't let him get up."

"I don't think he *can* get up," Amber said. "Jason, hurry."

"Don't worry," Jason said. "He'll be fine. Just keep talking to him and don't let him go to sleep or anything. I'll be right there."

Brett took the water from her, but he wouldn't look at her at all. She realized he was quite embarrassed about what had happened and when she said, "Jason is coming over. He'll be right here," he only nodded.

Amber took Brett's hand while they waited and she talked to him about her decision to go back to Wisconsin for the winter. "I just don't think I'm ready to leave home yet," she said. "I've had a great summer vacation but I really want to go home for my senior year." She knew that Brett wasn't really listening, that he was in too much pain to care about her or her problems, but she thought it was good to talk about something. She had the feeling that if she didn't keep talking, the gulf of embarrassment might widen between her and Brett to the point where they could never look at each other again.

Jason was there in ten minutes and Amber had never been as glad to see anyone in her life. She said, "It's really hot out here and he seems kind of funny. Do you think he could go into shock?"

Jason shrugged and bent down. He took his brother's pulse and asked him, "Where does it hurt?"

Brett pointed to his left leg and Jason said to Amber, "Get a pair of scissors and we'll cut his pants open. At least we can see if he's bleeding."

Amber jumped up and Jason mouthed the words, "Nine-one-one." She nodded and ran to the kitchen where she dialed the emergency number.

The paramedics were there in just a few minutes and Brett was so angry that Amber was really glad it was Jason's decision, not hers. He railed at both of them, crying and waving his fists as he was loaded onto a stretcher and carried up the stairs to the ambulance.

Jason just grinned and said, "Don't worry,

big brother. We'll be right behind you."

"My car is blocked in," Amber said. "We should have asked for his keys."

"It's okay," Jason answered. "We'll get them at the emergency room." Then he stopped and asked, "You don't mind riding with me, do you?"

Impulsively, she reached over and hugged him. "Of course not. I was never so glad to see anyone in my life."

Jason let her hug him and when she stepped away, he let her go without comment. She was suddenly embarrassed and said, "Brett was really weird. I think he was afraid I'd see him crying."

They were in the Corvette now, skimming down the highway toward Santa Monica Hospital.

Amber said, "He seemed more like a little kid."

Jason nodded and said, "Brett's an odd guy. He's always been sort of a loner. He had a really bad childhood, you know. I mean, he's okay now, but he's probably always going to be a little removed from the scene. I tried to tell you that."

"Why was his childhood any worse than anyone else's?" Amber asked. "Because his mother drank?"

Jason nodded. "She still does. My dad finally made a deal with her when Brett was ten to stay away from Brett, and he's lived with us ever since. He's had a lot of therapy and stuff but he's pretty closed up."

"What will happen to him?" Amber wondered out loud.

"He'll be all right," Jason said. "How did he happen to break his leg? You push him off the edge?"

"I mean what will happen to him *eventually*. He seemed so young and frightened down there on the beach. He seemed younger and more frightened than Kyle."

"He'll be fine," Jason said. "Brett's got his whole life planned. He'll be a history professor and marry someone like Sunny Perkins and live happily ever after. He may not take a lot of chances, but he'll be fine."

"You know a lot about people," Amber said. "Maybe you should be a psychiatrist or something instead of a filmmaker."

Jason laughed and asked, "Are you going to tell me what happened? How *did* Brett fall?"

"I've decided to go back to Milwaukee for my senior year," Amber said abruptly.

"I thought you would." Jason nodded as

though it was the most unsurprising thing he'd ever heard.

Amber's heart flip-flopped and she realized that she was hoping Jason would try and talk her out of it. I wouldn't change my mind, she thought, but I wanted him to try.

Chapter 33

Brett had to stay in the hospital two days and three nights because it was a multiple fracture and he had to have a pin put in the ankle to hold the bones together. Someone from the family stayed with him all the time. His father was there a lot and Madeline switched her schedule around so she could be there as well.

Jason stayed most of the time, playing checkers with Brett or just sitting beside him and reading while he slept. In the evenings, everyone crowded into the small room and Brett seemed very pleased to have all the attention. Amber decided that the broken ankle was going to be good for him because he would finally feel as though he was an important part of the family.

On the third day, Jason and his father picked Brett up from the hospital and drove him and his new crutches home. When they entered the house, Catty and Kyle ran out and yelled "Welcome Home!" and did a cheer Catty wrote especially for the occasion.

Madeline said to Brett, "I made you some soup — well, I had Cook make some soup. And I've had the maid make up a room for you on the first floor. That way you don't have to climb stairs."

"I'll be going back to the fraternity house soon," Brett said, but he smiled at his stepmother.

The heat wave had continued all the time Brett was in the hospital and the day he came home was the worst day of all. Amber and the kids spent a lot of time in the swimming pool. She taught Kyle to play water games and they laughed and splashed around so much that the others came out to watch them. For the first time since she'd been there, Madeline put on a swimsuit and actually got in the water, but she didn't stay long or get her hair wet. John Harvey, on the other hand, joined in the game of catch and soon he, Jason, Catty, and Kyle were wrestling and shouting at each other.

Lucia came over the day before Amber was going to leave and they decided it was too hot to do anything but hang around the swimming pool. They swam and talked all day. Amber told her all about her plans for the next year and then she said, "The Harveys invited me to come back next summer to work for them. They really want me to go to college at UCLA and live with them, too. They say their offer will still hold a year from now. I said I probably would take them up on it."

"Probably?" Lucia asked. "I guess I can understand why you wanted to finish your senior year at home, but you have to go to college the next year anyway. Why wouldn't you take a great offer like that? I thought you liked the Harveys."

"I do. I've really changed my mind about them. Or maybe they've changed. Or maybe I've changed. I'm not as sure about things as I used to be."

"So why wouldn't you come back?"

"Jason."

"Jason! I thought you said you were friends now?"

"We are friends," Amber said. "Ever since I called him when Brett broke his ankle, I've understood that he's the real glue of this family. The reason they all quote him all the time is that they really respect him. So do I. Jason's a great guy."

"I've told you that over and over again," Lucia said. "I'm glad you finally figured it out for yourself."

"But Jason doesn't really like me," Amber said. "He's been nice but very remote ever since that day. And when I said I was going to go home, he said he thought it was a good idea."

Lucia shook her head and said, "I hope I never fall in love. It is definitely bad for the brain cells. Did I tell you Tony is back together with Anna Lynne? And you still don't know that Jason is crazy about you, do you?"

"If he is, he sure has a funny way of showing it," Amber said, and then she changed the subject. It was her next to last day in California and she wasn't going to ruin it worrying about Jason Harvey.

As she drove Lucia home that evening, she said, "It really has been a totally awesome summer. I'm going home with a tan and some great new clothes and money in the bank. I've got it all . . . except . . ."

"Except what?"

"Except I dreamed I'd have this wonderful summer romance and I don't think Mike or Brett qualify for the boyfriend of my dreams."

"No," Lucia said, "but you did have a wonderful summer romance if you just think about it."

"You mean with Kyle? Yes — Kyle has

really come a long way. I guess I should be satisfied with that."

"I wasn't talking about Kyle," Lucia said. Then she laughed that deep throaty laugh of hers and said, "I'm sure you can figure it out if you just concentrate."

Chapter 34

Amber couldn't sleep that night, partly because she knew that Lucia had been talking about Jason and as she reviewed her summer, she saw that Lucia was probably right. Jason had never really been interested in Lucia, and he probably had been interested in her — at least until she blew it.

Thinking about her mistakes with Jason gave her insomnia and it made her sad. Also, she was excited about going home. The mixture of emotions made it absolutely impossible for her to sleep. By midnight, she decided she couldn't stand it anymore — she would take a swim and see if that helped her sleep. She slipped out of bed, put on her bathing suit, and went outside to the pool. It was still very hot and the cool water felt good.

Amber swam silently back and forth across the pool several times before she realized someone was sitting on a chair in the rose garden watching her. "Brett?" she called out. "Is that you?"

"It's me," Jason's voice came back to her.

"What are you doing here?"

Jason rose and walked over to the edge of the pool. He was wearing swim trunks. He squatted down beside the edge of the pool, trailing his hand in the water. "I had the same idea you did. I came down for a swim and after I finished I was just sitting there, drying off. You came down so I sat there and watched you. You're a good swimmer."

"Thanks." Amber wondered if her face looked as green in the overhead lights as Jason's did. She asked, "Do I look green?"

"You look beautiful," he answered her.

"I want to talk to you," Amber said. "I've been wondering when I could catch you alone. I want to apologize, for starters."

"Me, too." Jason smiled down at her and said, "You do look a little green — kind of a golden green but there's a definite green glint around the gills. Want to get out now?"

Amber smiled at him and raised her hand for some help. When she wasn't mad at him, she liked Jason better than just about anyone she knew.

He reached down and grabbed her arms.

She let him help her up onto the pool deck. As he pulled her up, she bumped into him and she laughed and drew back, saying, "I'll get you all wet."

"I don't mind." Jason pulled her close again and before she knew what was happening, he was kissing her. She sighed and wrapped her arms around his neck. Kissing Jason was such a wonderful experience, she just didn't feel like saying no. In fact, she felt as though she'd like to stay in his arms a long, long time. Eventually, he pulled back a little and said, "I'll get you a towel." Then he kissed her neck and added, "I'm really going to miss you, Amber, and I need to talk to you about that."

Amber let him go into the bathhouse and get one of the terry towels the Harveys had stacked in rows on the shelves. She let him put it around her shoulders. She smiled and said, "I'm going to miss you, too. No one else takes such good care of me, even though I don't want it. That's what you are Jason — you're a caretaker."

"Couldn't you think of a more romantic title for me?" Jason asked. He said in a quiet voice, "I really love you, Amber. I have for a long time."

"Why didn't you talk me out of leaving?"

"I wanted you to make your own decision,"

Jason said simply. "I think you made the right one, by the way. We've got lots of time in front of us and we don't need to rush things."

Amber sighed and said, "I *will* miss you."

"Here we are in this romantic setting. Boy and girl in love. Warm summer night, moon . . ."

"You'll never make it as a romantic hero if you don't stop describing the scene as you live it," Amber teased. "Would you mind kissing me good-bye again?"

He seemed very happy to oblige and they sat wrapped in each other's arms for a long time. Finally, Amber asked, "If you really thought you loved me, why didn't you tell me before this?"

"A couple of reasons," Jason admitted. "First, I was jealous. Second, I thought maybe you were too young for me. And then . . . then everytime I tried to tell you, you seemed to think it was Lucia I wanted. The trouble is, all those other guys were so handsome. I felt like the ugly duckling most of the summer," Jason said.

"All those other guys? What are you talking about?" Amber was laughing.

"Mike."

"Mike was never anything but a jerk. You didn't ever need to be jealous."

"Tony."

"Tony is nice but he's too old for me — besides, he's in love with Anna Lynne."

"And I'm in love with you," Jason said.

"And if you felt like the ugly duckling, I guess I felt like Cinderella. Catty told me you only liked brunettes and Carlyle had those dark curls and Lucia was so beautiful. You did always seem to like Lucia a lot, you know."

"I do like her a lot. I even like her brother now that I know you're not interested in him. But it's you that I like most of all. I really did try to let you know," Jason continued after he had kissed her again. "But you really didn't seem to understand. And then when you had that big decision to make, I knew I should let you make it without confusing the issue. If you think it's best for you to go home, then it's best. Our love doesn't really change that."

"It doesn't?"

"Not really. I can come out there at Christmas if your parents will let me." He kissed her again and added, "I've always wanted to have a real traditional Christmas. When I was a kid, that was my favorite daydream. Now my favorite daydream is kissing you."

She kissed him again and said, "You'll be welcome at Christmas and maybe you can come back during spring break. Milwaukee is nice in the spring. And there's my senior prom — that's in May."

"I can do all that," Jason promised her. "Then you'll be back here in June. It will all work out — you'll see."

Amber snuggled closer to him and said, "I guess it *will* work out. So far, things have worked out really well."

"But the whole thing is off unless you tell me how you happened to break my brother's leg."

"I didn't break his leg!" Amber pretended to hit him. "Besides, it's only a broken ankle and he more or less did it himself."

"Tell me about the more or less," Jason insisted.

Amber told him the whole story and Jason laughed and laughed. "Poor Brett. It will be years before he tries to kiss another girl."

"Don't you worry about your brother," she answered. "He's so handsome he'll have lots of girls who want to kiss him."

"I knew you loved me all along," Jason said. He took his glasses off and wiped them on the edge of the towel. "You steamed up my glasses. You really are a dangerous lady, aren't you?"

"I think I could learn to be," Amber admitted and she kissed him again. "I think I have a talent for this romantic stuff. Only up until now I didn't have the right partner."

"Don't you want to know how I knew you were crazy about me?"

"How?"

"When I talked to your mother that time. She tipped me off when she asked if I was the 'good' brother. I knew you must be saying nice things about me even if you weren't saying them to me."

"You talk a lot," Amber said as she snuggled closer.

After a while, Jason asked, "Know when I fell in love with you?"

"When?"

"When I first saw you. You looked so sweet and scared walking across that lawn with your suitcase. I was so mad at Madeline I could have wrung her neck."

"I thought you were mad at me," Amber confided. "In fact, I thought you were mad at the world."

"But now that you know me better, you know I'm a real sweetheart," Jason said.

"That's right." Amber agreed. "And you're *my* real sweetheart."

"So I am," Jason said and he kissed her once again.